MALCOLM AND ME

A NOVEL

MALCOLM AND ME

ROBIN FARMER

spark press

Published by SparkPress, a BookSparks imprint,
A division of SparkPoint Studio, LLC
Phoenix, Arizona, USA, 85007
www.gosparkpress.com

Published 2020
Printed in the United States of America
Print ISBN: 978-1-68463-083-7
E-ISBN: 978-1-68463-084-4

Library of Congress Control Number: 2020944806

Interior design by Tabitha Lahr

To my family

"I'm for truth, no matter who tells it."
—MALCOLM X

CHAPTER 1

"The penguin is in a wicked mood today," Geoffrey whispers, as he passes my desk in eighth-grade history class on the way to the pencil sharpener.

I sit in the back because it's mission impossible to see the blackboard from behind my hair, which has been inspired by social justice activist Angela Davis, my idol.

I'm in the last seat in the last row next to a bank of windows overlooking the schoolyard. Far from Sister Elizabeth's desk, it is the best seat in class. Big hair has its perks.

"Mr. Mulligan, share with the class what you just told Roberta!" Sister Elizabeth says, rising from her huge wooden desk at the head of the classroom.

Tall and ruler straight, she has unfriendly blue eyes under her horn-rimmed glasses—and zero patience. As with all nuns, her age is a mystery. We can't tell if her hair is gray or if she's bald under her habit. Unlike most nuns, she still wears the corny old-fashioned kind of habit even though it's 1973.

On the flip side of being scary, she loves to sing and has a butter-smooth voice and a laugh I rarely hear, but dig because it is so free and loose. So unlike her.

1

"Nothing, Sister. I just asked her to move her foot so I wouldn't trip," he says, the red splotches on his pale cheeks deepening. He shuffles to his seat up front by her.

"Unlike you, I am not uneducable. I told you earlier to keep your trap shut. I am in no mood for shenanigans today." Sister's voice sounds scratchy, like she's fighting a cold. She makes her what-smells-bad expression, snatches up an eraser, and wipes the board clean. "Let's return our attention to Chapter 6 in your history books. Review the five rights proposed in the Declaration of Independence, and then we'll have a discussion."

Scanning the room, her disapproving eyes linger on my gigantic halo of hair, which she called "distracting." My Afro is even bigger and bolder than it was when she made me move my desk out of alphabetical order and plunk it behind Mary Zito. Guess that's punishment for both my fast-growing hair and increasing Black pride.

Sister Elizabeth nods at my closed textbook, shorthand to start reading. Now, I had already jumped ahead and completed the review assignment yesterday, but I chill out. No need to wind her up. Two more classes and I'm heading home, where special birthday gifts await the new teen me.

Opening my textbook, I watch to see if she'll doze off like she's been doing lately during reading assignments. We wait for her habit to droop and jerk up before turning our attention to each other. After about ten nods, I receive a handful of birthday cards from around the room along with a pack of apple Now and Later candies, my absolute favorite sugar rush.

The candy is a gift from Donna Rapinesi, a Cher wannabe and eye-shadow junkie, who flirts with dimpled-faced Gary as Sister Elizabeth cat naps. His pearly teeth and green eyes framed by lush lashes make every girl in eighth grade, Black and white, agree that Gary is so fine.

Mouth watering, I scratch off the wrapper glued to the candy and gaze out the window just as a streak of lightning, odd for this time of the year, zigzags across the sky. I wait for a thunderclap that never comes. Rain falls in thick sheets from a sky covered by a gray veil, but not even this bizarre storm can spoil my birthday.

Besides, my English teacher Mr. Harvey has an announcement this afternoon about the annual writing contest. I've come close to winning it the two years prior. I softly tap my knuckles on my desk for luck that he'll say the contest will be another essay competition. I'd consider that news another birthday gift.

After a few minutes, our big mouths wake up Sister Elizabeth. She goes to the middle of the blackboard and writes with perfect penmanship: "Among its list of self-evident truths, the Declaration asserts that 'all men are created equal.'"

I perk up. History is one of my favorite subjects, so I slip the neon-green candy into my pocket.

Sleepy-eyed Sister Elizabeth turns from the blackboard and addresses us. "Who can tell me why Thomas Jefferson signed the Declaration of Independence when at the time he owned slaves?" She sits.

Geoffrey's hand shoots in the air. Sister ignores him and calls on her pet, Eileen, a wavy-haired brainiac with crooked eyeglasses whose dull essays somehow beat mine every year.

"He probably didn't have a chance to free them yet."

I mentally groan. For starters, that's incorrect, and two, Sister doesn't correct her.

Sister looks around the room and rests her eyes on me. "What do you think, Roberta?"

"Because he was a hypocrite."

Sister Elizabeth stiffens and blinks until her eyes become blue blazes. "What did you say?" Glaring, she rises from her seat, breathing as if she had just run up the three flights to our class. She peers out the window at the wind-whipped Old Glory on the flagpole in the middle of the schoolyard. Then she eyeballs me, fury curling her lips.

I swallow hard.

Without warning, she snatches her beloved yardstick and slams it against her desk with such power that it snaps. That seems to enrage her more. She pounds her desk with her fist, and points to the closed classroom door.

"Who do you think you are, Roberta Forest? Get out! Get out of my classroom!" she thunders, rocking in her stumpy black heels. "How dare *you* speak poorly about one of our forefathers who built this great nation." Eyes and mouth tight with rage, she wags her finger at me. "Get back in the boat. Go back to Africa. We never needed *you people* in the first place!"

My mouth drops open. All eyes shift from Sister to me. I glance at Stephanie, the only other Black student.

I cannot believe my ears or eyes. I know in my gut that something bad is about to happen. She is out of control. Maybe I am, too. I am so mad everything turns gray like TV static. My body feels rubbed raw. Gripping the edges of my desk, I am way more angry than afraid.

"I don't have forefathers, I have just one," I say, rising out of my seat. "I wasn't born in Africa, but my ancestors were, before they were enslaved by *your people*."

She's quicker than the Flying Nun. Sister Elizabeth's habit flows out like a cape, and her rosary beads clack as she rushes down the aisle. She towers above me.

"*You* get out of my room now!" she hollers, her warm spittle flying all around me.

Scowling, I wipe my face. I turn to leave when she swings her hefty arm with Muhammad Ali force and delivers a mind-blowing slap that rocks my cheekbone. I didn't see it coming and instinctively, I throw up my hands to protect myself. Pushing outward, I accidently strike the top of her armpit. The chain of her glistening crucifix scratches the knuckles of my retreating fist.

"Ooh, she just punched Sister," Eileen whisper-shouts. Gasps echo around the room.

I want to apologize, but Sister's second slap, stronger than the first, snaps my head sideways. And then, like *The Twilight Zone*, the unthinkable happens. Before I can catch myself, my hand deliberately curls up and blindly slams into a pillowy softness that makes me want to throw up.

Jesus, I just hit Sister in her titty. My stomach ping pongs with shame.

My wide-eyed classmates watch in shocked silence as Sister saves her best shot for last, a fury-fueled pop that makes my ears hum. Cradling my lava hot cheek, I jump back out of hitting range even though I want to bend her fingers back until they break. But she's a Sister. I can't.

Where is God? I wonder. *Because he's not here with me. Or in Sister Elizabeth's heart.* I glance at the crucifix on the wall above the blackboard. He wasn't there either, because this madness should force his son off that cross and between me and this monster wearing God's gold wedding ring. But it doesn't.

Tears nearly blinding me, I flee the classroom. Sister follows, tossing my book bag out behind me. Backtracking, I scoop it up as her screechy voice echoes in the hallway and draws curious teachers out of their classrooms.

"Go to Mother Superior and tell her you just struck me twice, you unbelievable miscreant! I never want to see the likes of you in my classroom again."

I brace myself, expecting a lightning bolt to zap my back as I wobble through the hallway and head down three of the longest flights of stairs in my life to report to the main office. I shiver right down to my bones with every step, knowing electrocution is better than expulsion.

CHAPTER 2

In the empty stairwell, dizziness gets the best of me. It's my thirteenth birthday and I just fed my homeroom nun two knuckle sandwiches. No doubt, I now have a reserved seat on an express train to hell. I cannot imagine the number of Hail Marys needed to out of this.

I feel like a let-go balloon. Loose, unsafe, ready to pop. *Wait, haven't I popped already?*

My parents didn't raise me to act like a juvenile delinquent. It's just that no one, not even my "girl, don't play with me" mother, had ever tried to slap the Black off my face before. Or, looked at me as if I were a roach in need of a big shoe.

I step out into heavy rain and covered my Afro with my book bag. Mind elsewhere, I step into a puddle. I fight the urge to scream F bombs in the schoolyard.

With soggy shoes, I move to the school's oldest structure, a gray stone building housing grades first through fifth and the main office. The yard separates the primary school from our church, which I'm tempted to bum rush to beg God to end this nightmare. But clearly I'm wide awake with wet toes, a stinging cheek, and an Afro shrinking from the humidity.

Rain hits my face sideways as I peer up at the glistening twin gold crosses. *Help me.*

I step into the primary school and linger outside the main office. Making the sign of the cross, I pray for Mother Superior to listen to my side.

I approach the counter. The office aide sizes me up. Her eyes dart over my empty hands, a sign I'm not here on an errand.

"Another one. Must be a full moon." Her disgust flattens her mouth.

"Sister Elizabeth . . . threw me out. My name is Roberta Forest."

She sniffs like I had forgotten my deodorant. Someone sure smells funky, but not me. She writes my name on a list. I plunk myself next to other student sinners awaiting their fate.

Fear bubbles in my throat. I calm myself by picturing the pink princess phone waiting in my bedroom. The idea of talking for hours almost makes me smile.

No telling what extra goody would be waiting for me from Daddy. He had already left for the trolley depot by the time I sniffed peppery scrapple frying and ran downstairs before my little brother, Charles, ate the crusty bits I crave. Mom said he left early so he'd be home for my birthday.

Now my birthday is ruined.

What happens to a nun puncher? Suspension or expulsion? I bow my head and squeeze my eyes shut, hoping God and I remain on speaking terms. There's only one way to find out:

Me: Dear God, Almighty Father, our Lord, sweet Jesus, I am so sorry! You know I did not mean for any of this to happen. Save me, please!

God: I know, my child. I will make it all go away.

Me: In time for my birthday party? It's only a few hours away. Bonnie is coming over. Fix it, please! I'll go to church every Sunday, and I'll be on time. Promise!

God: Stop pushing your luck. You struck a holy woman. You must suffer the consequences. I will save you from being suspended and expelled, and allow you to get your birthday gifts. Say ten Hail Marys, apologize for your transgressions, and really mean it.

Me: Thank you, God.

Opening my eyes, the bright lights in the office of doom make me blink. Hope that filled me seconds ago gushes out like air escaping a punctured tire. God knows what I feel. It's the fiery knot of anger that balled up my fist. Something burns in my chest, too. I am furious at Sister for hurting me in places I cannot see. I seesaw between anger and guilt.

It doesn't help that in the hour it takes Mom to arrive, I freak myself out from all of the punishments I imagine await me if I'm expelled.

When Mom appears in the doorway, her mouth is a thin line. Someone is about to get a verbal beat-down. I hope it's not me.

"Come out in the hallway, Roberta," Mom demands, holding the door open.

The aide, typing with her back to us, turns around. "She can't leave until Mother Superior sees her." Her tone is appropriate for a student or clueless sub, not for my mother.

Mom arches an eyebrow and tilts her head as if she misheard. "I don't need anyone's permission to speak with my daughter. I am Dora Forest and you are . . .?"

The aide pushes her glasses up. "I'm sorry, I didn't know she's your daughter."

No headline news there. My caramel complexion, super thick hair and full lips have nothing in common with Mom's sharp features, ivory skin, and wavy, sandy hair. People are often surprised to learn she is Black. She's quick to set them straight.

I shuffle into the hallway and widen my eyes to look innocent.

"What the Sam Hill is going on? I take off to get your phone connected, and you're up here acting like a fool. Boxing nuns?" She throws her hands up. "You know I had to fight to get you and your brother in here. Now, you may get expelled! Then what? You're not setting foot in any public school with those gangs, fights, and fast girls. We'll ship your butt down South."

My Uncle Wayne's tired, dusty farm? *What?*

"Sister is prejudiced. She told me to go back to Africa! Then slapped me three times." My voice gets tangled in the web of hurt lining my throat. "I defended myself."

"She said *what?*" Mom leans in to hear better.

I share the ordeal with Mom, whose stony expression crumbles with every word.

The aide pokes her head out into the hall, motions that the principal is ready.

"I wonder if your father was called?" Mom says.

In the office we sit and face Mother Superior, who looks at me with disappointment. "I'm sorry Mr. Forest could not join us as we discuss this serious infraction."

Mom's shoulder jerks. "Did you call him at work?"

"We were informed that he's off today."

Mom's eyes narrow. Daddy took off at the last minute for my birthday, I figure.

Mother Superior faces me. "Did you or did you not strike Sister Elizabeth?"

Her question stings like more slaps. I'm not sure what happened. I didn't mean to. *Right?*

Unwilling to wait for me to squeak out a response, she turns to Mom. "As you know, hitting a member of our faculty can result in expulsion."

"Roberta will be punished." Mom speaks in a formal tone she uses when controlling her temper in public. "But Sister Elizabeth smacked my daughter three times after telling her to go back to Africa in front of the entire class. Will she be reprimanded as well?"

We wait in uneasy silence until Mother Superior clears her throat. "Sister Elizabeth was pushed too far by your impudent daughter. Roberta has a tendency to be too prideful and mouthy."

Mom turns to me, anger knotting her face. "Go wait out in the office."

Twenty minutes later Mom exits the office, a half-smiling Mother Superior on her heels.

Our principal takes me by the shoulders. "Your mother wants the best for you. I can't say that for all our . . . students. However, this is serious and I have no recourse."

I stare at my damp shoes, heart thumping in my ears and sweat pooling behind my knees.

"I'm suspending you for three days and you have a week of detention."

I'm so relieved I could do a *Soul Train* split. But then an instant twitch kicks in and I go back to feeling turned inside out. After suspension, then what? There's no escaping Sister, who teaches two of my advanced classes.

Outside, approaching Mom's car, I ask, "Why didn't you talk to Sister Elizabeth?"

"Apparently, she's not feeling well. We'll meet tomorrow. I'm ready to read her the riot act, so waiting is probably a blessing in disguise."

Right on, Mom! Closing the door, I reach for the radio dial. Mom smacks my hand away.

"Ouch! What's that for?"

"Hit another teacher, and I'll knock you out, hear? You're not grown."

"Wait! What did I say that was wrong to get slapped and humiliated?"

"It's not what you said today, it's your behavior lately. Mother Superior said Sister had planned to call us about your conduct. Again."

Blood rushes to my face. "I thought you were on my side. I should have known."

"Call Bonnie on the house phone. Tell her she can't come over. You're on punishment."

"Huh?"

"I didn't stutter. And I told you about saying 'huh.'"

We ride in silence until Mom parks by the supermarket. She rushes to the hardware store down the block.

After a few minutes she returns with a small paper bag. Opening it, I squint at a padlock tiny enough for a jewelry box. I refuse to ask what it's for. It doesn't matter.

Sister makes my spirit groan. Mom can't hear it, but Daddy will.

<hr>

I sulk on my bedroom floor with Daddy's *Autobiography of Malcolm X* on one side and the be-all and end-all of all phones on the other. It's perfection in a bubble gum shade with a dial pad doubling as a nightlight. And here I sit, unable to rap with Bonnie, my bestie, about my life yo-yoing out of control.

Sighing, I pick up Daddy's book with a holy card of the Virgin Mary sticking out of it, my makeshift bookmark. Suspension means I'm free to read it all day tomorrow. How ironic that Malcolm X also had an encounter with his racist eighth-grade teacher. I recently read that he was the only Black student in his class back in the day when racist monsters roamed unchecked, before Black Power and all. No wonder he became so militant. His book is unlike anything I've read. His autobiography electrifies my mind and sets my soul on fire. And I'm just on the second chapter.

I slide the book back under my bed and peek into the hall. Mom's on the phone with the door shut. Closing mine, I use a pillow to muffle my dialing of a number I've called since age four.

"At the tone, the time will be 3:15 and 20 seconds," a voice says. My alarm clock is right. At the beep, I hang up. Never has a secret one-sided conversation pleased me more.

A car door slamming draws me to the window with a grin. *Daddy's here, finally.* Instead, a stranger inspects a tire on his station wagon parked in my father's spot.

Chest tightening, I grab my poetry book. Just the crinkly sound of turning pages to a blank one starts to relax me. Before I know it, working on a poem has me breathing easier. An hour later, I've found the right rhymes after counting meters on my fingers.

If God is our father, aren't I his child?
One to be embraced, not slapped and reviled
I'm not a science experiment gone wrong
with bushy hair you see as ugly and wild
If you're married to Jesus
aren't I your child?
Sister, before answering, I must say
there were awful lessons I learned today
My soul is scraped like a bike without a kickstand
after you tried to slap me into no-man's land
You just proved you're a two-faced, religious crank
who thinks answers to some questions are best
left blank

The last line fills me up. Writing is my superpower. Just like that, I no longer feel misunderstood or misheard. I'm shiny and sure—the confident and smart me.

In front of my mirror, I pretend I'm reading in class. A portable 8-track tape player blasts an oldie: "Say It Loud, I'm Black and I'm Proud." Sister's eyes twitch as the class claps to the beat. I turn the music down and all motion stops. Shoulders back, head high, voice loud, I read, "If God is our father, isn't hating and slapping—"

The door opens, bumping my big behind back to reality. Mom barges in without knocking as usual, her lips heavy with fresh attitude.

"I'm reading a poem," I say, "not talking on the phone."

Ignoring me, she studies the finger wheel of the phone. Suddenly, she whips out that shrunken padlock and hooks it around the first finger hole of the dial pad, clicking it shut. I can't make a call now, even if I were that sneaky. Shocked, I drop my poem.

"Glad I didn't get the new push button version," Mom mumbles.

"It's my birthday! That's so unfair!"

She turns in the doorway. "You forget you came close to being expelled?"

When her feet hit the squeaky floorboard at the bottom of the stairs, I run in the hall. I yell, "Swear to God, I can't wait for Daddy to get home!" Then I kick my door shut.

After that, I spill my sorrows to my well-worn diary until shortly before dinner.

My homemade chocolate cake begs my fingers to dip into its gooey icing. But Mom, adding shrimp to a frying pan of popping Crisco, shoos me away. The phone rings.

"Hello. This is Mrs. Forest."

I leave to set the dining room table. Charles is already waiting with a comic book. Minutes pass. Clearly, the caller is clueless it's my birthday, as messed up as it is.

I peep into the kitchen. Spatula mid-air, Mom stands rock still.

"So awful. Please call when you know more." Mom hangs up and casts a hard sideways glance at me.

Gripping the messy spatula, Mom plops in her dining room seat. She fails to notice the grease dripping on our special occasion tablecloth. Charles gapes at Mom's odd look.

"It won't stop." Mom's bottom lip quivers. She drops the spatula. "That was Rita McNabb. She heard Sister Elizabeth went to the hospital an hour ago. Sister Elizabeth," Mom swallows hard, "had a massive heart attack. She may not make it."

Thou shall not kill.

The Sixth Commandment pops in my head and turns my skin clammy.

I whirl around. My world looks the same, only a bit hazy. My eyes sting at the sight of my second-place writing awards in Mom's prized cherry curio in the living room.

The distant wail of an ambulance twists my stomach.

The thought of me as a possible felon makes it hard for us to breath. Charles can't stop coughing. Smoke rushing from the kitchen knocks Mom out of her state of shock.

Fanning the scorched air, she bolts into the kitchen before a grease fire makes my birthday a bona fide real-life horror movie.

CHAPTER 3

We race toward the kitchen windows, raising them as high as they can go. We wave dish towels to fan the smoke outside until Charles's hacking coughs force Mom to shoo us away.

In the dining room, I stare at a Creamsicle sky. The sun is running out of time. *Am I?*

Behind me, plates clink against the table. I wait for Mom to get the cherry Kool-Aid I mixed earlier before sitting. Her anger I'm used to; her quiet terror, not so much.

I sit across from Charles at the table now missing Mom's plate. Wish I could skip dinner. Slumped over like thirsty plants, we pick at our food. *So much for my last supper.*

Ignoring me, Mom sets the pitcher down. I feel lower than an earthworm.

"I hope you're not arrested," Charles says after Mom leaves.

"Don't be silly," I sniff, watching my arm hairs rise at the idea of leaving in handcuffs. The screen door opening startles me. I jump. *Are the cops here already?*

The front door swings open. In walks Daddy. He'll wrestle King Kong to keep me from being fingerprinted or thrown into a reform school with heathens.

"What's burning?" Nose scrunched, Daddy carries a gift-wrapped box roomy enough to hold a record player. He sets the box down and drops his keys on top. I sprint into his arms as Mom rushes over, newly energized like a toy with fresh batteries.

"Happy birthday," he says, kissing my cheek. I study his smooth chocolate face, dark happy eyes, and new mustache. Like me, his smile reveals a right dimple. Seeing him happy and handsome in his blue and gray SEPTA public transportation uniform makes it feel like my birthday.

Mom zaps the magical moment. "Chuck, talk to her. Motor mouth almost got expelled for getting into it with a nun, who," she rubs her forehead, "I just learned had a heart attack."

Daddy's dimple disappears in slow motion. He freezes. Shame, along with my father, grips me.

"How can they blame Roberta for that?" Daddy removes his arm from my waist.

"Sister slapped me, and I sort of hit her back in self-defense," I mumble.

"What? You struck your teacher?" Dad starts to unloop his belt.

Mom wedges herself between us. In thirteen years, I've only been whipped with a belt a handful of times because Mom did not want us beaten like she had been. "Adults should never touch a child when angry," she would always say, her eyes fierce and distant.

"Hold on," she said now. "You'd have known if you'd gone to work. The school called you first."

An odd tic flickers across Daddy's face. "I did go to work."

Mom does a double-take. Guilt covers his face like Noxzema covers mine at night. Something weird between them hangs in the air like burnt toast.

Dad turns to me. "Why were you fighting your teacher?"

"Roberta called the slave-owning Thomas Jefferson a hypocrite," Mom says.

"And what's incorrect about that?"

"Let me finish?" Mom huffs. "Sister didn't like her answer and told her to go back to Africa." Mom pinches her lips. "Then she proceeded to slap the crap out of her three times."

Daddy flicks the light on, studies my cheek. It's not sore but I wince as he rubs it.

"Is that what happened?" His tender tone reminds me how raw I still am.

"Yup." Tears well.

"The nun set her up," he snorts. "What other answer suffices? I told you that damn place was full of nut jobs. I'm going there, right now."

"Going where? The damned school is closed!" Mom screams.

"I'm going to the damn convent!" Daddy hollers, grabbing his keys off my gift box.

"I'm going with you." Mom snatches her pocketbook from the coffee table.

"Will Roberta be arrested?" Charles asks, jumping up.

"No!" they scream, rushing out the door and slamming it.

Charles cries, his tears mixing with a gooey stream of snot, which knots up my stomach. I slouch next to him, understanding his bewilderment. An almost fire. An almost fight between our parents. A sister headed to the pokey for possible murder. Having just mastered the multiplication tables, this is all too much for Charles. It was for me, too.

"Is this what happens when you become a teenager?" he asks, rubbing his eyes.

"I hope not. September 26, 1973, is going down in history as the worst day of my life." My head thumps like a drum on a party record.

"We didn't even sing 'Happy Birthday'!" Charles says, wiping his eyes. "Want me to call Bonnie and tell her to call on your new phone? It still works, you just can't dial out."

What a great little brother. I nod. If anyone can make me smile, it's Bonnie Haley, my gossipy best friend since she arrived in second grade and kept me from being the only Black girl in class.

"Eat the rest of my shrimp," I offer to reward him, scribbling my number on the *TV Guide* cover. In the kitchen, I cover Daddy's plate in aluminum foil and stick it in the fridge, then cut a fat wedge of cake to chow on in bed. "Call her now," I say, licking my fingers and zipping upstairs. Bonnie, whose popularity thankfully rubs off on me, can sort through this confusion.

Waiting for her call, I alternate between gorging myself with cake and picking the lock on my phone with a bobby pin the way it's done on TV. I stop when the phone rings.

"Girl, it's a wild house over here," I shout. "Guess you heard what happened."

"Yup. So you drove Sister Elizabeth over the edge. Short trip, right?" Bonnie snort-chuckles. "I would have pulled off her habit so we could see she's bald."

"Bonnie, Sister Elizabeth had a heart attack not long after—"

"Girl, stop playing!" Bonnie interrupts.

"She might not make it!" My voice cracks. I death-grip the phone.

"You don't think it's your fault, do you?" Bonnie squeals. "She's about forty. Old people have heart issues. Something's wrong because she falls asleep. That's not normal."

"If something bad happens, I might get expelled or worse."

"Look, let's pray for a miracle," Bonnie says.

"Dear God—"

"If we had that Black nun with the Afro this wouldn't have happened," Bonnie interrupts.

"You're the only one who has seen—" A car door slams. Peering out my shade, I spot my newest neighbor. "Gotta go! If Mom calls from a pay phone and gets a busy signal, I'm dead."

"Girl, Sister is too mean to die. Happy birthday! I'm sorry Sister ruined it. Later."

"Later." I white knuckle the phone long after the line goes dead.

I felt better until she said "die." I eyeball my flowery wallpapered room with glossy pinups of Michael Jackson, Kevin Hooks, Foster Sylvers, and other famous crushes, maybe for the last time.

Dropping the phone in its cradle, I flop against my bed with palms pressed. "Dear God, please let Sister Elizabeth live. I swear I'll never ask for another favor."

Churning in my stomach forces me to sit up. Great, I'm nauseated on top of it all.

"Daddy will fix it," I say to my Michael Jackson poster. I imagine Michael nods. My father has the gift of gab with women. I guess his charm works on nuns, too. But what if Daddy is too late? What if Sister dies?

Mom says God hears you better when you're on your knees. I kneel.

"Dear God, forget the hot pants and the Schwinn 10-speed for Christmas. All I want is for Sister Elizabeth to live and not get expelled. I—"

A car door closing stops me. Out my window, Daddy strolls ahead of Mom with quick, long strides.

Is Sister hospitalized or heaven bound? Or in purgatory? *God, I did not mean that in a bad way.* I feel clammy and dizzy.

The front door slams. I dive into bed and bury my head, faking sleep. My stomach hula hoops as heavy footsteps rush upstairs.

"Roberta, get up," Daddy shouts. "You need to hear this!"

His grim face tells me the verdict. My stomach heaves as if I just rode a roller coaster in an endless loop. The bedroom spins. I clutch my woozy belly.

"Daddy, I'm sick! I need to go to the bathroom."

I try to push past him, but he grabs my arm and pulls me close.

"Sister Elizabeth is . . ." He stops, as I lean over and spew chunks of shrimp and birthday cake down one leg of his trolley uniform and all over the pile of dirty clothes on the floor Mom told me to pick up days ago.

He grabs the wastebasket, holds it under my gagging mouth. "What a terrible birthday for my baby."

Jesus, he still calls me his baby after what I've done?

"Dora," he yells downstairs. "Roberta is sick. Get some soup and tea going."

Mom races upstairs. She sidesteps my vomit and touches my forehead.

"What a day," Mom grunts, glaring at Daddy instead of me. "I'm not sure how much more I can take before I blow." She looks back at me. "You feel warm." When she leaves, her zombie shuffle is gone.

"Sister Elizabeth is fine. That nut who called is the one always blabbing to the weekly newspaper about the neighborhood going to pot. Why your mother would listen to her mystifies me. The ambulance was for another nun with chest pains. Sister Elizabeth went with her to the hospital."

I kiss his cheek. He pretend-gags. By the time I return from the bathroom, he had cleaned up my mess, and Mom had left steaming tea and soup on a TV tray. I promise my father I will never hit another adult no matter what.

Daddy leaves and returns, carrying my new record player, even though I can't play it until I'm off punishment. I'm grounded for a month, and my parents will ask for weekly reports. I'm so relieved Sister is alive, I don't feel that sorry for myself.

"You know you're stuck with her since she teaches Track 1 classes," Daddy says, examining his pant leg. "The first sign of trouble, tell us so we can address it. I'm not having anyone beating on my kids when I don't."

"So you and Mom are meeting with her, right?"

"Yes, indeed, tomorrow afternoon. We pay tuition, and if she has a problem teaching Black kids, we need to find a remedy."

"Daddy, she lied. This country needed Black people to help build it."

"Pumpkin, that won't be the last lie you'll hear. The Bible is full of them."

He reaches under my bed and pulls out his copy of *The Autobiography of Malcolm X*, which he spotted during Project Vomit Removal.

"I wondered where this was," he says, opening the book to my bookmarked page. "I had been rereading it until it disappeared. It's deep. Unclear about anything?"

"Nope. It's so good. I just read the part where his teacher called him a nigger."

"I remember that."

"Sister didn't call me that, but she implied it."

Daddy rubs his chin, which means he's about to drop some knowledge. "I am livid about what happened. She's the adult, and she lost control. Big time. But you have to control your temper, too. Technically, she could have filed charges. So promise me when someone angers you, count to ten and think hard before reacting. Cool heads think better than hot ones." He fingers his paperback. "Brother Malcolm said some of our best revolutionaries are teens. So speaking up matters," Daddy says. "I'm proud of your answer about Jefferson. Malcolm would've been, too."

His words and kiss comfort all of my hurting hidden places. Leaving, he presses the edges of the *Shirley Chisholm for President* bumper sticker on my door and turns.

"Happy birthday, dear Roberta," he sings, his rich voice soothing my heart. Then he says, "Happy thirteenth birthday to you, Pumpkin."

"Love you lots."
"Love you, too."

―――――――――――

Banging and yelling wakes me up.

"I'm not a toy. Don't play with me," a voice screams. "You're a liar, Chuck!"

I look out my window and gasp. Clothes rain down on Daddy's car parked beneath my window. Poking my head out, I see Mom's arms tossing it all out of their window. *What in the Sam Hill is going on?*

My parents spot my head at the same time. "Go to bed, Roberta!" they yell in stereo.

Fat chance. I jam my feet into slippers and zip down the steps and out the door. I run to my father, who holds an armful of clothes.

"Daddy, don't go!" I whisper. "Come inside, this is so embarrassing." Porch lights from other houses turn on. I realize I'm in my nightgown. I fold my arms across my braless chest.

"Roberta, we'll talk later. This is between grown folks. Go in the house."

I snatch up garments the wind has scattered from the curb to the middle of the block.

"Roberta!" he barks, "I said go in the house. Now!"

I shuffle a few steps then scamper back. "Is it my fault? Did I make you fight?"

Under the streetlight, his jawbones clench. He shakes his head, pecks my forehead.

"Roberta!" On the steps, Mom glares at me with a madwoman scowl. "Get in the house!"

Heading in, I spot a shoe in a shrub. I lay it on the landing. "Here's the other one."

Mom's head whips around like she needs an exorcism. I run into the house and go in Charles's room, expecting to find him crying. Instead, he smiles in his sleep.

The front door slams so I sprint into my room and close the door. Dad's car peeling away makes my throat feel like I swallowed a bowling ball.

I sniff my nightgown. I smell like shrimp, heartbreak, and failure. How can I sleep with a thunderstorm in my heart? *Is God punishing me for hitting Sister?*

It's 12:07 a.m. My birthday is gone. A new day begins and it promises to be as sucky as yesterday. My parents just had the worst fight ever. *Outside.* My gut tells me it involves Dad's whereabouts when school called. Isn't it obvious he took off to get my gift? So if they get a divorce, it all boomerangs to me by way of Sister Elizabeth, enemy No. 1, followed by Mom, enemy No. 2. Wait, scratch that. It's a tie for these two disgusting hypocrites.

CHAPTER 4

Anger, confusion, humiliation, and guilt pin me down in my twin bed. I can't move. Not that I have anywhere to go anyway.

I kick off the sheet and hope my funky feelings go with it. Can't spend time feeling sorry for myself when I need to figure out how to reunite my parents and pass eighth grade without getting expelled or arrested.

I just turned thirteen, and I feel old as fossil dirt. I'd give anything for a gigantic do-over—a normal birthday instead of a terror show at school and home. Instead, I'm a suspended nun-boxer with a tyrant as a mother and a missing father.

I click on my transistor radio. The new Concorde airplane broke a record yesterday by flying the fastest time nonstop from D.C. to Paris, the DJ says. I broke one, too: Most screw-ups achieved in a day.

Images pop into my head. Sister's rage. Mom's bark. Daddy's aching eyes. What was the common denominator? Me.

Daddy skipped work to buy my special gift and got caught in a white lie. So what? He likely got it hot from the barber shop since Mom always nags about his spending.

I'm floored at how Mom acted after my awful day at school. She never even sang "Happy Birthday."

I feel worn out and the morning is fresh.

"Roberta! Breakfast is ready." Smelling like pancakes, Mom stands in my doorway with droopy eyes. She's dressed in a white blouse and striped pants for her job helping people get on welfare. *Wish she'd help me.* She hurries away.

I raise the shade, peer out. Daddy found all his clothes in the dark. *Hurray!*

In the hallway, I nearly collide with Charles rushing from the bathroom smelling like Daddy. Inhaling the musky cologne pinpricks my heart. But I say, "I'm telling."

"Daddy said I could wear a little."

"Is he downstairs?" I whisper.

"Nope. Mommy said he left for work already."

"Go ask Mom what time Daddy left. I'll give you my lunch money."

He sprints downstairs as if his room is on fire. Leaning over the railing, I strain to hear. Normally Mom's loud, but now her words are hushed. *Hmmm.* I slam the door.

"I've a headache!" Mom yells from the kitchen. "Slam one more door, hear!"

I whip open the medicine cabinet door, stare at Dad's cologne.

Charles knocks. I crack the door. "Mommy said Daddy left before we got up."

"Get the dollar off my dresser."

Mom lied. I blink at myself in the mirror. My face is my father's except for a ski slope-shaped nose combining Mom's high bridge and his wide tip. Fury bubbles up in my throat like a hot pepper soda. I squeeze my eyes to keep the heaviness behind my lids.

Downstairs, Charles chews with his mouth open. Reading a paperback, Mom fails to notice. "Don't use the phone, go outside or have any company in this house," she tells me.

"Who would be home?" Sarcasm colors my voice.

Mom's head snaps up. I look away, and she resumes reading.

Turning toward Charles, Daddy's scent unsettles me, and everything goes gray. "What time did you say Daddy left this morning?"

Charles's eyes bug out. "I just told you upstairs Mommy said before we woke up."

"Oh, really?"

Mom aims her book at my head and scores. She leaps up and gets in my face, her forehead vein pulsing. I lean back so far I nearly tip the chair.

"Don't provoke me, Mouth Almighty."

"Am I supposed to sit here and pretend you didn't kick Daddy out last night?"

"I'm sick of your incessant back talking. Shut up. Now!" Turning to Charles, her voice and face instantly soften. Because he's her favorite. "We're taking a break. It doesn't mean we love you or your sassy sister any less."

Charles's face crumbles. That's no news to learn way before recess.

"We'll talk about it in the car." Mom turns to me. "One thing for certain and two things for sure, you are working my last good nerve."

They leave me all jumbled up like the *Soul Train* scramble board. I feel like tossing my clothes out the window. Instead, I dial my grandma.

"Praise God." Mom-Mom's sugary voice, one you can hear smiling, soothes my broken parts.

"Hi, Mom-Mom."

"Hi, lamb. You don't sound sick. Why are you home?"

"I got in trouble for fighting." The words tumble out before I can tug them back.

"Who hit you? A mean girl or hard-headed boy?

"Ummm, neither one."

"What? How can that be?" Mom-Mom's voice squeaks in confusion.

"I got into a fight with my teacher." I squeeze my eyes and hold my breath.

"Precious Lord, Father God!" she hollers. "What is happening to you?"

"Mom-Mom, my teacher is wicked unfair. I guess Daddy hasn't told you, yet. Is he there?"

"What? Isn't your father at work? Why would . . ." I hear rustling. I picture her grabbing one of her church fans since I upset her equilibrium. Daddy said it's delicate. "First, what do you mean you fought your teacher?"

I explain what happened.

"Africa? Will this keep you off the honor roll? How many days are you out?"

"I don't know and three days."

"Hot tot-tot-tot!" My sin has her speaking her holy ghost dancing language. "What's this about your father's whereabouts? My heart can't bear all this."

I give her a few details but edit the fight since one heart attack scare is enough. "Please don't tell Mom I told you," my voice breaks. "I'm in enough trouble."

"Telling the truth ain't easy, but you gotta do it." She blows her nose and coughs.

"You okay?"

"Yes. Fixing to ask the Holy Ghost to protect y'all. Call me later, lamb. Love you."

"Love you, too."

Heart thwacking in my throat, I hang up. I riled her up for nothing and still don't know where Daddy is staying. As we say in Spanish class, *No bueno*. I bolt into my room and grab my diary. I think best by writing, which is easy. It's like riding a bike. Where I end up often surprises me.

Not now. I stare at the blank page until tears dot it. Maybe that's all I need to say.

I turn to my Michael Jackson poster. His adoring chocolate eyes lock on mine. Can he see the cloud of failure following me? I press my hands together.

Me: Dear God, why am I in the middle of everything wrong?

The silence pokes holes in my gut. I look heavenward even though I can't see past the ceiling, where water spots resemble coffee stains.

Me: Are you there, God? It's me, Roberta. I need you badly.

I wait, heart open. Street traffic is all I hear.
Just when I think life can't get sadder, it does.

Reading the Malcolm X book beats out the game shows and soap operas I'd normally watch when not in school. I feel awakened from the inside out by this great leader. Unlike Dr. Martin Luther King Jr., he didn't believe in turning the other cheek. I so dig that.

Like me, Malcolm attended a predominantly white school. He was the only Black student in his class. Popular and smart, he was elected by his fellow students to be class president. While initially flattered, he considered his election tokenism. I recall my growing unease over the years when paraded around as a good example for my race at HSB. As the only Black second-grader in "smart classes," I gorged myself on sugary praises to fill up the emptiness that often gripped me. Whenever we lined up in pairs for recess, church, or to go just about anywhere, I stood alone. I listened to chatter about birthday parties I never was invited to.

When outgoing Bonnie showed up mid-way through the year, I clung to her like static on a slip. Honestly, we clung to each other. By the end of fourth grade, whenever teachers praised us for being articulate and able to "go to a Black college and do great things for your people," we responded with eye rolls. We knew they believed we weren't smart enough to attend a white college. Such slick talk sometimes came from classmates.

In sixth grade, Sam Burns, who I thought was cool, stood mere feet away from me in the schoolyard fussing with his pals about two "niggers" who dared to walk on his block. Everyone knew that word triggered an automatic fistfight.

"You nuts? Don't you see me standing here?" I huffed.

"You're not a nigger."

I cartoon blinked at his boldness. His friends snickered. "And you say it, again?" I scanned the yard for Bonnie, nowhere in sight. If I hit him and his pals jumped in, I was toast. Stomach knotting, I moved nose-close with a dead-eyed stare and rapid hold-me-back breathing, a winning combo for quashing beefs with most white kids. Mom called it selling wolf tickets you hope your butt won't have to cash. "Take it back!"

Sam swallowed hard and the fire in his eyes went out. *Whew.*

"Blacks and nig—" Beet-cheeked, he licked his lips. "The meanings are different."

Henry, who walked with a scaredy-cat hunch, tugged him away.

"What's the difference?" someone yelled when the group moved a few yards away.

Sam cupped his mouth and shouted, "My dad says Blacks know how to act."

At dinner, when I told Daddy about the incident, his mouth twitched.

"Racism is racism like a rose is a rose. Calling it by another name won't change it. Saying you're different, you're not like other Blacks, that's just complimentary racism."

"Like when white people say I'm articulate?"

"Nothing slow about my Pumpkin," he gloated. "You'll never hear a white person call another white person articulate. I'm not knocking being articulate, but some compliments fool you into thinking you're something you're not. Some doors I can't walk in no matter how articulate I am. Your generation? Get your toe in and knock 'em down."

So sad teen Malcolm's dad wasn't alive to give him advice. If he had, Malcolm may have graduated high school and become a lawyer despite what his teacher said.

I reread a paragraph Daddy underlined at the end of the first chapter about Malcolm lacking mercy for a society that unfairly squashes people and then punishes them for being unable to bear the weight.

⎯⎯⎯

That's what happened to me yesterday. Sister saw me as a rebel who needed punishing. Would she feel the same way if I wore my hair pressed and curled like it used to be? I saw the way she frowned at this book the other day. Did she consider Malcolm a radical threat? Did she fear what I would learn? Then I better read more!

I get a soda from the fridge and resume reading about white people who flocked to Harlem at night to watch Black entertainers perform. I bet my allowance they wouldn't want any of them as neighbors, no matter how talented. Seems white folks feel like they've done something wrong if they live next to us. White families in droves are moving out of our parish as more Black families move in. *Love thy neighbor.* Guess the second commandment is too hard. *Hypocrites.*

I brush Tastykake crumbs off the book that should top Holy St. Bridget's reading list. Malcolm evolved from a criminal into an incredible leader despite a terrible childhood. Racists murdered his father. His mother ended up in a mental institution, which broke up his family. He briefly lived with foster parents until he moved in with family in Boston. Malcolm is a real life "Metamorphosis," a much more interesting one than the guy who wakes up as a cockroach in a short story by Franz Kafka.

I'm eager to rap about what I'm learning with Daddy. I set the book aside. At this rate, I'll finish too soon. The worst thing about a good book is turning the last page.

Besides, I've tons of homework to do, including reading the short story "The Ones Who Walk Away from Omelas" by Ursula K. LeGuin for Mr. Harvey's class. But I'm inspired. I reach for my poetry book. I write:

Fill me with wonder,
Shake me like thunder
With your different way of thinking
So bold, Black, and unblinking
Our greatest preacher
My first Black teacher

The title pops in my head. Smiling, I jot at the top: "Dear Malcolm."

The grandfather clock chimes. Spanish is next. A pang of longing kicks in. Then dread. It's bad enough I have Sister for religion and history, but homeroom, too? One that has the fewest Black students. Shy Clyde, spacy Karen, fraidy cat Stephanie, and quiet Vietta, who tries hard to go unnoticed with an eye-catching skin condition. Her fudge complexion has splashes of white skin, like someone erased the coloring around her lips, cheek and hands. People bullied her when she came to our school last year, but Bonnie ended that.

Bonnie would have stood up for me, too. Man, I miss having her in my classes.

I flip to the calendar in the back of my speckled copy-book. Eleven weeks remain until Christmas. In the living room, I snatch the glossy Christmas catalogue buried under an avalanche of *Ebony* magazines on the coffee table. Chuckling at the heap not spilling over, I rip out the pages with the white 10-speed, which will make my life complete, and a green plaid jumper perfect to wear to the awards ceremony to accept my first-place writing prize. Zooming upstairs, I slip them into my mirror's edge as reminders, when picking out my 'fro, about why I need to chill if Sister Elizabeth drives her danger train nonstop to my desk.

CHAPTER 5

A tired-looking Daddy arrives with Chinese food, a Sister Elizabeth update, and the newspaper, which I grab from under his arm.

"So she apologized for her comments at our meeting," he says, lining up several cartons of food on the dining room table. "Her brother was rushed to the ER the night before, and she said she was up all night. I told her that was no excuse," he pauses as Charles hands us a paper plate, "for what she said or how she acted."

Listening hard, I pass around the egg rolls and grab a carton of shrimp fried rice. Daddy isn't sounding as mad as I imagined.

"I can tell she's a piece of work. She didn't look so saintly when I told her she overreacted to hearing the truth from my smart daughter." He laughs and I join him, relieved he gets what I'm dealing with.

"What did Mom say?"

"Her work schedule changed. She'll meet with her later."

My face falls along with all hope in the free world. I can't even fake the funk. Mom meeting with Sister Elizabeth is a gathering of Benedict Arnolds.

Daddy gives me a weary once-over. "Stop fretting. Your mom will handle her. Let's eat and then we'll talk. Gotta make a call first." He heads upstairs with his plate.

Picking at shrimp fried rice, I read my horoscope in the newspaper. It says my talents will help solve a problem. *Yeah, right.* Scanning the headlines, I see a fourteen-year-old boy was stabbed outside a public school not far from us. The gang problem is growing in the city. Mom says when it hits closer to home, we're out. The last thing I want is to move to the corny Black suburbs.

Charles bangs the table. "Earth to Roberta, come in, come in."

"What?" I snap.

"Daddy called you. He wants to talk about," he whispers, "you know what."

"I'm the oldest. Why am I going first?" I snap a fortune cookie in half.

"I'm still eating," he whines.

The fortune reads, "Your win will solve everything." Reading the white strip in my hands, my brain and body tingle. I perk up like I always do when I'm on the verge of a good idea.

I push my plate to Charles. "Yours if you go first."

Charles zips upstairs, leaving me to mull over my messages and try to make sense of them. I rush to the curio cabinet in the corner of the living room, our favorite spot to pose for photos because it's always neat, and remove my second-place plaques from writing contests won in sixth and seventh grade.

They glimmer in the sunlight streaming through the porch. Rubbing my fingers across "Roberta Forest" engraved in the brass nameplates removes the cobwebs of ick trapping me since the fight with Sister. I see myself again. If one thing is certain and two things are for sure, I am the answer to the problems I caused. I *know* how to reunite my parents and prove to Sister

Elizabeth I'm smarter than she thinks. I'll win the eighth-grade writing contest if it's the last thing I do. It's meant to be. Why else would two separate messages say the same thing? Daddy has a cool expression: "Same suit, different tailor."

"Your turn," Charles says.

I practically skip into my room. Leaning against the window sill, he turns. He looks tired. My bed creaks when we both sit on it.

"Wish I could spend more time with you two but I got a double shift."

"Why don't you take a nap?" *I won't tell.* Something flickers in his eyes. Sadness? *Man, I can't stand Mom.*

"I'm glad your brother didn't see," he gestures at the window, "all that foolishness last night. You, okay?" He rubs my cheek, and suddenly I'm undone. The cockiness rediscovered minutes ago vanishes and my deepest fear comes clean.

"Are you two going to dddi . . . vorce?" Saying that horrible word makes the possibility of it more real, which makes me collapse into a bawling heap. Lately, pain clings to me like gum on a shoe.

"Ssssh, no one wants a . . . that." Daddy avoids my word. "I'm not going anywhere." He pats my eyes dry with his hanky. "Focus on getting along with that nun and winning—" Angling his head, he snaps his fingers. "When's that contest?"

My heavy heart lightens up with a quickness. The hope that fortune cookie and horoscope gave me minutes ago balloons back. Daddy mentioning the writing contest is no coincidence.

"February and I'm taking gold this year," I chirp. "First place or nada."

Grinning, he stands and stretches. "I can see it." He snaps photos of me with an imaginary camera as I pageant wave. "Even if you take third or get an honorable mention, we'll be there rooting."

"We?"

Daddy tilts his head as if he misheard. "Your family, what other we is there, silly?"

"W-e doesn't work without y-o-u. When are you coming home?"

Daddy looks down at the floor then back at me with bright eyes. "Soon. We had a disagreement that blew up. Our biggest problem yesterday should have been stomachaches from too much cake." He flashes a dimpled smile. His eyes say everything will work out. "I'm sorry you saw us acting like that. I love your mother. Call me at Uncle Jimmy's if you need me."

That's where he is. My stomach stops feeling like a pretzel.

We step into the hall and find Charles sitting on the top step, clearly eavesdropping.

"Find a movie you two want to see this weekend." Daddy hugs us at the bottom of the staircase.

Squeezing his waist, I realize winning a first-place medal four months from now will do more than prove I'm the best writer in eighth grade. It's the ticket to reuniting us. And proving to Sister my words matter.

We follow Daddy outside, where he says he'll stop by tomorrow and check on us.

"Yay," I say, "because we didn't talk about Malcolm X. I'm learning tons."

"There's a documentary about him that was nominated for an Academy Award last year," Daddy says. "It's at Uncle Duke's community center next month. Maybe we can go."

"I'd love that." I beam at him.

He slides into his Roadrunner, honks twice, and drives off. I vow that when he stops by tomorrow, I'll work up the courage to ask what happened. Bet he tells me to keep what he says between us. We have other secrets. What's one more?

Mom walks in minutes later. She probably waited until Daddy drove off.

"Daddy just left. How long is he staying at Mom-Mom's?"

She shrugs, hands me the newspaper. I trail her into the dining room as she glances at mail. Her blank expression when I mention my father bothers me.

"How long is he staying at Mom-Mom's?" I repeat.

"I don't know." She pauses to cast a side long glance. "Why didn't you ask him?"

"He's not staying with Mom-Mom."

She crosses her arms. "So why ask questions when you know the answers?"

I swallow the scream forming in my throat. "What did Sister Elizabeth say?"

"That you have a tendency to be mouthy, which I know to be true."

"I did nothing wrong. I honestly answered her question. You see how big she—"

Mom shushes me with a raised finger. "We spoke by phone. I couldn't leave work."

"Oh! My! God! You *have* to meet her face to face to see what I'm dealing with."

"I made my point. There will be no round two." She frowns at Daddy's newspaper spread out on the table.

"What's Uncle Jimmy's number again?"

"Why do you need it?"

"To call Daddy."

Mom's shoulders tense. "It's at work. He changed it. I'll give it to you tomorrow."

She's a few feet away but it feels like we are worlds apart. Mom clears her throat.

"What your father and I are dealing with is grown folks' business." Her eyes narrow. "So stay in a child's place, nosey. I told you to stay off the phone, motor mouth."

"You told me to stay off *my* phone."

"You'll be on punishment until you stand on your head and spit wooden nickels."

Her ridiculous sayings rival Sister Elizabeth's. Talking to her is as useless as eating soup with a fork. She hates when I suck my teeth so I do it super loud and hurry away, taking comfort in knowing she's freshly annoyed.

The next day I sleep until mid-morning because I can.

For hours after I wake up, I lose myself in Malcolm's fascinating story until I crave a sugar rush.

I head out (after being careful to take the phone off the hook), passing row houses dotted with "For Sale" signs. Above me, telephone wires bear several old sneakers and a few gray rubbernecking pigeons. I cross the street to avoid bird crap dropping in my hair. Dad calls pigeons "rats of the sky."

Mr. Hostetler's face lights up when I enter the basement candy store. Even though the Hostetlers smell like mothballs mixed with lotion, we dig them. They were the first white neighbors to welcome us when we moved in. How long their store remains open is unclear. Their family wanted them to move like yesterday since most of their customers are Black kids.

"My sweet Roberta, school let out half a day?"

"I had an upset stomach. I feel better." With their old hearts, fibbing works best.

I get butterscotch Tastykakes and Mallo Cups. I hand him a dollar, but he winks.

"Thank you, Mr. Hostetler."

"Feel better, Roberta. Tell your parents I said hello."

I hurry home and hang up the phone so calls can get through. It rings. It's Mom. Perfect timing.

"Get your father's suitcase ready. He'll swing by."

"Mom, when do you think—"

"I'll bring pretzels home for dessert," she says, cutting me off. "See you soon."

Then Daddy calls. "Hey, Pumpkin." He exhales, and I picture the cigarette in his fingers. "I'm working double shifts. I'll pick up my suitcase when I take y'all to the movies. Okay?"

"Okay." I try to swallow questions bubbling up. About being Black and Catholic. About divorce. About Malcolm. About what to do when your heart thunders. I chew my lip, but the most pressing question slips out. "What happened?"

A deep sigh follows his quiet breathing. "You know better than to ask me that." His tone is clipped like with Mom sometimes. It pushes me away. "I gotta go. Listen to your mom. Love you!"

"Love you, too."

The calls ends, but I stare at the receiver's greasy holes, wishing they offered clues.

My parents' marriage is a lot like Bible stories. The details don't make sense. Mom nags Daddy, who always works overtime, about money so much that she now works. That infuriates him since he says her job is to stay home. But two paychecks don't seem enough.

During one fight that forced me to turn up *The Brady Bunch*, Mom screamed that we better not get the lights turned off again and reminded Daddy we had no heat for a week. She didn't mention if he was gambling on card games.

Daddy stayed with Mom-Mom after fights. But not always. I overheard Mom on the phone say she drove over there one night while we slept. His car wasn't there. She also said she's hiding money just in case. In case of what, I do not know.

Lies and secrets, like the holy spirit Mom-Mom sent through prayer, fill our house.

CHAPTER 6

I'm nervous about returning to class tomorrow. Unable to discuss it with Daddy who stays working, Mom will have to do. But as soon as I step into the kitchen, she sends me to the store for detergent.

Heading toward the avenue I recall how I landed on Sister's hit list long before, on the third day of school. Thinking back to that day gives me a stitch in my side.

That day, I ran into the schoolyard, which was empty except for Stephanie sporting two fluffy Afro puffs. Her hair looked like two servings of brown cotton candy attached to her head.

"Love it." I squeezed a springy puff. It bounced back to its original afrotastic shape.

"Mom did it," Stephanie said. "She was in a good mood after trashing her girdles."

We giggled like first-graders as we rushed inside and took the stairs two at a time.

"I never want to wear one, even though my butt is big," I said, chuckling.

"You have a cute shape," Stephanie said fingering her right puff. "I tried to wear an Afro, but my hair won't stand up in the middle."

"Your hair is pretty like that." Her stick figure required no comment. "I'm sick of my press and curl," I said as we round the landing. "I had an Afro this summer. Boys called me *fine*. White folks said my hair was soft..." I giggled. "...like cotton."

Stephanie chuckled wryly along with me. "I bet it was pretty. You have good hair. So what—" Two seventh-grade boys racing up the steps nearly knocked Stephanie over. But so could a hearty breeze.

"Girl, you better stand up for yourself."

"Boys are stupid, I don't care," Stephanie said. "Whatcha do over the weekend?"

"My dad took us to the drive-in. We saw *Billy Jack*."

"You like it?"

"Yup, except when Charles farted in 3-D. Girl, it was a struggle to breathe!"

We laugh as I remember the worst part of the night that had started with Daddy whacking the metallic box attached to his window.

"The speaker is real raggedy," he said as it hissed and crackled.

Mom frowned at the speaker and fished out a cigarette and a pack of matches. She was about to strike a match when Dad whipped out his lighter and lit the end of her Salem.

"Look at you! Listening to all these no-men-having women libbers killing chivalry," Daddy said. "You used to wait for me to light your cigarette. Don't want men opening doors, pulling out chairs, treating you well." He shook his head.

Charles and I rolled our eyes. We knew this argument well.

Mom blew a cloud of smoke that took its time exiting. "I do want that, but I need you to help me carry the load, pay bills. How about that?"

"Daddy, can you turn up the volume?" I asked.

"I guess next you'll be telling me you're going back to school," Daddy snorted.

"And?" Mom softened her tone. "You know I wanted to teach."

"Mom, I didn't know that," I said, leaning forward. "What happened?"

"You!" she said.

Full-throated laughter filled the car. It didn't last because Daddy continued. "I say, 'Hey, let's take the kids, do something fun as a family.' But," he thumped the steering wheel, "you just have to put a hard-working brother down."

"Chuck, you started this nonsense over *me* not waiting for *you* to light *my* cigarette."

Charles gave me a do-something nudge. "People are staring!"

I slumped.

"I'm doing the best I can," Dad said, pausing to light his own cigarette. "We have a roof over our heads, three meals a day, two cars, kids in private school—"

"Which reminds me. Tuition payment is late, the one you were *supposed* to pay last month," Mom said. "We keep being late, and they will kick us off the payment plan."

"Stop listening to women talking about not needing a man. I take care of mine."

"That and a dime gives me a whopping ten cents," Mom muttered.

Daddy responded by slapping the steering wheel and accidentally honking the horn.

"Nothing I do is good enough!" Daddy yelled.

"Lower your voice," Mom hissed.

"I will say what I want, how I want and when I want. None of these damn people pay my bills!" Daddy glared at Mom and the air sizzled. Then he turned to us. "Popcorn?"

"Yes!" We responded with relief.

Slamming the door, he made the speaker work. We watched the film in silence.

I told Stephanie a happier version. We beat the late bell and entered homeroom smiling. At my then front-row desk by the door, I removed from my book bag textbooks in glossy covers instead of grocery bags cut to fit. Everything felt new-school-year fresh.

I peered over at Sister to see if she still looked like her feet hurt when I noticed that she looked more pained than usual while watching Stephanie load books into her desk.

Later, in history class, Sister kept eyeballing Stephanie as if she stole something.

"When you get your pop quizzes back, most of you will be rendered speechless by your dismal performance. I suspect your brains went to mush over the summer."

I aced it so I asked to be excused.

Returning from the lavatory, I wasted time retying my shoe outside the class door. That's when I hear Stephanie whine, "I like my hair this way."

In full Nancy Drew mode, I pulled my thick curls back and peeked into the classroom.

"Why do you want to look like the least common denominator?" Sister asked. She towered over Stephanie, who looked like she was melting into her desk. "You're a pretty girl, but that hairstyle is not becoming?"

Maybe it was from reading Malcolm X's book, which I had just started. Maybe I felt bolder with the record number of Black students this year, about 300 out of 1,200. Maybe it was Stephanie shrinking at being told her beautiful hair was anything but.

Breathing fast, I rushed in and blurted out, "Her hair has nothing to do with the least common denominator. Our natural hair is beautiful."

Sister cupped one hand behind an ear. "Excuse me? Was I addressing you?"

"I'm just saying—"

"That you eavesdropped on a conversation that," she glanced around the room, "as students like to say, was between A and B, so C your way out."

"Good one, Sister," Geoffrey said.

Laughter from the class set my jaw on edge. I slid into my desk, cheeks warm at Sister's effort to be hip at my expense.

I raised my hand. Sister looked skeptical as she nodded for me to speak.

"Is there a rule against wearing our hair the way we want to?"

"No, as long as it's clean and you don't impede your classmates' view."

The next day I showed up with my humongous Afro, which is what got me reassigned to the back of the class and put me squarely in Sister's crosshairs.

Thinking about Sister's antics almost gets me hit by a car on the way back from the store.

I wait until we do kitchen chores to express my fears. "I'm worried what Sister Elizabeth may do to me," I blurt out as I sweep up Charles's crumbs. "What answer do you think she expected?"

Mom stops stacking dishes. "Don't be. She won't put her hands on you again. You know I asked about Jefferson. She said his views reflected the times. I said people even then knew slavery was wrong. Some things are black-and-white. He was definitely a hypocrite."

"Right on, Mom!" My pulse quickens and the air feels lighter.

Mom grins and squeezes dish detergent into the sink.

"She lied when she said Africans weren't needed. Black people built this country."

"You got that right." Mom turns on the faucet as I empty the dustpan into the trash.

"Did you know Malcolm X's teacher called him a nigger when he was my age?"

Mom's smile fades. "I read his book years ago. When did you start?"

"Last month. We have something else in common. He couldn't stand hypocrites."

"Interesting that you've been using that word a lot lately."

"Mom, look up hypocrite, Sister's and Jefferson's faces will leer back at you."

"Who gave you permission to read that book?"

"Huh?" I stop wiping the table. "I didn't know I needed permission."

"Thirteen isn't grown, miss. You can't keep taking things. I saw it in your room while picking up the dirty clothes I keep telling you to put in the hamper."

"You take Daddy's book while I was out?"

She nods. Something closes up in me. Chewing the inside of my cheek to hold my anger in, it escapes anyway.

"I can always go to the Free Library and borrow a copy, Mom."

"Oh, so you're going to do what you want and have the gall to tell me to my face?"

"You encourage us to read and now you're banning books? That's censorship."

"It's called parenting. I didn't say you can't read it, I said get permission."

"Daddy and I talk about it all the time," I huff, gripping the broom handle.

"Then why was he looking for *his* book all last week?"

What's really going on? Is she mad she failed to toss his book, too? Hand to God, she gets the silent treatment until Daddy returns. Super glue can't seal my mouth tighter.

"I have Daddy's permission."

"But you don't have mine."

Nope, not asking either. All the nopers in Noperville say nah. I look away. The scorched wall from the grease fire is ugly and crumbly like our relationship.

"Think you're grown? Be grown then. Wash and dry." She wrings out the dishcloth and slaps it down. "You better not touch that book without my permission." She bolts.

If someone had to leave, why not her? Guilt instantly slaps me upside my head. Now I'm breaking part of the fifth commandment: *Honor thy father and mother.* I'll be in confession for a year at this rate.

Rubbing the dishcloth too hard against a glass stained with Mom's lipstick, I crack it, nicking my finger. I hold it under the faucet and watch the blood wash clean. Why am I the only one in pain here?

CHAPTER 7

Carrying all my books weighs me down. Still, I sprint the last few blocks to school. Can't be late on my first day back. I wipe my brow, it's a steamer of a day.

At the traffic light, winded, I catch my breath and watch a few stragglers jaywalk toward the four gray stone buildings that dominate the entire block. The rectory anchors one end with the lower and upper schools in the middle and the church on the other corner. I kick an empty milk carton. It skips across the road and lands with the other trash lining that curb: stomped-on cigarette butts; broken soda bottles; hoagie, cheesesteak, and Tastykake wrappings; newspapers. Litterbugs everywhere. As much as I love my hometown, Philadelphia really deserves its "Filthadelphia" nickname. Too bad I can't throw my worthless feelings onto the trashy heap.

My watch tells me that the late bell will blare in two minutes. Coming to my senses, I dart to the annex and up the steps. I glance up at *Veritatem Cognoscere*—Latin for "Truth and Courage"—engraved in the gray stone above the entrance. Pigeon droppings on it make me snort.

Stepping into the emptying hallway, my nerves flutter. Wish I could go home. The late bell rings. Dashing up the stairwell, I see Donna lingering by the window fixing her makeup.

"Wow," I say, "I'm glad to walk in with you instead of by myself."

"Yay! You're back. My mom said you should have been expelled, but I defended you." She pauses from applying mascara to flash an I'm-on-your-side grin. Her mother's comment irks me so I turn the doorknob. In the doorway, I glance back to see her zipping her mascara in her pencil case. I wait.

"Did you see Cher's feathered outfit on TV last night?" Donna searches my face as we move down a shiny hallway I missed so much. "My boyfriend thinks I'd look better in it."

Unlike Cher, Donna's thin body has all angles and no curves. Cher has a waist while Donna is built like a rectangle. Because we're so late, I don't have to answer. We give each other a here-goes-nothing shrug and enter class.

The air is full of invisible razors. I hold my breath. Sister Elizabeth looks us up and down, but says nothing. Her eyes ride my back as classmates greet me on the way to my desk. Someone has carved a tiny heart into the edge of the wooden top of my desk. I cover my mouth, exhale, and mentally note to report it ASAP to avoid blame from the slap-happy demon.

Loading my books under my desk, I'm disappointed that being back feels less than expected. Maybe I'm numb to keep from being scared. Or angry. Not that anyone can tell. All I have to do is look down and hair is all anyone can see.

I look up into Sister's glare, which could cut concrete. *Here we go.* I study my protractor while listening to rustled papers and whispered conversations. Time stretches.

"Let us begin the school day in prayer," Sister Elizabeth finally says.

Our desks creak as we stand mindlessly, making the sign of the cross over our torsos. "Our father who art in heaven, hallowed be thy name."

Repeating the "The Lord's Prayer" for the millionth time,

my mind drifts. My favorite part is "forgive us our trespasses as we forgive those who trespass against us." I'm not sure why.

Next, we turn to the flag and recite the Pledge of Allegiance with our right hand over our hearts.

I overheard Daddy say that after he read *The Autobiography of Malcolm X* the first time, he stopped reciting the Pledge or standing for the national anthem. I haven't read yet what prompted that. When I remember Mom taking the book, my chest tightens more.

Malcolm feeds my mind with heaping portions of awareness, confidence, and pride for my heritage. I'm starved for such information at HSB, where four years earlier Mother Superior came on the PA with an odd request. I recall it as if it were yesterday:

"Will all the colored students please report to the main office immediately?"

Bonnie and I exchanged curious looks. We were the only ones in our fourth-grade class of fifty-two students.

The PA sputtered off. I wondered what all of us had done wrong?

We scurried to the office and squeezed in with about forty other anxious students.

Waiting, I stared at the wall of honor noting our best attendance record set ten years earlier when 169 students were absent out of 3,000. That's when HSB could brag about being one of the largest parochial grammar schools anywhere.

We have way fewer students now. Some sisters and lay teachers say enrollment is dropping as the neighborhood changes. They look like their teeth hurt when they say that.

"Please take this home. It's about a meeting regarding your future here." Mother Superior handed each of us a sealed envelope and promised damnation if we opened it.

Handing Mom the letter later that day, I repeated what Mother Superior said.

Mom read the letter silently, then said, "This is a school run by God's people?" Mom held the letter as if it reeked. "This shit burns me up. They won't send their kids to a crappy public school, but they want us to."

Mom never told me what the letter said. All I know is she attended that meeting, Charles and I are still enrolled, Black kids are still coming, white folks are still moving, and Malcolm X can help me understand why reciting the Pledge of Allegiance shouldn't be part of my school routine.

". . . with liberty and justice for all," we say.

Desks groan and a few skid as we settle down. An ambulance wails in the distance and most of us make the sign of the cross.

"Roberta, do you have something to give me from Mother Superior?" Sister Elizabeth's face and vibe are February cold.

Ah jeez, here we go. "No, Sister Elizabeth." I take in her joyless expression, then return to fiddling with my protractor. She frowns like she just remembered she left the oven on in the convent.

"Step into the hallway."

Now I'm light-headed with rubbery legs. Am I heading for another showdown? Sister trails me to the door then whirls around to evil-eye the class.

"Challenge yourself not to sound like a convention of wild boars."

Sister tugs the windowed door shut behind us. She steps away from the door, motioning me to follow. I'd rather have witnesses while we talk, but okay.

She clears her throat for me to meet her eyes, which appear normal at the moment.

"We will start over and wipe the slate clean. Bear in mind, I will not put up with your smart aleck attitude. I blew my stack, which is most unfortunate. I—we—behaved badly. You're a smart girl. Don't throw your future away."

I'm back to staring at the shiny black and white tiles.

"Let's get one thing clear. If you think the world revolves around you, here is a news flash: It doesn't."

Huh? I lift my head and meet her sour gaze. She waits, lips pursed. Seldom are nuns good looking, which may be why they decide not to date. Sister Elizabeth has two exceptions in the looks department: To-die-for electric blue eyes and an eye-catching Hollywood complexion that looks like makeup. More golden than white, her skin is downright pretty, which I'll never say out loud. The rest of her face is bland with teeth the color of ancient piano keys and a nose shaped like President Nixon's.

Sister pushes her glasses up, juts out her chin, and pockets her hands. "Do you have anything to say for yourself?"

I will my mouth not to hang open. *She expects an apology?* She's four cents short of a nickel. Heat rises from my cheeks. Why can't adults admit when they messed up? I think of our fight, my parents' fight, the fight with Mom last night. *I better count to 100.* Studying the water fountain, I count backwards. I'd drink poison before apologizing to her.

"All righty then."

Her I'm-done-frown makes me reach for the doorknob. Throat clearing turns me around. Her shark eyes glint.

"A wise man is like a nail," she says. "His head keeps him from going too far."

A tight smile escapes me. "Yes, Sister Elizabeth."

She cocks her head at my sudden perkiness, clueless that her words of wisdom shape a payback strategy I didn't even know I had until now. I will strike back for everything she's put me through, just not with my hands. And not yet. I've Christmas gifts on the line. Dora and Chuck didn't raise a dummy.

I feel confident, calm, and guilt-free as I glide to the best seat in class.

CHAPTER 8

When Sister finishes taking roll after our talk in the hallway, she looks up directly at me.

"Roberta, you need to get your permission slip signed right away for the field trip next month. Get it off my desk on the way out." Her eyes and tone are tight and harsh.

All of my cool flies out the window. I'm stuck with her for nine more months and I'm no match for this prejudiced monster who not only humiliated me and refused to apologize, but busted up my family. *Temporarily though, right, God?* Just like that, my chest tightens, again. I'm trapped in an icky web of powerlessness.

The first period bell rings. Taking the permission slip on my way out, I avoid eye contact with her. In the noisy hallway, in a sea of bodies, my breathing eases. I exchange quick hellos and hurry to speak with Mr. Harvey before English class, where I always feel welcome.

Balding with thick glasses and a runny nose, Mr. Harvey's looks have *muy poco* to do with us considering him the hippest lay teacher ever. Cool without trying, he lets us know our opinions matter. He talks with us, not at us.

On the first day of reading class, he stood on his desk with a globe in one hand and a stack of books in the other. "Books let you travel without moving your feet. And, oh, the places we'll go."

Coordinator of the annual writing contests for each grade, I had already dubbed him my favorite teacher before I set foot in his class. He called me a gifted writer after I won second place in the sixth-grade contest for my short story about two friends with gang-banging brothers.

Inspired by my desire to keep my brother Charles safe, the story was a no-brainer. The newspaper is full of articles about Black teen males dying from gang activity—corner guys with dangerous smiles who boxed each other with fancy moves instead of studying. Boys like Charles, who loves religion and science, are considered sissies by them.

Mr. Harvey sent my story to the newspaper. It wasn't printed, but he impressed my parents. At a PTA meeting, he told them I marched to my own beat, quite a compliment because he hadn't taught me yet. He protested when I lost the writing contest last year, too.

"Hey, Mr. Harvey."

Hunched over a test checking off incorrect answers, he flips it facedown so I can't see whose test it is. Unlike most teachers, he respects our privacy. We do the Black Power handshake. His execution is water ice smooth.

"Welcome back. All caught up?"

"Yes. I heard there are some changes to the writing contest."

"Indeed. It's open to the archdiocese. Top school winners will compete for huge prizes. There may be other rule changes. I'm fairly sure it will be an essay contest."

I pump my fist in the air. "Yay! Wish we could pick the topic. I'd like to write about race relations!"

Mr. Harvey clasps his hands behind his neck, leans back in his chair. "That's provocative. We have many racial issues with policing, community—"

"No, Mr. Harvey, race relations here, in this parish." My voice quivers.

Usually when I've got a deep problem, it pops up at the worst time. Like now. Before I know it, I'm two seconds from boo-hooing like a kindergartner.

"Let's step out," he says, rising.

Students stop streaming in to allow us to exit. Once we're out there, Mr. Harvey holds out his hanky. I shake my head. He's a chronic nose-blower.

"Sister Elizabeth hates me. I'm stuck with her."

"Kiddo, I'm sorry about what happened with you and Sister Elizabeth." His voice is butter soft like Daddy's when something bothers me. "You know you can always talk to me. Come find me during recess."

The bell rings.

"Thanks, Mr. Harvey." I put on my game face as we enter class.

English may help. There's no better Band-Aid for a wounded soul than disappearing into a world of words. Sister just reminded me I am Humpty Dumpty in living color, only nothing rhymes and I just look fixed. Everything, even breathing, still feels broken. At my desk, in my favorite teacher's class, I dump my feelings into a lockbox where my heart used to be. Being numb and silent protects me.

I hide behind my hair listening to the discussion about our assigned reading, "The Ones Who Walk Away from Omelas." It's a short story about a Utopian society that functions due to a cruel requirement. One poor kid has to be kept locked up in a windowless room. That child's mistreatment keeps everyone else happy.

Mr. Harvey keeps glancing my way: probably concerned I'm not chiming in as usual. At this moment, I feel like the poor kid in the story. Glancing around, I bet my allowance no one's world here was rocked like mine in the last week.

Heck, I'd wager against anyone in HSB. Better yet, the entire archdiocese.

———————

I feel less yucky by recess. For the twenty Black girls in the eighth-grade class, recess means jumping double Dutch until it's too cold outside. It's the best activity we can do without messing up our hair. Plus, I get to see Bonnie, who I desperately need and miss. This is the first year we no longer have the same classes.

Bonnie's grades nosedived last year after her father became ill—didn't help that she refuses to wear her glasses. Despite serious squinting, she has trouble seeing the lessons on the blackboard. Even with ugly glasses, she's cute with a reddish complexion, amber colored eyes, and a curly ponytail. It's hard to hide pretty. Boys like her sassy personality, too—even a few white ones. Boys don't matter more to me than making the scholar roll, which beats the honor roll, thank you very much. I dig being on top.

In the yard, I'm the buzz. Duking it out with Sister boosted my popularity, from the nerds who fantasize about hitting anyone to the girls who mistakenly think I struck a blow for feminists to the scowling boys destined for juvie who consider me an honorary hoodlum.

I wind my way through admirers. A few boys jab the air as I approach.

"You so bad they don't even throw you out of school for knocking Sister's block off," says Douglas, fifteen and in eighth grade. He isn't a sociopath, yet. But he'll get there.

"Make way for Cleopatra Jones," says pasty-faced Ben, who expects Black students to act like the stereotypes he sees on TV and in movies. *He must be thrilled with me.*

Their approval of my fight with Sister feels like rubbing against a wound that hasn't scabbed over. I'm a nun-boxer by accident, not design.

Geoffrey spots me and ambles away from his buddies playing wall ball. He raises a clenched fist at me. His friends snigger at his Black Power symbol. "Bet Sister will think twice before correcting you. Black Power is no match."

"What are you talking about?" Confusion contorts my face.

"You decked her. You know, by any means necessary, all that Black Panther stuff."

I try to count to ten and give up at five. "Black Power doesn't mean violence. The Black Panthers did a lot of good in the community. By any means necessary is something that Malcolm X said about justice—"

"I watch the news. Those Black Panther X guys carried guns," Geoffrey says.

"They also carried law books."

Geoffrey squints at me. "My dad says they were thugs. Anyway, how come you didn't get expelled?" He smirks. "If you'd been white you would've been."

"If I were white the fight wouldn't have happened."

Bonnie swoops over and pulls me away. "Forget him, he's cruising for a bruising. Guess he doesn't come to school with enough black eyes and busted lips."

"He said my fight with Sister was 'Black Power.' He saw the whole thing." I suck my teeth in frustration as we head toward our rope crew.

"He's harmless, but Sister Elizabeth isn't. She's beyond mean. Sabrina had to take a note into the faculty room and overheard lay teachers talking about her. They said her brother is really sick, but she only visited the hospital once."

"I bet it was while I was suspended."

Bonnie nods. "Her sub was a pushover. We dug him."

"So she took her frustration out on me."

"Just remember that Sister is" Bonnie snaps her fingers, "the human version of period cramps."

We giggle-choke as we round the grotto of the Blessed Virgin Mary.

On the other side of the stone alcove, smiling faces and jump ropes slapping the concrete greet us. Exchanging hellos, my mood lifts. Every Black eighth-grade girl is here, even Vietta, although she doesn't know how to jump. It's the one time I see everyone. My girls are as smart as me, but for some reason they're in the lower tracks. We claim this corner of the yard. Black boys come, too, especially the few loudmouths who stare and make lewd remarks about our bouncy body parts.

"You're up first," Bonnie says, cutting her eyes at Derrick, the one we all agree is a bad influence on the rest. I tie my sweater around my waist to keep prying eyes off my jiggly butt.

Rocking my body to the *pit pat* rhythm of the overlapping ropes, I feel the groove and time my entry just right, jumping in with knees high. Steadying myself, I execute spins and fancy footwork. Out the corner of my eye I see more boys approach, whispering behind their hands.

The longer I jump, the less I care. About fresh boys. Geoffrey. Sister. Mom. My reputation, just everything. Jumping loosens the tightness in my back and brain. Frees me. Every time my feet clear the ropes with precision and pizazz, I'm feeling more like my old self—a girl enjoying spending time with her friends at recess; a girl who loves school and looks forward to her afternoon Spanish class; a girl who doesn't hurt to be me.

CHAPTER 9

Double Dutch and reading Malcolm's riveting story has kept me sane for the past few weeks. Three more and I kiss punishment adios.

Turncoat Mom returned *The Autobiography of Malcolm X* a week after she took it. She's been trying to bribe me by bringing home soft pretzels and bean pies. I mumble thanks, which is one more word than I usually say to her. I just can't connect with Mom. Our family is in a free fall she triggered. Talking to her means crossing enemy lines.

Daddy has checked on us a handful of times and always while Mom is out. I miss him so much my throat hurts. Mom stopped wearing her wedding ring and band, claiming she misplaced them. I pray for no divorce, but if God listens, I no longer hear him. I do hear Mom crying at night. She thinks we're asleep, but I'm up even later than usual rereading Malcolm's words.

My connection to his story has hooked Bonnie, who finally started reading the autobiography and loves it as much as I do. Discussing it after school is a daily highlight. On the way home yesterday, we talked about how Malcolm's education took off in prison. We chuckled at the irony of him feeling freer to learn behind bars than he did in school, where his racist teacher dashed his ambition to become a lawyer.

Malcolm helps me better understand why I sometimes feel like an outsider in my school, church, neighborhood, and even my country. He also questioned the hypocrisy of religion as well as the U.S. Constitution, which counted Black men as three-fifths of a person while the Declaration of Independence said all men were created equal. He's dead and still a better teacher than Sister Elizabeth.

How I ached for Malcolm when he learned the man he called the Honorable Elijah Muhammad was anything but. The Nation of Islam leader was a hypocrite, having fathered children with several young women. Malcolm's father figure, who preached discipline and virtue, lied big time. That betrayal devastated Malcolm. I'm dying to talk to Daddy about this shocker.

The grandfather clock chimes, reminding me the trolley arrives within minutes. We're finally hanging out with Daddy downtown, and Charles lollygags upstairs. Grabbing the latest issue of *Right On!* off the coffee table, I hurry to the staircase. "Your science experiment can wait," I yell. "Let's go!"

Huffing from chasing the trolley, we step on board and deposit our tokens. We sit up front because our parents said we fought too hard not to. Charles fidgets on his cushiony seat in anticipation. I'm psyched, but stay cool. I'm thirteen. I open my magazine.

"Look, that store got tagged." Charles points. Out the window we stare at black spray-painted letters in squiggly lines. We strain to decipher it. The graffiti popping up across the city in recent years is new in this stretch of the avenue.

"Slanted bubble letters in bright colors look more artsy than like vandalism," I say.

Leaving Charles on graffiti watch, I read my magazine. Nothing beats immersing myself in the world of celebrities whose lives I'd love to write about some day.

The trolley jerks to a stop and the magazine leaps off my lap, opening to a centerfold of Soul Train dancers—a portrait of 'fros, tight tops, bellbottoms, and chunky platforms. The trolley door wheezes open as I snatch the magazine off the grungy floor.

"Look at all that hair!" says an older woman at the fare box. She approaches me and leans in so close I smell her Dentyne.

I like her vibe so it's okay when her hand plunges into my thick, huge Afro—a foot high and wide (I know because I measure it). She chuckles as the hair she just mushed down springs back into place. We chat about my hair care until she gets off at her stop.

I wave to her out the window and watch the trolley glide through neighborhoods alternating between Black and white residents. Few stay mixed for long because of what my parents call "white flight." I admire the area we are in now with its roomy three-story row homes with lush lawns. It's clear money people live on these postcard-pretty blocks free of litter lining the streets and graffiti scrawled on walls.

Philly is funny like that. Go six blocks in one direction and the neighborhood takes on a new flavor—bright and fresh like a butterscotch Tastykake or as tough and unappetizing as a week-old pretzel.

Daddy meets us at the last trolley stop, which always smells like Lysol, urine, and cigarette smoke. He hugs us, and the smell of his cologne makes me giddy.

"Daddy, can you buy a new pick for my hair?" I ask, side-stepping a mysterious puddle on the steps leading to street level.

"Sure, let's check out the brothers' tables, if the police didn't run them off," Daddy says, referring to the vendors with thick dreadlocks the color of rusted nails hanging to their waists.

"Why do they run them off?"

"Because they can. You read the papers; you know about police brutality."

Cops infuriate him. When they arrested the Black Panthers several years ago at night, police lined them up outside even though they were nude or in their underwear. Cops tipped off the newspaper so it could run a front-page photo, Daddy said.

"Are the Black Panthers still active here? I don't read much about them."

"Not like they used to be. The FBI saw to that."

"I recently had to school a classmate. He said the Black Panthers were only known for violence."

"Give me dap," he says.

We bump our fists together so the knuckles touch. I float up the stairs. Exiting the subway into a bright afternoon, my body tingles with the pulse of downtown, its noisy traffic snaking past hulking skyscrapers and gobs of people rushing somewhere. I glance up at the William Penn statue atop City Hall. The founder of the colony that became Pennsylvania is a bad dude. No building in Philly can rise above his statue.

At the corner, waiting for the green light, Daddy tugs my elbow. "Write about the Black Panthers for your contest. Scare the nuns." He winks. We cross the street laughing.

"You ever think about joining the Black Panthers back in the day?" Charles asks.

"I did for a hot minute until I got hired by SEPTA. Had to slow my roll after that. Tell your classmate that the Panthers' ten-point program will be as meaningful fifty years from now as is it today."

"In fifty years I'll be an old lady, Daddy. We won't need it," I say.

"Let's hope not. As a betting man, those are odds I wouldn't take," he says as we turn into a block where merchandise-packed tables line the sidewalk. On each table, pungent incense sticks resembling brown caterpillars produce a sweet aroma I adore.

At a vendor table, I pick up a metal rake comb with a black plastic fist on top. Charles selects a sew-on peace patch.

"How is school?" he asks us, pulling out his wallet.

"Fine," says Charles.

"I'm staying out of trouble," I say.

"How are you getting along with your Mom?"

"I'm staying out of trouble," I say.

"You are your mother's daughter." He hands a bill to the vendor, whose long twisted, natural hair fascinates me. Daddy deposits his change into our eager hands.

"I'm more like you." I smirk. "Even though you don't believe in heaven."

"Look, I know I am going to hell. Your mother is, too." Charles gasps and I freeze.

"In fact, everyone I know is going. You two will be there. We'll have a heck of a party," he says laughing. Realizing he's joking, we join in, although Charles looks uneasy.

"Daddy, how can you not be religious growing up with Mom-Mom?" Charles asks.

"That's exactly why." His cartoonish cackle makes strangers within earshot laugh.

When it comes to religion, our mother sits halfway between my atheist father and zealot grandmother. She is religious enough to make us eat fish on most Fridays and say grace before meals. Mom no longer nags us to attend weekly Mass, but ensures we slip in every other week and attend all of the holy days. She's not exactly a Bible thumper.

"Y'all hungry?"

"My stomach is as empty as a slinky," Charles says.

That tickles us to no end. We hoot while waiting in line at a hot dog cart with an aroma of onions and chili that has us drooling. We chow down in silence.

Finished, I lean back on the park bench stuffed. "Did you see it coming, Daddy? That Elijah Muhammad was a fraud?"

He tugs at the small goatee he's grown since he left home and studies me. "A wise man once told me if you don't die a hero, you will live long enough to see yourself turned into a villain. People aren't perfect, Pumpkin."

"That's deep, Daddy, but it's not true. You're perfect in our eyes."

Mouth full from his third hot dog, Charles nods in agreement.

Daddy's face gets squishy, like a water ice left in the heat. "Elijah's lies caught up with him." He looks away.

He misses us. Even when he smiles, there's a hint of sadness. I'm dying to ask when he's coming home. Instead I blather on about Malcolm. "There's so much I want to say in religion class these days, but I can't risk Sister flipping out and getting a bad report."

"Malcolm's perspective on Christianity may not be the best topic to discuss right now," Daddy says, checking his watch. "He wasn't a fan, as we know."

"There's a lot I want to say in history class, too, especially when we discuss current events. Malcolm wouldn't be surprised by the Watergate mess, which comes down to a lying president abusing his power. He was criticized for saying the chickens came home to roost after President Kennedy's assassination, but what he meant was taken out of context." My words run together since I'm on a roll. "Our government, which approved of slavery and killing Indians for their land, is hypocritical and corrupt. I wish I was old enough to vote."

"You preaching to the amen corner, Pumpkin. I'm all for you speaking up, but maybe slow your roll a bit. Let's give your mother one less thing to worry about, okay?"

I nod. As Charles heads to the trashcan down the block, I seize my chance. "Will all your overtime . . . make Mom happier?"

His smile tells me the answer. "I'll be working a lot in the next few months." He pinches my cheek. "Everything will work out."

So their fight was over money. He's gambling, again.
Mom's fault for nagging.

"Do you think—"

He gives me the not-now glance as Charles ambles within earshot. "Thank you, son. Who wants to get dessert at Wana-maker's?" Daddy asks.

"We do!"

We bounce-walk to the fancy downtown department store that fills an entire block. Known for a soaring Grand Court, it's home to the largest pipe organ in the world. Passing its sparkly display windows on the way to the entrance, I gape at a blue-and-green jumper falling mid-thigh on a skinny mannequin. I imagine myself in it, flashbulbs blinding me as I strut across the stage to accept my first-place prize for the essay contest.

Stepping inside, I crane my neck at endless columns as we approach the legendary bronze eagle sculpture. The humon-gous eagle serves as everyone's meeting spot. I waited there at age seven with crybaby Charles when we were lost during the Christmas holidays. It happened after we rode the monorail for kids that looped above the eighth-floor toy department, which allowed us to gaze down at a toy wonderland. I never confessed that I saw Mom coming and ditched her after we exited the tin cars. I wanted to explore the store on my own. When I slipped into the crowd, Charles tagged along.

"Charles, we'll catch the Christmas show this year." Dad smirks at me. "I guess you're too old to come with us."

"Y'all better not leave me."

Unlike Mom, he doesn't mind me using slang. I haven't said y'all since he left. I haven't felt like this since he left. Gath-ering here for the stunning light show is a Christmas tradition that started long before I memorized the alphabet. The idea of returning as a family makes me grin so hard my cheeks hurt. It's the be-all and end-all of "y'all" events. Grinning from ear to ear at my father, I'm the happiest I've felt in weeks.

The trolley lurches to a stop, forcing me to scribble on the poem I just wrote on the back of a flyer. I nudge Charles, who stops reading my magazine. I hand him my latest creation. In a quiet voice he reads:

My final year here, at HSB
I'll win the top spot, little old me
My name will be engraved in the trophy case
That'll restore my reputation in this place
And bring my family together again
For me that will be my most important win
My family will be happy and proud while I'm aglow
Cause I'm adding a first-place prize to Mom's curio

"Wow." He flashes me a thumbs up. "I could never write like you."

"You know it, I'm a poet."

Charles laughs as if he's never heard this before. Hanging with Daddy has us both in a cheery mood.

Rereading my poem, I smile non-stop because a) Charles praised it, b) the syllables for aglow and curio don't match, c) hope, MIA lately, hugs me, and d) all of the above.

CHAPTER 10

" **Y**our decorum," a beaming Sister Elizabeth pauses, clasps her hands, "and excellent questions during our visitor's presentation was such an unexpected delight that you've earned free time."

Half the class blurts, "Yay, Sister!"

Stephanie looks at me and we do a Vulcan mind meld: Sister is sleepy.

"Settle down. Please spend your free time quietly," Sister says with a half smile.

Geoffrey's hand rockets up. "Can I do a cool 3D project using construction paper?"

Our collective groans actually make Sister laugh. A smile changes her face into something pleasant to look at.

"If you prefer that to read quietly, then do so. If you want to work on a craft project, that's fine, too." She nods in my direction and points to the gray steel supply closet against the wall behind me.

"Roberta, get the colored construction paper. Look in the blue bin."

A smirking Geoffrey turns, mouths "teacher's pet." I shrug. Girlfriend is just trying to keep the peace. Sister is, too. *Praise God.*

Anyway, I'm eager to explore the packed shelves of a storage closet usually locked. Inside is a goldmine of steal-worthy goodies jockeying for space—new scissors, fresh tape dispensers, crisp folders, and packs of jumbo rubber bands. Everything gleams.

Nosey, I rummage through a bin marked 1965–66. It's stuffed with old rosters, pink laminated hall passes, and a class photograph. In it, Sister wears different glasses and a radiant smile, maybe due to the lack of chocolate chips in her vanilla class. Under the photo, an illustration pokes out. It's a white (as in European white) baby on a bench feeding three other Black, yellow and brown infants to represent they were from Africa, Asia, and Latin America. Pagan babies. The white baby has a halo. That makes it a saint feeding the poor colored infants sitting at its feet. Suddenly I recall the classroom collections to save unbaptized children in these other continents. The drawing belongs to a certificate issued to our school in 1966 for the adoption of a "pagan baby" named Maria.

The picture is all kinds of wrong. Sourness and shame gurgle up. In third grade, I saved my allowance and bought in the last fifty cents needed for our class to baptize a pagan baby. Allowed to choose the baptism name, I selected Diahann after Diahann Carroll, the first Black woman to have a TV series where her role was an educated professional. Sister said Diahann wasn't Christian enough and she selected Grace. What an overeager try-hard I was back then, so blind to this racist crap in the name of religion.

"What's taking so long, snoopy?"

Sister's hunky-dory voice eats me from the inside. I count to 10.

"I found a Pagan Baby certificate." I turn, wishing I could unhear what I just said and go back in time and take my money back.

Stepping forward, I hold up the certificate to the class. My hand shakes. I avoid Sister's face since my temper feels nine cents short of a dime.

"Oh, I remember Pagan Babies," someone murmurs, voice syrupy with affection. A few others with ear-to-ear grins nod with fondness. *Jesus, Joseph, and Mary.*

"Roberta, stop lollygagging."

Getting off punishment means not saying what I want to.

I replace the certificate and snatch up the stack of construction paper. Why did she have to call on me?

Humming, clueless Sister takes the papers from me. Inside my head, I'm screaming like a banshee while I wrestle with this racist religion of mine.

Back at my desk, I make a commotion digging into my school bag and plopping the Malcolm book down. *Please ask me what I'm reading. Just saying the title would make me feel heard.* Instead, Sister dozes.

Thumbing through it, I reread passages where Malcolm argues that whites used Christianity in hypocritical ways to oppress Black people. I'm halfway through a chapter when a spitball darts across the row and lands in Eileen's curls. "Ewww, stop it!" Her response wakes Sister.

"Class, clean up around your desks before the bell rings." Sister scans the room.

Donna and I arrive at the trash can at the same time.

"I wonder what happened to our Pagan Babies? My second-grade class adopted three."

"I wonder what happened to all the money we sent them," I snap, as the bell rings.

Her eyes widen in surprise as she watches me yank my book bag up and rush away.

I storm into my bedroom and reach deep inside my bedroom closet. Its stale air makes me cough. I've outgrown all the clothes on hangers, which are crammed together like lines on a ruler. One day, I'll give them away along with my huge Barbie collection.

I pull out a tiny, lacy white dress and matching veil. This communion dress once made me feel like a holy Cinderella with its matching fancy socks and white patent leather shoes. The silk sash slides across my fingers, and my desire to trash it blinks. Sure, I was a brainwashed kid who used to save pagan babies and wore this dress with pride to eat the body of Christ for the first time. I wore it again later that year during the May Day procession to the statue of the Blessed Virgin, where I wasn't picked to climb the ladder and place the crown of flowers on Mary's concrete head. I so wanted to. I toss the dress in my trashcan. Still fuming, I grab the latest *Right On!* and rocket downstairs.

At the kitchen table, Charles mouths a catechism answer he's trying to memorize for his upcoming confirmation. I mimic him. He ignores me. Aiming my magazine at his Bible, I let it fly across the table. It bounces off the Bible and knocks over the salt shaker.

"Cut it out!"

"You're the one reading like a first grader. Let me help you before the bishop slaps you stupid. What is man?"

"Man is a creature of—I mean, composed of a body and soul, and," he struggles to remember, "made in the image of God."

"Close enough. Not that any of it makes sense anyway. Dig this: What you're reading brother dear." I throw out my arms and sing, "It ain't necessarily so."

Horror fills Charles's face as he sits frozen, his Bible held mid-air. "What's *wrong* with you?" He looks like he wants to throw holy water on me.

I can't stop laughing.

Mom walks in, turns on the faucet, and adds dish detergent. I join her at the sink to dry dishes and put them away for an extra $1 a week in allowance.

As the sink fills with soapy water, I sing with Aretha Franklin gusto: "'The things you are reading you best stop believing.'"

"You better stop," Charles says, making the sign of the cross.

This causes me to double over in hysterics. Coming up for air, Mom gives me a hard glare.

"What I do? Come on, think about the stuff in the Bible."

Charles watches me with suspicion.

"Do you really think it rained forty days and nights? That Noah really built an—ouch!"

I jump back from Mom's pinch.

"Leave your brother alone. If you don't, the Bible says I can smack you and your water bucket head into next week."

"He—we are being brainwashed."

"I said zip it."

Infuriated at losing my constitutional right to freedom of speech, I act mute. Mom tries to chop the tense silence with questions about school, as if she's not getting weekly reports, and the Malcolm book, which I only discuss with Daddy. So there.

Fed up at my back-to-back shrugs, she turns to Charles, who packs up his books. "Wait. I want to review the questions with you."

"Okay. Mom, want to hear a joke first?"

Mom pauses from rinsing a glass to glance at me. "I could use one."

"Why is six afraid of seven?"

Exhaling like a drama mama who ran for the bus and missed, I say, "Because seven—" Mom plucks my arm to shut me up.

"Because seven eight nine!" Charles says, and snort-laughs. Mom joins in. Just another sign that Mom loves him more. My heart knows.

Mom helps Charles with his canned religion answers until I store away the last dish. Annoyed by their mutual admiration society, I take another karate kick at religion to get them hot and bothered like I am.

"Mom, how did you know I wanted to be Catholic?"

"What?" She pauses from signing Charles's religion homework to give me a legendary frown. Charles squints in disgust. 'Cause, Tweedledum and Tweedledee.

"You baptized me before I knew what a compound sentence was. Shouldn't I get to decide my religion?"

"I'm your mother, I decide for you. You decide when you're older. How's that?"

"Forget it."

"Good, go pick up your clothes off the floor."

Great talk.

Back in my room, I press my diary to my heart. It's the only thing that gets me. No one here comes close. I open to a clean page and bleed out in ink. I write:

The pagan babies are no longer round
They no longer sit and eat on the ground
They've grown up tall and lean
Smart with their own gleam
And they are demanding to know
Where did their Pagan Baby money go?

I call it "Another Question for Sister Elizabeth." I belly laugh to the moon. Mom barges in.

"You were laughing so much I thought you were . . ." She glances at my phone.

"People, knock."

"I'm not people, I'm your mom."

"Well, Mom, something's been bugging me. Why didn't you ever go and meet with Sister?"

"Are you in trouble again?"

"No."

"I get weekly reports and we've talked on the phone several times. I don't need to stare in her face. I'm shocked that your father meeting with her wasn't good enough." She walks out and leaves me steaming.

The field trip tomorrow is a blessing in disguise. Between dealing with Mom's nonsense and clamming up in religion and history classes with Sister Elizabeth, I'm ready to blow up like a box of firecrackers.

CHAPTER 11

I dread our field trip to Independence Hall with Sister Elizabeth, but welcome any day away from school. But like yesterday during our discussion about President Nixon's decision to fire Archibald Cox, I'm keeping my mouth shut. Like Daddy says, Stevie Wonder can see something is wrong when Nixon fires the special prosecutor investigating him and attacks his own justice department.

Independence Hall sounds like another trip down Hypocrisy Lane. The Founding Fathers? Those white men aren't my daddies. Well, maybe one of them *could* be a forefather if they were all like Thomas Jefferson. Our Virginia relatives said he had children with a slave.

A paper airplane crash lands on my Afro and tumbles to my lap. I whip my head around. Geoffrey's cheesy grin is a dead giveaway. Before I can mount a counterattack, Sister, sitting in front of the bus, shoots daggers at Geoffrey. His face transforms into a portrait of innocence.

Sister isn't fooled.

"Geoffrey, it's not too late to turn this bus around and cancel the field trip. Use your single brain cell to behave. And Roberta, do not encourage Geoffrey's clowning."

I mentally affix a halo atop my head and try to look angelic. Sister glares at Geoffrey and then gives the bus driver unneeded instruction on how to get to a tourist attraction he could find blindfolded. Looking in the rearview mirror, I see him rolling his eyes.

The school bus bounces past City Hall, and I try to window shop at Wanamaker's when we stop at a traffic light. It's not yet Thanksgiving, but I'm already compiling more must-have gifts for an already lengthy Christmas list. I'm also trying to fill my checklist balance sheet with a lot of "nice" to offset the one big "naughty."

But making nice and keeping my lips zipped will be a chore in Independence Hall. Sister told us this was where both the Declaration of Independence and the Constitution were adopted, as if every Philly kid didn't have that drilled in us from Day One. But if Thomas Jefferson was the king of hypocrisy, those documents were its Magna Carta.

We hold these truths to be self-evident, that all men are created equal, that they are endowed by their Creator with certain unalienable Rights, that among these are Life, Liberty and the pursuit of Happiness.

Those words from the Declaration: What a crock! All men are equal? Many of the men who signed on to those words owned slaves. Even Benjamin Franklin owned slaves! I was punished for telling the truth about Jefferson's dishonesty. Now my nose was being rubbed in the lies.

"Roberta, why are you all frowned up?" Stephanie whispers. "Don't you know a field trip is like playing hooky from school? You need to learn to keep on truckin' and stop letting Sister and idiot Geoffrey work your nerves."

Stephanie's right. I can't change history, but I can change

my attitude. I'm not going to fight battles that I can't win. My mission, should I choose to accept, is to get through this without making waves. I imagine a tape recording going up in smoke like on the TV show *Mission: Impossible.*

The bus rolls to a stop in front of a red brick building topped by a white steeple. I've passed by it countless times but never been inside. Mom has never brought us down here for a tour, and Daddy calls it the usual whitewash that passes for American history. Whitewash. It's the only time the word "white" seems like a bad thing, unlike "black," which hardly ever means anything good.

"Okay, young ladies and gentlemen, single file and quiet please," Sister shouts at the front of bus. "Let's be on our best behavior. You are representing not only yourselves, but our school."

A petite, sandy-haired woman wearing glasses, a bright smile, and a brown uniform meets us at the entrance to Independence Hall.

"Hello, boys and girls. My name is Betsy Goodman. I'm a ranger with the National Park Service. I'll be your tour guide today. Welcome to Independence Hall, the birthplace of American liberty. It was here that the Founding Fathers debated and signed both the Declaration of Independence and the Constitution."

With a wave of her hand, she summons us inside. In a loud whisper, she asks, "Who can tell me how many signers of the Declaration of Independence were from Pennsylvania?"

Silence. None of my classmates have a clue or care enough to respond. I raise my hand, even though we aren't in class.

"Yes, Roberta," Sister says, her sour expression suggesting that she expects the worst, like me calling Ben Franklin a hypocrite.

Actually, Ben seemed pretty cool, even though "Early to bed and early to rise" is one bit of advice I'm not down with. But his flying that kite in the lightning storm to discover electricity was pretty cool.

"Nine," I say. "More than any other colony."

The tour guide's eyes widen with surprise, then narrow with curiosity. I know that look. *Who is this smart black girl?*

"Can you name them?" Her voice strikes me as more challenging than friendly.

"Benjamin Franklin, Benjamin Rush," I say, counting them off on my fingers. "George Ross, George Taylor, George Clymer. James Smith, James Wilson."

Memorizing them had been easy because so many of their names were similar. Two Bens, three Georges, two James. Was there a name shortage in the colonies? But now I'm stuck.

The tour guide gives me what looks like a smile of relief. "The last two are Robert Morris and John Morton."

Ah, the M's. How could I have forgotten them?

"Who was the author of the Declaration of Independence?" she asks, locking her eyes on me, as if we are holding a private conversation. Hmm. Maybe I've misread her. It occurs to me that she might enjoy having an engaged student on the tour. Maybe most kids go through the motions, pay her no mind, or act—as Mom says—like they just escaped from the Philly zoo.

I know the answer. She knows I know the answer. But I'm not going there today. Thomas Jefferson has landed me in enough hot water without me taking another swan dive into that boiling pool. If I can't say something nice.

Donna, excited, raises her hand. "Oh, I know! John Hancock?"

I chuckle to myself. Not a bad guess, Donna. Hancock signed that paper like he owned it.

"No, young lady," our guide says, shaking her head. "Thomas Jefferson of Virginia was the primary author. He would go on to become our third president."

We walk toward the Liberty Bell, which I'm actually looking forward to seeing. The crack in that golden-brown bell sums up America in a nutshell—flawed from the start. The weight of the nation's hypocrisy—land of the free, home of the slaves—was too much for the bell to bear. The men who wrote that Constitution declared that people who looked like me were only three-fifths of a person.

I'm ready to go all Patrick Henry and say as much to the tour guide and the class, even though I know it will bury me like a bone beneath Sister Elizabeth's doghouse. We'd learned about Henry, a Virginian, in history class. "Give me liberty or give me death"? Henry owned slaves, too.

The bell, as far as I'm concerned, is a symbol of the imperfections and outright lies that hang over this nation like a dark cloud, ready to burst. But my inner rage is interrupted by the words of our tour guide.

The bell, she tells us, was largely forgotten before being embraced by abolitionists as a symbol of freedom. Abolitionists? Weren't they the people who wanted to free the slaves? Long before we learned about him in school, I remember Daddy telling me about Frederick Douglass, an enslaved black man who beat up his master, escaped to freedom, wrote an autobiography and became a leading abolitionist. Douglass even became friends with Abraham Lincoln! "That dude sounds badder than John Shaft," Daddy said, referring to the cool action movie about the Black private detective.

Our tour guide tells us that the bell is made of copper and tin and weighs more than a ton. I read its inscription, which is from the Bible, Leviticus, 25:10.

"Proclaim Liberty throughout all the land unto all the inhabitants thereof," it reads.

Hmm. No qualifiers there. No three-fifths compromise. No citizens requirement. "All the inhabitants thereof." That would include Black people and American Indians, too.

Maybe the bell didn't crack because of the weight of hypocrisy. Perhaps it couldn't bear the tension between what America is supposed to be and what it is.

Often, these days, I feel like that bell, like I'm about to crack. The gap between the truth and the world around me is too much to bear.

CHAPTER 12

On a wet fall morning, happiness whispers in my ear, then shouts: hang time with Daddy!

First up: watching the Malcolm X documentary narrated by James Earl Jones. It's at the community center in Uncle Duke's neighborhood, which is known as a hotbed for militant activists. Then I'm riding with Daddy on his trolley route.

I'm pacing my tiny room since he's ten minutes late. Peering out the window and biting my nails, I count the fallen leaves until a familiar car noses around the corner.

I grab my poetry book, fly down the steps, and yell bye to Mom. In record time, I'm snuggled inside Daddy's car smelling his stinky car deodorizer.

"Hey, Pumpkin." He kisses my cheek, lowers the volume on the 8-track and honks the horn twice. Instead of peeling away, he waits. Mom comes to the door, and Daddy's face lights up. He gestures for me to roll down my window.

"She get all her chores done?"

Mom steps out, leans on the railing, and nods.

"Just checking."

A why-not-ask-me look takes over my face. Doesn't matter. Daddy's love radar only checks for Mom. They stare googly-eyed. I sigh like someone stole my jar of coins, which I've been saving for five years. Daddy shooshes me. In my head I scream.

Then I feel bad.

I prayed for the icy block between my parents to thaw. But right now? I'm set to jet. Plus, why waste gas in the middle of a gas crisis everyone was talking about? Mom rides her blue 10-speed to work now because she refuses to pay fifty-five cents a gallon.

"Talk to you later," Daddy sing songs to Mom.

"Sounds good." She pauses. "Have fun, Roberta." She says it like I'm an afterthought. I am.

"Later, Mom." I lazy wave and lean back.

Instead of putting the pedal to the metal, a finger-snapping Daddy turns up the 8-track playing one of their favorite Motown songs. Mom sways and Daddy bops his head. *Jesus, Joseph and Mary, I'm going to have a heart attack if we are late.*

After what feels like forever, but is actually two minutes and seventeen seconds, we pull off. Daddy eyeballs Mom in the rearview mirror like she's a snack.

He continues warbling nonstop with back-to-back begging love songs. So much for us catching up. Irked to no end, I doodle so hard in my notebook I poke a hole in the paper.

To keep from blurting out something inappropriate, I edit some new poems. When I glance up, we're zipping along the accident-prone expressway, where everyone acts like drivers in the Indy 500. Another good sign? Daddy stopped singing.

I reach to turn the radio on to my favorite station, WDAS. Daddy shakes his head.

"Don't ever mess with a man's music when his jam is playing," he teases.

"They're all your jams." I pretend-gag.

He turns the volume down. "What's wrong?"

"Nothing, I just miss you and thought we'd talk."

"Baby, we got all day! Don't we? After Uncle Duke's, you're riding shotgun with me, right?" He pinches my cheek, and his thousand-mile stare returns.

Turning the volume back up for him, I lean against the window, wondering what's up with me. Cause if I'm honest, I felt jelly over the attention he paid Mom. That's not only weird. It's kind of sick.

We squeeze into the packed space, grateful Uncle Duke saved our seats. Stinks we're so close to the projector screen, but that beats standing in my blue platform shoes. These leather tie-ups were too small when Mom-Mom bought them, but I refuse to wear a size nine.

So amen to Uncle Duke, who bear-hugged me then told us he had to step outside to handle a situation, the kind he specializes in. Both of his girlfriends showed up. I'm not amused. I hate that Daddy stays with someone with a bunch of girlfriends. I see why he's separated.

We barely avoid stepping on toes on the way to our seats in the middle of a crooked row of folding chairs. The smell of Afro Sheen nearly chokes me. Almost everyone sports a glistening bush, but just one—on the head of a mixed-looking girl—overshadows mine.

A lady grumbles about my hair behind me as I settle on the hard seat. I feel bad, but not bad enough to move. Sorry.

Daddy hands me a chocolate bar. I notice his wedding ring. "Mom misplaced her diamond ring."

"Misplaced or pawned?" Daddy chuckles.

Unsure if he's joking, I test him. "Maybe she needs another one?"

"Maybe so," he says. "Maybe someone can help me pick it out?"

I nod, beyond thrilled. I did not see this coming, and I feel like I just played a part. Even if he had planned to replace the ring, my encouragement at least cancels out the weirdness I felt toward Mom earlier. Right?

The ceiling lights go down, and the documentary starts with a black screen. An unseen Billie Holiday sings "Strange Fruit." The lyrics embed themselves into my brain. I can barely see but I write: ". . . blood on the roots."

Then Malcolm, my fiery, intelligent, and brave hero whisks me away me on a ninety-minute trip. I watch, mind blown. Based on the book, I already knew the story. That's not what matters. In this crowded room, it's just Malcolm and me. He's alive, wowing crowds and angering critics. He pumps me with pride and wonder until I get kicked in the guts seeing him dressed in all white and lying soulless in his coffin. Like Silly Putty, my feelings are easily pulled in many directions during the viewing.

When the lights come on, other people wipe their eyes, too. Daddy pats my back. His face says he knows what I'm feeling.

"You, okay?"

I sniffled. "I can't imagine knowing I'm going to die and still trying to make a difference every day."

"I'm sure brother Malcolm felt fear. Courage is about being fearful and still doing what you have to do." Daddy rubs his eyes, yawns, then sits with his head in his hands. I guess that's how he's buying the ring—with all of his overtime.

I write "courage" in my book and fret about the lack of rhyming words. Throat clearing makes me look up. I'm blocking everyone in. I nudge Daddy, who briefly dozed.

"We're sorry, good people." Daddy jumps up embarrassed. We shuffle out the row toward the nearest exit door.

Outside the rain and high wind pulls my umbrella inside out. Because rain shrinks my hair like nobody's business, I'm so preoccupied with protecting my hair with my notebook that I slip on a patch of leaves. Daddy catches me before I tumble.

"One reason the season is called fall," he says. Opening the car door, he smirks.

"Sorry, I was thinking about how great a writer Alex Haley is. That documentary wouldn't exist without his book." I spill inside and reach over to unlock his door.

"True. Hellava writer." Daddy dries his face with his hanky. "But so are you. Pumpkin, who you gonna write a book about? 'Cause you got the chops."

Daddy has a way of complimenting me that makes me feel good deep down into my corpuscles. While driving to Uncle Duke's, we discuss the old Malcolm who viewed whites as devils versus the new Malcolm who rejected those beliefs. Daddy changes into his SEPTA uniform when we get there.

Daddy finds out he got reassigned to a hilly route in the northern part of the city. He frets over his assigned trolley, a known lemon. I use some fast talking mixed with pleading to keep him from having Uncle Duke drive me home.

On the way to the depot, we resumed talking about Malcolm.

"So the house slaves did in Malcolm?"

Backing into a parking spot, he nods. "With help from the Man," he says. That's adult code for the establishment. Charlie is another code, as in "don't act the way Charlie expects you to." Fooling the Man and his cousin Charlie lives in my brain much like the command "no babies unless married."

"Self-hating Negroes can be the worst. Some of us believe the white man's ice is colder," Daddy says, cutting off his engine. He gestures to the convenience store across the street from the depot. "Get me a pack of gum and whatever you want." He hands me two dollars.

By the time I board the trolley, Daddy and several men are holding a spirited debate about the match between Billie Jean King and Bobby Riggs, which everyone in the free world watched. Mom and I agreed the match was dumb. Billie Jean was nearly half Bobby's age. I won a $5 bet against Daddy.

Wanting no part of their conversation, I head for the middle of the trolley to write in peace. I hunt for a leather seat without any rips spilling its yellow spongy guts.

"You all right back there?" Daddy asks.

"Yes, I just want to work on something."

"My daughter, she writes poems when she rides with me." Daddy puffs up. The two men near him, one Black with a mustache and the other bald and white, smile at me then continue railing against feminists.

Two young white women with waist length hair sit across from me. They eye my hair, but don't ask to touch it. Good. I'm not in the mood. I open my notebook to work on a poem I felt coming on since Billie Holiday's first note. I write: "Lies in the Bible."

The words feel flat on the page. I think about our conversation in the car and the voices around me fade. No one believes it, but sometimes I just push the pen and the words appear. The sensation is like biking down a steep hill—it's fun as long as I hang on and don't stop too soon. I write:

He left us pining for his greatness, longing for his voice
Hurt by misguided people who robbed us of our choice
of a great man unwilling to break, but so willing to grow
A realistic role model, one every Black student must know
He educates with a global reach and challenges my mind
His words of truth and pride, help me see I was once blind
To my power, to my story
To my history, to my glory
I cried today that he died at the hands of Black men

The kind like crabs that pull you back down again
Let's be real family, why can't we see
We are sometimes our own worst enemy

I squint at the page, as the trolley rattles. Close, but not entirely there yet. I add a tentative title: "Wake Up." A smile bubbles up for my handiwork, and then the silence registers. Looking up, the men near my father sit on the edge of their seats watching Daddy pump away on the emergency brake, and we're not slowing down.

Every trolley has three sets of brakes, which I learned one winter day when the electrical brakes and track brakes failed. To slow us down that afternoon, he used the sander, which sprays sand on the undercarriage to increase traction.

Out the front window, businesses whip by as we pick up speed barreling downhill. At the bottom of the drop, a line of cars waits at the red light. We're maybe twenty seconds away from a collision.

I'm making the sign of the cross when Daddy says something low to the men. He rings the gong then faces us.

"Roberta, everyone, please get down behind the seat and hold on tight. Brake troubles. I got one more option." He leans over his seat to open the front doors.

The women near me exchange panicked frowns then huddle behind the seats while the men yank off seat cushions. I refuse to crouch until I see Daddy's plan. To my horror, he moves toward the steps of the open doors, and, gripping the railing, leans out and looks down at the track.

"Daddy!" I choke out in shock. Not only may we collide with a vehicle or two, the trolley could jump the track.

The mustached man feeding cushions to Daddy whips around. "Sweetheart, we're not going to let your father get hurt. Sit down."

Tears spring to my eyes. Daddy's fate lies in the hands of strangers. I step into the aisle and grab onto an overhead strap to keep my balance as the trolley slides downhill fast. Daddy tosses cushions right and left. But the seats fail to jam the wheels; they just bounce off the trolley and whiz past the windows.

"Get down now." The mustached man's voice drips with authority. I obey, bending low behind the seats, hands pressed, fear hammering my heart.

"Dear Lord," I pray, "we need a miracle."

Something under the trolley catches and drags. We're slowing down. Clearly God still hears me. Yay! I peek as Daddy races up the steps toward me. The men follow.

"Hold on, we're going to have impact," Daddy says, then he crouches next to me. A few seconds later, a big thump rocks us as metal grinds and glass shatters. The trolley finally stops after ramming into a double-parked car. Smoke fills the air. Outside someone screams.

———

I hang up the phone and struggle to open the folding doors of the raggedy phone booth at the edge of the gasoline station. Uncle Duke is coming to take me home while Daddy waits for a tower trolley.

Half a block away, several cop cars with flashing lights block the entrance to the intersection. Two officers reroute backed-up traffic, and two bulkier ones talk to Daddy. Their body language troubles me. Both cops stand wide-legged. One has his arms folded across his chest, and the other has his head cocked.

I cross the street and head back to the accident scene, praying Daddy will not lose his job. Seeing how the passengers huddled around him and patted his back and shook his hands, he shouldn't. Plus, no one is yelling "whiplash." Daddy said that's what some passengers immediately yell whether injured or not.

A cold drizzle falls, but I'm not worried about my hair. Just my father. Up ahead, another officer jots notes while talking to the two men who helped with the cushions. When I get within earshot, they stop talking and watch me approach.

"Roberta, right?" asks the Black guy. "You okay? Need a ride?"

"I'm fine, my uncle is picking me up. Thank you."

"That's his kid," the other guy says.

The cop nods at me, and I keep walking. When I'm close enough to hear Daddy's booming voice, I prep myself for a scolding.

"I have to say that I was just about sick when the sander didn't work. These leaves are treacherous on the track this time of year." Daddy gestures to the trees lining the street. He spots me and frowns. He told me to wait at the phone booth.

But I need to make sure the cops eyeballing me now know Daddy is a hero. As Mom-Mom says, I'm here to bear witness.

CHAPTER 13

I scrawl a big X across today's date in my copybook calendar, marking the third week of Project Keep Cool with Sister. She's at her desk calling us up one by one to return our report cards. On the surface, where I live these days, if I had graded myself, I'd get A+ for getting along with Sister since the fight. If I weren't a fake pretender, I'd have an F like she gave me in conduct and effort.

Opening my report card, the offensive grades stare back in Sister's perfect cursive. Suspension meant automatic Fs in those two non-subject areas, which still kept me off the honor roll for the first time since second grade. Good thing the trolley miracle occurred because this latest punishment from her for telling the truth would have made me flip out.

Zeroing in on the comment section, above Mom's signature, Sister wrote in red ink: "Roberta's classroom demeanor is more nuanced and thoughtful." Translation: "She keeps her big trap closed. Hurray!"

Sister summons me. She checks Mom's signature and smiles. "Keep up the good work and you'll be back on the honor roll."

Jeez, wonder why I'm not on it now?

Daddy says my face tells everything straight with no chaser. I'm an open book. Not lately. All Sister Elizabeth sees is a blank face. I got that on lock. Christmas gifts are on the line. Back at my desk, I snicker at how it's at home where I really flunked conduct and effort. Before the trolley accident, I fought any effort Mom made toward acting nice. At least my limited responses cut down on arguing. Only the good weekly reports from Sister Excrement worked in my favor and kept the allowance coming.

At school, I'm all drama mama, fooling Sister big time. And because I pretend like I don't despise Sister or think she's lower than pond scum, she treats me like a human being instead of a dark mistake.

A few times, she had me sell pretzels in class, a job usually reserved for her pets. It's a cool gig that involves trust since I count pretzels and collect the nickel payments.

"Roberta, collect the homework," Sister Elizabeth says.

"Yes, Sister," I chirp. Students forward their papers to the person in the first seat. Handing me papers, a smirking Geoffrey mouths, "Brown noser." He whispers, "You're as useless as a nun's nipple."

I scurry away, hoping Sister won't demand he repeat what he has said. Geoffrey can bad-mouth Sister all he wants. My guns will not be loaded anytime soon. Yes, Sister has been buddying up to me, and I'm all about a truce. I'm real clear about why I want one. Sister, not so much. I don't understand her at all. How can she treat me with sweetness now and such hellish scorn weeks ago? Where did she come from? Who raised her? She is such a mystery.

Earlier, when I ran back upstairs to fetch my umbrella out of the closet cubby hole to keep my Afro shrink-proof on the way to lunch, her singing spilled out into the hallways. I stood, trancelike, feeling each note of her version of "Yellow Bird," a Caribbean song we learned in fifth grade.

Sister Elizabeth doesn't sound like any off-key nun I've ever heard. Her throaty voice rivals the choir ladies in Mom-Mom's church, where ushers dress like nurses and people wearing their best get the spirit and dance in the pews or fall out on the floor.

"Those women can *sang*," Daddy said when we attended on special occasions. "They make a brother step in here every Sunday morning after partying all night."

Daddy was right as usual. That tambourine-backed singing, along with soulful sermons, reached deep inside and settled in, compared to my church's high-pitch and dry warbling and sleepy Gospel readings and homilies. Aside from the impromptu boogeying freaking me out, Mom-Mom's small storefront church pulled me closer to God than mine. Sure, our huge church offers jaw-dropping beauty in spades, from life-sized marble angels and museum-like columns to enormous stained-glass windows and an altar with real gold. But I spend more time twisting in the pew admiring its beautiful sights than getting anything out of priests reading with all the excitement of dial tones.

"Close your textbooks," Sister Elizabeth says, taking the papers from me. Her cheeks arch toward . . . a smile. "I am astounded by the quality of last night's homework and your decorum all week," she says to the class. "So you have the rest of this period to spend in free time. Just do it quietly."

I raise my hand. Sister nods.

"Can we sing 'Yellow Bird?'"

The class murmurs in agreement.

"I love 'Yellow Bird.' That was my favorite song in fifth grade!" volunteers Donna.

"Can we use the maracas?" asks Stephanie. "I know where Miss Dillon keeps them."

"'Yellow Bird'?" Sister seems puzzled but pleased by our request. "That's one of my favorite tunes, too, but don't you want to sing something more contemporary?"

"'Yellow Bird,'" several students say in unison.

Her eyes sparkle at our enthusiasm.

"Okay, settle your horses," she says, laughing with ease. Even her laughter, wiggles of ear joy, is musical and as gleeful as her glorious singing. "You young folks never cease to amaze me. Know-it-alls one second and," she scans the class, "sweet kids the next. Get the box of maracas." She claps her hands. "Let's travel to the islands through song, shall we?"

The vibe from Sister is crazy cool and we *dig* it. She beams from the inside.

Her brother must be doing better, I thought. "Sister, can you sing it first?" I ask. "Please, pretty please."

Chuckling, Sister points to her high stool nestled in the corner next to the locked supply cabinet. Geoffrey is up and heading toward it before Sister can ask, trying to muscle in on her good graces. He carries it to the front.

Sister perches on the stool, adjusts the folds of her habit. Eyes closed, she takes several deep breaths and I lean in.

The stirring voice that fired up my soul earlier pours out. I shake my maracas up and down, pretending they're drumsticks and I'm striking a tin drum to produce a calypso beat. The swishy rattle of maracas tuck around Sister's throaty voice, transporting me to an island in my mind. In a new purple bikini, I lay on the beach watching palm trees dance with my family. Under an umbrella, we wiggle our toes as Sister's voice serenades us. Rare moments like this feel like the old carefree days.

Flashing teeth, Sister says, "Class, now sing to me." Sister conducts as we belt out the "Yellow Bird" lyrics. We sing with enthusiasm but fall way short of her mastery.

"Take it away, Sister Elizabeth" Geoffrey says.

Looking endlessly happy, Sister actually winks at him. Eyes closed, she sways and snaps her fingers as classmates lacking maracas clap to the beat of the lyrics. Judging by

Sister's voice, she has a heart. No one can sing with such emotion without one.

"That's it," she says, with a clap of her hands. "The bell will ring in two minutes, and we need to return the maracas and straighten the desks."

We applaud Sister for her unexpected performance. Times like this, I sort of like her—until I remind myself I can't. I remind myself that three people eat dinner in my house instead of four. That Fs sit on my report card. Every time I do, sparks of anger poke through, reigniting a fire I refuse to let burn out.

The next day, a seminarian visits religion class. Brother Richard is a hardcore bore fest. Still, a few brown nosers ask questions to impress Sister. Brother Richard leaves midway through class, and our good conduct earns us more free time.

I held my tongue during his visit to keep the peace, but I was dying to ask: Why is Jesus always shown with white skin? When Malcolm was imprisoned, he pointed out to his chaplain that Jesus, as described in the Bible, was not white. Malcolm also said the Bible was used to justify slavery. Sister would have a heart attack for real if I bring any of that up.

Donna and other students get into a conversation with Sister Elizabeth, peppering her with questions about some of the changes that resulted from Vatican II, which we discussed earlier with Brother Richard. I am content to daydream, but Donna calls me over.

"We are called to engage with the modern world," Sister says as I join the huddle. "There are competing perspectives on how best to do that. That's one reason some nuns and priests speak out against the Vietnam War and," she glances at me next to Donna, "support civil rights."

"My grandmother says she preferred priests facing the altar during Mass instead of looking at church members," Donna says.

Face aglow, Sister turns to me because she mistakenly thinks we're friends. "I'm sure Roberta will have an interesting question or two."

Daddy says you can say anything, it's how you say it. There is something I've wanted to know for a while, so I went for it.

"Sister, why do you still wear the old-fashioned habit? Don't you get hot keeping your hair covered or not wearing something shorter?"

"I guess I'm rebellious," she says. She winks, earning cool points.

When will the aliens return Sister?

"It's a choice," Sister says. She forms a teepee with her hands. "As a girl, I was attracted to the nuns in their splendid habits, which led to an attraction to the lifestyle. I believe in tradition. It's a privilege to wear a more traditional habit and veil. Being a nun for as long as I have been means I get to choose."

I raise my hand. Sister looks impatient.

"We're talking, Roberta. You don't need permission to speak."

"Is your preference for tradition the reason why you don't use colored chalk like some of the other sisters and lay teachers?"

She taps her hands against her nose. "I prefer white, it's so clean against the blackboard."

The word "clean" rubs me the wrong way. I count.

"It's easier to see. It has a better contrast. And yes, it's traditional."

Glancing at the floor, I remember how in first grade when the black-and-white tiled flooring was new, we were told to walk only on the dark-colored floor tiles to keep things looking clean.

Sister pushes up her glasses to better see me frown. "Are you trying to make this a race thing, Roberta?"

"No, Sister. It's just that you said about white being . . . so clean. It makes me wonder why white has to represent everything that is good and black is the opposite." As her eyes narrow, I add, "In the general sense."

"Technically black and white are not colors. But Roberta, I'll give you the floor. Continue," she says, sitting.

Everyone stops and listens.

"So you have the white knight on the white horse, good cowboys wear white hats, brides wear white, purity is white, communion is white," I say. "Angels are white with white wings. Doves symbolize peace. And *black* is dirty and sinful, you know, a black mark is bad. Then there's blackballed, blackmail, demons are dark. Bad guys wear black. Black cats are bad luck."

Titters erupt. Sister's raised eyebrows act as stop signs. I lean back on my desk, satisfied.

"My habit, which I love, is mostly black," says Sister, who rises and paces the front of the room. "So is the robe for a judge. A starless night is black, and without it we would not have daylight. Coal, a precious resource, is black. We know that black is beautiful."

"Preach it, Sister," says Stephanie.

My cheeks burn, mainly since I am caught off guard by a) Sister's response and b) brown-nosing Stephanie all up in her amen corner.

"Roberta, one of the most powerful tools is a blackboard. Teachers all over the globe use white chalk and a blackboard to teach students." Sister taps the white chalk against the board. "Black and white together can be so powerful. Let's focus on that."

She's deliberately ignoring my point. My temper shoots up like an escaped balloon. I picture the 10-speed I asked for Christmas and speed count to twenty.

"Are you finished making your point?" Sister asks.

I nod. *For now.* Sister responds with a huge grin, a sight as rare as Halley's Comet. The bell rings. I file out to recess, feeling beaten at a game I expected to win. Who knew she'd checkmate me with a Kumbaya moment?

———

"Hey Roberta, I got a great joke for you." Geoffrey stops me.

I think to myself, *the joke is you.* Sister cracked me up yesterday when she told him "some village is missing its idiot" and that he was "allergic to common sense."

"What's black-and-white and black-and-white and black-and-white and black-and-white?"

I shrug, scan the yard for Bonnie and wait for the cornball punchline.

"A nun falling down the steps." He collapses into hysterics.

He wishes. I roll my eyes so hard I hope they don't get stuck and head toward the rope jump crew.

"What's that clown hooting about?" Bonnie asks.

"He always has such stupid jokes. He's a flake," I say.

"You usually like them."

"I'm not in the mood. Sister made me mad. I make a point about how the color white stands for everything good while black represents everything bad and she acted like I didn't know what I was talking about."

"Girl, she knew what you meant."

"Yup, which is why my first book of poetry will be called *Angel Dressed in Black.*"

"Love it. Now, let's go kick some Black butt," says Bonnie, laughing.

Donna ambles over as we wait our turn to jump. She's one of the few white students comfortable enough to walk over by herself to our section of the yard.

"What's so funny, you two?" she asks.

"Sister Elizabeth," I say.

"Oh, I thought Geoffrey told a joke about an angel."

"Oh, that's the title of my first book, *Angel Dressed in Black*."

"I'll buy it," Donna says. "You're a great writer."

A grin takes over my face and a buzz shoots through my body. I smile at the coolest white girl I know as I wait to jump rope with the coolest Black girl on the planet.

CHAPTER 14

Clouds shaped like gigantic dumplings float overhead on a warm, sticky fall day so humid my Afro shrinks in half. This weather makes me long for carefree summer days of playing jacks or riding the trolley with Daddy while reading *Right On!* cover to cover. Afterward, we'd eat steaming crabs.

Instead, I'm bored out of my mind in music class. No one is singing today. We're learning how to read music—shoot me now. I turn my attention back to Sister Elizabeth, who, with a few exceptions, has behaved like a normal teacher for weeks.

Wouldn't it be fun to play Nancy Drew and learn more about her since she's filling in for our music teacher? I bet she's from down South.

My hand shoots up. Sister nods.

"Sister Elizabeth, how old were you when you discovered you had a good voice? Were your parents also singers?"

"What interesting questions. I was, maybe in sixth grade. And, yes, both of my parents have lovely voices. Much lovelier than mine."

"Were they professional singers? I bet they were. You could have been if you weren't committed to the Lord and all, which is more important than a singing career."

Sister throws back her head and laughs. "I think I made the right decision with my life. I love to sing, but I love doing the Lord's work more."

"Are your parents happy you entered the convent?"

Her smile trembles for a nanosecond and her eyes reveal a faraway gaze. She knits her eyebrows and tilts her head. "Yes . . . they were very surprised." Her voice sounds odd, unsure mixed with something I can't quite pinpoint. Her whole vibe changes before my eyes. As the seconds pass, she appears . . . less Sisterly? More like a regular person time traveling in her mind. Unaware of the present, she seems just focused on what had been.

The room grows quiet. We've never seen her like this. Falling asleep? Sure. But right now she's wide awake and still not really with us. *Tell us where you are?*

She's so still I can see her bottom lip is slightly chapped.

"Did you want to be a nun as a little girl?" Donna asks.

"Not until I was about fourteen or fifteen."

"Was it hard to give up your name?" I ask.

Sister shakes her head. The faraway gaze remains.

"How many siblings do you have? Any enter the priesthood or convent?" I ask.

"There are five of us, four sisters and one brother." She says *brother* with tenderness. They must be close like Charles and me. "He's the youngest. And for you Curious Georges," she says, chuckling. "I'm the only Rucker child who gave her life to the Lord."

Heads swivel. We look at each other with surprise. Nuns never tell their last names to students. Sister is clearly in a way-back-when trance.

"Is your brother doing better?" I ask.

If a record had been playing, my question would have made it skip and scratch. Sister's eyes snap open and her body jerks as if the devil poked her back. She adjusts her glasses and studies me as if seeing me for the first time. Those dreamy eyes seconds ago transform into a dead-eyed stare. She grimaces as if I'm an experiment gone wrong. Even the air in the room changes. *Me and my big mouth.*

"Excuse me, Miss Forest? What do you think you know about *my* family?" She shares her dagger gaze with the class and then pierces me to smithereens with it. "I give an inch and you demand a mile. I try to be nice and you ride roughshod. Don't ask me another question unless it's tied to the subject at hand. Got it?"

I nod, parting my lips to say I'm sorry.

"Not another word."

What did I do? I feel low, dirty and desperate. All I know is this: I gotta fix it. One bad report and Christmas is toast.

My stomach gurgles while I try to figure out how to convince her I meant no harm.

After everyone files out, I approach Sister. She ignores me while searching desk drawers as if gold is buried in them.

"Sister Elizabeth, may I speak to you, please?"

"What is it?" She looks at me from head to toe then searches inside a drawer.

"I meant no harm, I promise. Geoffrey told a bunch of kids that your brother was sick. I've been praying for him because I would want someone to pray if my brother became ill. I wasn't trying to be ugly, I swear."

"Don't swear." Sister stops rummaging. Her eyes appear softer. "And take my advice: stop listening to Geoffrey. You can't straighten an old crooked tree. You'll get hurt in the process. I'll talk to him about not spreading rumors like a fisher wife."

"Yes, Sister." I scurry toward the door.

"Roberta," she calls after me.

I turn, holding my breath.

"Thank you for the prayers."

"You're welcome." My smile is real as I hurry into the hallway. That was close. Good thing I can think on my feet.

I nearly stepped on a verbal landmine. Sister's reaction reminded me that the body snatchers can return to the old version anytime. I let my guard down. She's still the same crooked tree. Stupid me.

I charge into the house to find Charles watching cartoons and chowing down on a huge bowl of butter pecan ice cream topped with cookies.

"Did you leave me any?" I hurry into the kitchen and find a spoonful and two broken cookies left. I march into the living room and block the television. "You're not the only one who lives here. Please stop eating us out of house and home."

"At least I did not break up our family."

I step closer. "What did you say?"

Charles's nostrils flare.

"Take it back on the count of three," I demand, using my fingers as I countdown. "Three, two, one." He watches me like I'm a circus animal. "Why you say that?"

"I'm not stupid. I can figure things out."

"I know you heard Mom say it on the phone."

"Mommy didn't say it. And I hate the way you treat her."

"You're really going to hate the way bullies treat you from now on. The next time someone picks on you, don't come crying to me."

"Don't worry," Charles says, shoveling what should be my portion of ice cream into his whale blubber mouth.

"Give me the rest of that ice cream." I lean in to grab the bowl as he spins away.

He places the bowl at the other end of the coffee table and tosses his glass of milk in my hair.

"Oh no, you didn't," I sputter.

I leap onto the sofa, pinning him against the cushions. I yank him up by his collar as beads fly everywhere, some bouncing off the coffee table or rolling across the floor. Charles becomes hysterical and surprises me by cuffing my cheek with unexpected force.

"My rosary beads! You are gonna burn in hell, Roberta," he sneers. "You only care about yourself. You make me sick."

I let him up. He crawls after the scattering beads, picks up a few, then puts his head on his knees and cries. Now I'm bewildered as I look around for his inhaler. "Why are your rosary beads around your neck?"

"I always wear them when I am praying for something big."

"Your spelling test?"

"No, our family."

My mouth goes dry. I feel dumb. "Stop crying before you make yourself sick. Where's your inhaler?"

He points to his stuffed book bag. I dig out his inhaler, and, after handing it to him I collect scattered beads. Nestling them in a napkin, I spot a few more beads in the bowl.

"I'll be back." I take the steps two at a time and grab my never-used rosary beads out of a drawer. In the mirror I glimpse milk weighing down a section of my Afro. I grab a T-shirt from the floor and pat my hair dry.

Downstairs, I drape my beads around his neck. "I'm sorry," I say, helping him up from the floor. I pull him close and nuzzle his nose. "Charles, let's pray real hard that we spend Christmas with Daddy. If that happens, it's a matter of time before he comes back home."

We kneel on the green shaggy rug and silently pray.

"I'm sorry," Charles whimpers.

I clean up the milk, and we share the ice cream blessed by rosary beads and watch cartoons that make us laugh out loud.

When Mom walks in, I make it a point to not scowl and dash away. I talk to her for the sake of my brother, who beams at me. He'd purr all over the place if he were a cat.

I realize if I can be civil to Sister Elizabeth, then Mom deserves no less.

"I'll be back," I say to Mom and Charles.

In my room I pull out my diary and scribble myself in one word at a time.

I write: "What a weird day. If it had a theme it would be, 'The trouble with brothers.' Sister freaked out when I asked her about her sick brother. She's so guarded and not just against having a good time. Clearly, she has something to hide. Word around school is she has seen him once in the hospital and he's been there for weeks. Hearing that made me appreciate Charles a little more. 'Cause when I came home, he freaked out on me for being mean to Mom. And you know what? He's right. I'm going to do better. Promise."

CHAPTER 15

Picking the crust from my eyes, I toss my blanket and relish the victory warming my insides. After my fifth good weekly report, I'm off punishment. Done. *El fin*. Mom even threw in a sweet peace offering: Bonnie is spending the night.

We will play records and read magazines without any interference from Charles, who's spending the night with Daddy.

I yawn, having stayed up until after midnight spinning my favorite records. I replayed Jermaine Jackson's "Daddy's Home" so much that I expected Mom to tell me to stop. That she didn't is a great sign.

I hop out of bed and roll up the shade. Afternoon sun floods the room, revealing my bureau mirror smeared with God-knows-what. I study my teeth, assessing their whiteness. On a scale of one to ten, mine rank an eight. I want to score a ten before Thanksgiving, which is a few weeks away. Extra brightening drops are in order, starting today.

I make a mental note to clean my room before Bonnie arrives.

I smell bacon as I head into the bathroom.

Downstairs Mom has cooked so much bacon that when Charles heaps a handful of strips onto his plate, he barely makes a dent in the pile. He eyes me with suspicion as I grab my share.

"What are you and Daddy doing?" I chirp.

"He's taking me to the Franklin Institute," he says, talking with his mouth full.

"Awww, I want to go!" I joke. The interactive science museum hooked me from the moment I walked through its giant, thumping "heart" exhibit during a third-grade class trip.

"No, it's just me and Daddy." He frowns at me like he's doing his math homework.

"Whoa, calm down. I thought we made up, what's bothering you besides being a crybaby?

Charles pokes his lips out far enough for me to cross the Schuylkill River on them. "I'm telling Daddy how horrible you act all the time."

"Stop teasing him," Mom says.

I jump. I didn't hear her walk in.

"Didn't you just get off of punishment?"

"He started it. I came down here in a good mood, and he's acting all funky."

Charles hits the table and runs out, leaving his food.

"Is someone bothering him at school?" I ask Mom.

She purses her lips and pours bacon grease into a can. "You know he's sensitive. You're so self-absorbed. He misses your father as much as you do."

I'm fresh off punishment so I'm not reminding her she can make her children real happy by allowing their father to come home. At least things are better. Daddy comes to dinner almost every Sunday, and Mom is much more pleasant these days. But deep down I can't help but wait for the other shoe to drop.

"I'll stop teasing him. Promise."

Mom sighs then resumes washing the frying pan.

"Can I go downtown to Wanamaker's with Bonnie?"

"Just be home before dinner. I have extra tokens in my bag," she says.

———

We pay our fare and scout out two adjoining seats. Bonnie and I move down the narrow aisle past bright-eyed adults. During the week, most grownups look miserable going to or returning from work. I never want a job that makes me look like that.

We settle in seats near the rear door exit. We pour over the Christmas catalogue I swiped from home when the trolley jerks to a stop.

We hear a loud-talking, gum-smacking passenger before she boards. "I know that's right, girl," she yells to someone in another zip code. "Later." Her raspy voice sounds familiar.

I glance up as she deposits her fare. Popping gum, she's slender with enormous breasts and a huge Afro. A Foxy Brown wannabee. Heads snap, swivel, and lean back as she passes. I can just picture their eyes bugging out of their sockets.

"Whoa, Foxy Brown's Afro is bigger than yours," Bonnie says with awe. Her smile fades as the woman wiggles closer. "Nah, it's a wig," she mumbles.

I turn the page to a powder blue suit perfect for Easter when the gum chewer stops by us.

"Youse Chuck's daughter, right? That has to be you under all that beautiful thick hair."

I look up, search her face. The mole on her cheek and her top heaviness seem familiar.

"It's me." I try to remember her name. Her flowery perfume itches my nose.

Bonnie nudges me with her knee. Men up front are turned in their seats, checking out the rear view of her tight jeans.

"Your huge, pretty bush influenced my new look." She shakes her wig.

"That's sad," Bonnie whispers.

"How's your daddy doing?" Her smile reveals lipstick-stained teeth. I recall not liking her when Daddy introduced us when I rode with him before, around the time school started. Nothing has changed. I rub my nose.

"My father is fine. My mother, too."

Bonnie covers her chuckles with coughing.

The woman raises her eyebrow at Bonnie. She sits across from us next to a grandfatherly dude who studies her bodacious boobies.

"Like I was *saying*." Bonnie's rude tone makes me giggle.

We go back to studying the catalogue until throat clearing distracts us. I look over at her.

"I don't know what your momma looks like, but you the spitting image of your father."

She's annoying, like a fly buzzing around my dessert. "I'll tell him you said hello. What's your name, again?"

"Miss Wiggy Titty," Bonnie whispers.

"He, my friends call me Peaches," she says with a knowing smirk. "And he calls you 'Precious.'" She snaps her fingers, squints in concentration. "Nah, it's 'Pumpkin,' right?"

I flinch. Her voice annoys me like squeaking chalk. "My name is Roberta."

"Well, Roberta, if I see your daddy, I'll tell him I ran into you." Her blazing smile is pure evil.

Bonnie's mouth hangs open. Hairs on my neck rise. This hussy acts like she knows more than she's saying. Could this be the woman Mom was talking about on the phone a few summers ago? My heart clenches like a fist. I need to connect some dots.

"Oh, you live near Uncle Jimmy?"

"No, sugah," she says, smiling.

"Wow, something stinks on this trolley," Bonnie says, fanning her nose.

Peaches tilts forward in her seat to directly eyeball Bonnie, who stares back.

"I'm not a toy, don't play with me, little girl." She lifts her chin and pops her gum.

I nudge Bonnie to look away. Peaches starts talking to the man next to her who I suspect wants to be her Living Bra.

"I can't wait to tell Mom about this chick," I whisper to Bonnie.

"Nah, she has nothing on your mom except weight and a wig," she cackles.

Whispering and giggling nonstop, we invent a slew of wickedly funny insults about Peaches. She rolls her eyes so hard at us, we cross our fingers, hoping they get stuck.

When I tell Mom about Peaches, I study her reaction. Nothing changes on her face, not even a hint of concern. Her movements are loose and easy as she reads a recipe.

"You know your father is a big flirt. But some of these fast women out here think his attention means more than it does."

"But she seemed like she was insinuating something. Right, Bonnie?"

"Yes, Mrs. Forest. I wanted to tell her and her funky breath off. She reminds me of something my grandma says—it don't matter how good looking the salad is if the dressing is bad."

We chuckle at Bonnie's indignation. I'm glad she's staying overnight. Having her here lessens the tension between Mom and me.

Color-struck Bonnie, who never saw a light-skinned person who was ugly, is my Mom's biggest fan. Mom tops her list of beautiful people.

"Don't get in trouble over me," Mom says, hugging Bonnie. "I'll call you two when dinner is ready." She shoos us out of the kitchen.

———————

I'm sprawled on my bed with a book. Belly down on her sleeping quilt devouring the latest issue of *Right On!* magazine, Bonnie squeals and points to a headline: "Upcoming Contests in 1974."

"For Black History Week, they are holding a national essay contest. You should enter."

My dismissive wave couldn't be more lazy. "You know how many of their stupid contests I've entered? I can't even win a free subscription."

"Girl, this is national. But I know your heart is set on our contest. I hope you beat Eileen this year. I'm sick of her winning everything."

"I better. Want to play some more records?" I say as Mom pushes the door open.

"Hey you two, have you ever seen *The Trouble with Angels?* It's coming on now."

Nodding like a dashboard bobblehead, Bonnie pops up from the floor and dashes out the door to accept Mom's invitation without even asking me if I want to see the stupid movie.

"I think you'll like it," Mom says, waiting in the doorway. "It's about these two Catholic girls who are known trouble-makers getting into all kinds of mischief." Mom smiles. "Sounds like some people I know. I believe part of it was filmed in Ambler."

"How does it end?"

"Come see. I'll make some popcorn and root beer floats."

I wanted Bonnie to myself, but Mom is trying hard to connect. I force myself downstairs to watch one of *her* favorite movies with *my* best friend.

Two hours later we watch the credits roll in silence on the sofa, Bonnie wedged between Mom and me. What started off a light-hearted story about two friends who stayed in trouble with their nuns took an unexpected turn when the most rebellious teen decided to become a nun. The biggest surprise for me is she kept her decision a secret from her friend until after graduation.

"Wow, I did not see that ending coming. You're right, Mom, it was good." I keep to myself how moved I am. If Bonnie wasn't here, I would have cried a couple of times.

"They should make a Black version and star us." Bonnie laughs and reaches for the bowl of popcorn. She grabs a handful and passes the bowl to Mom, who doesn't respond.

"Mrs. Forest, are you okay?" Bonnie's face creases with concern.

I look at Mom, who brushes away tears. Is she crying over Daddy?

"What's wrong, Mom?"

"I love this movie. It always gets to me," she says, with a sheepish grin.

Whew! I slouch back with the popcorn bowl.

"My grandma does the same thing when she watches sad movies," Bonnie says, laughing.

"I love the friendship between the girls and the way Mary changes. Just shows you can't give up on people." Mom sounds wistful. *Is she talking about Daddy?*

"Yes," Bonnie says laughing. "Don't give up on Roberta."

We laugh as Mom searches in her pocketbook.

"If they made a Black version, they should get the Black nun with the Afro to play the Mother Superior role," Bonnie says.

"What Black nun?" Mom asks, pausing.

"The one that is a figment of her imagination," I answer. "She's the only who saw her."

"Mrs. Forest, cross my heart and hope to die, I saw her several times, although not in recent years."

"I believe you, honey," Mom says, chuckling. She hands me a dollar. "Get some more popcorn. The root beer floats will be ready when you return. Watch whatever you want when you get back. I'm going upstairs to read."

It's a chilly fall night. We wait on the corner under the street light for a car missing a muffler to pass.

"Can you believe she became a nun at the end?" I say.

Bonnie responds with a lopsided twist of her lips, short-hand for "hell no." She's quick to do that when she doesn't feel like talking, and it irks me.

"It caught me off guard, but it makes sense," I say.

Bonnie suddenly becomes fascinated with her chipped fingernail polish. We know each other all too well. She knows that I know she is deliberately ignoring me when she knows I am trying to make a point I want her to agree with, even though I know she has already made her mind up. Best friends can work your last good nerve like no other.

"Mary Clancy kept watching Mother Superior remember? She felt a connection, maybe sensed they had more in common than she originally thought. That's why they clashed," I say as we round a corner.

Bonnie whips her head around, narrows her eyes, and shoots me an "are you nuts" look. "If you are confessing that you suddenly understand Sister Elizabeth and you are planning on becoming a nun instead of a writer, I might have to call you out for a fair one and knock some sense into you right here, right now."

I unload a playful jab to her arm. "In case you forgot, we both wanted to be nuns back in first grade."

Bonnie cackles, pauses, and turns serious. "Before we realized how much fun sinning is."

Laughter from deep in my belly pours out. The kind that feels best when laughing at something one shouldn't.

We giggle-snort as we enter the new corner store owned by Mr. Whitby, an older Black man everyone adores. We stop at the Tastykake rack.

I finger a package of butterscotch Krimpets, then chocolate. Mentally I bite each snack and compare. Bonnie bumps me back to reality.

"Don't tell me that you're going soft on Sister."

I grab the Krimpets and head toward the register, Bonnie trailing me. "She ruined my life. What do you think?"

CHAPTER 16

"I'm coming in with my daughter, so watch the language." Daddy tucks a warning into his words as we enter the crowded barbershop.

"Ah, she's as pretty as can be. Must look like your wife," says Jerome, the bald shop owner I met last summer. He grins so hard I see all his teeth.

"Thank you, Mr. Jerome. Hello, everyone." I pick up several *Jets* to read while Daddy waits for a chair to get his Afro shaped up.

Greetings come from every direction in the shop. I recognize Ricardo, who plays chess, and a gap-toothed barber named Bennie. I spot a couple of fine boys with glorious cheekbones and perfect Afros watching me. Good thing I'm not light enough to blush. They're so cute it hurts to even glance at them.

Daddy sits next to me with his Malcolm book, which I finally returned.

"We were just talking about Malcolm," says Jerome. "You just reading his book, Charles? You kinda late brother."

"I'm re-reading it. Roberta just read it for the first time."

"Pretty *and* smart," Jerome says.

"And you know it. So what's the debate?" Dad asks.

"Listen to these fools and see if you can figure it out," says a pretty mother waiting with her young son. She smiles at Daddy. I lay my head on his shoulder.

"As I was saying, with all due respect, Reverend Doctor, the Bible also says an eye for an eye!" Bennie says, sharpening a long razor blade against a shiny black strap. He presses the blade against Reverend Doctor's neck and scrapes off the hairy white foam. The shaved skin looks butter smooth.

"That's Old Testament," the reverend replies. "The Bible of Jesus Christ and his disciples is what we should live by. Malcolm X wasn't a Christian. We need to put that Black Muslim foolishness aside and—"

"Reverend Doctor, the white man's Jesus kept us in chains," shouts a young man wearing wrap-around sunglasses, jeans, a worn denim jacket and a T-shirt with the words "Ready for Revolution." A bushy Afro and beard frame his handsome ebony face. I remember seeing him at the Malcolm X documentary.

"Bennie, you need to take them whiteys off your wall. Black folks always crying about JFK, but he didn't do nothin' for black folks. And Bobby and J. Edgar Hoover spied on Martin!"

"There's no need to disrespect Malcolm," says Jerome, as he snips the loose ends of a teenager's Afro with a pair of scissors. "You're talking about the old Malcolm. I just read his autobiography. He did a pilgrimage to Mecca and concluded that all men are one in the eyes of Allah. He became El Hajj Malik El Shabazz, embraced brotherhood, and rejected separatism."

"And what did that change of heart get Malcolm but a bunch of bullets?" asks Ricardo. "Black folks still catching hell, white folks dishing it. And you're talking about nonviolence? I'll be damned."

"Fool, men as Black as you and me killed Malcolm," Jerome says, spreading his arm. "Yeah, maybe the CIA was involved, but Black men pulled the trigger. I'm more afraid of these crazy brothers out here than any white man."

He raises his chubby frame from his seat and stomps toward the soda machine. He drops a coin in the slot, pulls out a Yoo-hoo chocolate soda and takes a long swig.

"I'm gonna tell you the truth, man," he says to no one in particular. "I like the old Malcolm better."

I watch this play out in awe. The barbershop is a place where a man can hold a blade to another man's throat and no one thinks twice of it, even as the men argue. A young man can go toe-to-toe with one of the community elders without being put in his place. Here, everyone seems equal, and everyone has an opinion. But where I stood in this debate, I wasn't entirely sure.

It takes forever for Daddy to get his hair clipped. We miss the matinee and have to go to a later show. Then we walk in and learn Mom-Mom isn't feeling well, so we're spending the night. She goes to bed shortly after dinner, and we pull out the Scrabble game. I love having Daddy to myself.

"That was a great conversation about Malcolm and religion in the barbershop," I say.

"Yup," he says, flipping channels. He settles on a sports program. Ugh. I scramble to think of a question that requires a discussion.

"Why didn't you want us to go to Catholic school?" I blurt.

"Your mom and I disagree about the whole school issue," he says with a bemused smile. "She will not budge," he fingers his goatee, "one iota. She thinks desegregation makes a difference. I say the goal should be equity of educational opportunities. While we march for equality, the white man builds equity." He shrugs. "But what do I know? She got some college in her." A wide grin lights up his face. "You think that trumps my PhD in street sense?"

I burst out laughing. "All the nopers in Noperville say nope."

Daddy laughs.

I grow serious. "A teacher wouldn't scream at me to go back to Africa in an all-Black school."

"Maybe not. But you're kicking butt academically at a mostly white school. It's preparing you to compete with them at an early age. For that, I gotta give your mother credit." He studies my face with listen-to-me eyes. "Cut your mom some slack. You two fight because you're just alike." He heads into the kitchen.

"I'm nothing like her," I huff. "I don't look like her, think like her, or act like her."

Daddy chuckles as he opens the refrigerator. "Stubborn like her, too. Two peas in a pod."

I'd rather talk about something else. Or watch something else. Searching the *TV Guide*, I find gold. "Daddy, there's a Western on. It started a few minutes ago."

"Let's get this party started! Want some ice cream?" he asks.

"Yes, please." I turn the channel, wishing this night would last forever.

Daddy returns with two bowls, chocolate syrup and a container of ice cream. "Has your mom talked about Thanksgiving plans, yet?" Dad scoops my ice cream first.

"No." I tense up.

"I'm working and may miss dinner. But we will celebrate Christmas together. I got a big surprise. Keep that between us."

Yay. I jump up and Soul Train dance as Daddy eggs me on. I'd dance on the moon if I could get up there. In recent weeks, Daddy started dropping by for dinner a few times a week. Guess all of his overtime pay pleases Mom. She's been downright pleasant. Clearly, he gave up gambling. I think he learned his lesson, and Mom learned hers. *Thanks be to God.*

Winded, I snuggle next to Daddy in a state of bliss and pretend to watch the Late Show Movie. Mom-Mom's TV is old and full of static. She doesn't know it but we're getting her a new one for Christmas.

The black-and-white movie has Daddy's full attention so I daydream about Christmas. Daddy says money can't buy you happiness, but it can buy a Cadillac big enough to pull up next to it. I think if we're all in the Cadillac and it's stuffed with gifts, then that's a fine saying. Christmas is everything, and for the longest I thought it would be ruined if we didn't celebrate together. Now we will.

At this rate, Daddy may even be home before the writing contest! Still, I need to win it. I dream about strutting across the stage as the best writer in the entire school. Maybe the entire archdiocese.

"For the writing awards program, I'm wearing red, black, and green."

Fixated on the staticky screen, he shushes me then adjusts the antenna. During a commercial, he faces me. "What was that again?"

"For the awards program coming up, I think I want to wear red, black, and green."

"The writing awards? Oh, yeah. Good idea," he says, reaching for his bowl. "My baby, or should I call you Little Malcomvina, wants to wear the colors of Black nationalism. Do you know the story behind the flag?"

I shake my head and wait for him to finish enjoying his scoop of ice cream.

"Marcus Garvey is the man behind it. About seventy years ago, there was a popular song called, 'Every Race Has a Flag but the Coon.' Ain't that something?"

I suck my teeth. *Devils.*

"That's where the term 'coon' comes from in reference to Black people." He pinches my cheek and winks. "I'll wear the colors, too. All of us will."

"Do you think you'll be back home before then?"

"You can bet on it," he says, winking.

The movie resumes, and I lose his attention to old actors on horseback. I'll get it back soon enough. Any second, the sheer joy I feel will ooze out of my pores like melted butter and cover the squeaky plastic covering Mom-Mom's sofa. For now, just sitting next to him, watching him hoot and holler and occasionally adjust the antenna, ends wrapped in foil to clear up the fuzzy images, is enough. Happiness whispers in my ears. It's been fifty-six days since we watched TV together. That I can stop counting soon is enough to shut me up. At least until the commercials.

CHAPTER 17

"**M**erry Christmas, Daddy!" We yelp in happy unison. We sprint into his arms. I bury my nose in his new red wool scarf: my gift. The vibrant color is a nice contrast next to his chocolate skin, making him look even more handsome and dashing.

I glance at Mom to see if she notices. Head tilted, Mom grins at our three-way hug fest. She tucks a wavy lock of fresh-cut hair behind her ear.

"Daddy, are we riding together to Mom-Mom's?" Hope makes Charles's voice squeak. We study Mom for the answer.

"We will ride together." Her voice is soft and light like her makeup, which she started wearing recently.

Dad hugs and kisses Mom, who blushes. "Merry Christmas, baby," he says.

"Merry Christmas, Chuck." Mom smiles and so do our hearts.

"I got you a little surprise," Daddy says, opening his shopping bag of wrapped gifts.

"You already gave me my gifts when you dropped off the kids. I don't need you spending any more money on me. Christmas is just one day and—" Mom stops when Daddy hands her a small wrapped box with an oversized bow. He presses his finger to his lips.

"Shhh. No fussing on Christmas. Repeat after me." He looks at us for back up.

"No fussing on Christmas!" we eagerly repeat.

Mom says it, too. Softly. She unwraps it to reveal a ring box. Taking a deep breath, she opens it. "Oh!" She steps back when she sees the diamond ring.

"Chuck, you shouldn't have—" She pauses as Daddy holds two fingers to his mouth.

"I wanted to upgrade your lost engagement ring. One thing for certain and two things for sure, I bet you won't lose this one." Daddy chuckles and we do, too.

"Mom, it's beautiful." I wink at Daddy.

"It really is," Mom says, peppering him with kisses. They snuggle for what seems like forever. *Yay!* Mom slips the ring on. "I really need to do my nails." She admires the glistening stone on her slender finger.

I shoot Charles an enthusiastic two thumbs up. Apparently my constant playing of Jermaine Jackson's "Daddy's Home" worked.

"You want some coffee? I know it's freezing out there," Mom says.

Nodding, Daddy watches her until she disappears into the kitchen. He surveys the dining room and rubs his forehead. "Every year it looks the same way, like Christmas threw up all over."

"That's funny, Daddy. Very descriptive." I remove my new black maxi coat from under the tree and model it.

"You sure you want it that long?" Dad cocks his head at the ankle-skimming coat.

"It's the latest style, thanks to *Superfly*."

Daddy groans. "I don't know if that's good or bad." His smile disappears. "You haven't seen that flick, have you?"

"It's rated R!" I hold up a blue V-neck dress with tiny flowers from Mom-Mom. "It's perfect for a special occasion." I twirl. "Like an award program for essay *winners*."

"Baby, you won? And you're just telling me?"

I shake my head. "Not yet. The contest is in February, remember?"

"I thought we were wearing red, black and green," Daddy says with a wink. He peers at my awards in the curio. "We need one more win, the big kahuna, to make our collection complete." The way he says it makes me feel like I won already.

"Whether it's first place, second, or honorable mention, do your best. When it comes to school, that's what we expect," he says, admiring Mom in the kitchen.

"This time the top winner will get a trophy instead of a plaque and have their picture placed in the school's trophy case."

"We'll be there to see it happen," Daddy says.

"We wouldn't miss it for the world," Mom says, returning with a steaming cup of coffee.

I bask in the moment, thrilled over the repeated use of the pronoun "we."

Mom remains fuss-free during the thirty-minute drive to Mom-Mom's. As always, her happiness has a domino effect on Daddy, whose mood is so Super Cheerios that he fails to grouse when it takes ten minutes to find a parking spot.

We exit into the brisk air feeling toasty with holiday cheer. Charles, carrying a stack of my 45s in a bag, races up the steps of the apartment building. I walk between my parents, a gloved hand held by each of them. I couldn't care less if I appear dorky or too old for handholding. I prefer holding on to being torn apart.

As soon as we step off the elevator into the narrow, dim hallway, a scrumptious aroma guides us to Mom-Mom's apartment. I fight an urge to drool. Daddy pretends to loosen his belt.

"Lord, Almighty if I could bottle that," Dad says inhaling deeply, "I'd be a millionaire."

The door swings open. Mom-Mom, clad in a gravy-stained apron, greets us with her throaty laugh. "Hello, precious lambs." A parade of mouth-watering scents rushes out and smacks us, in the best possible way, all over our faces.

Mom-Mom pulls us in for a wet kiss. This means we take turns being buried in her massive bosom. After she releases me, I peer down at my own smallish breasts and pray they will not grow another freaking millimeter.

"Everyone is here," Mom-Mom says, her eyes welling at us choking the entrance. I guess it's been a while since she's seen us together.

I scoot into the frilly living room, take my records from Charles and set them on the doily next to Mom-Mom's ancient record player.

"You two know you're supposed to hang up your coats. Give them to me," Mom says. I wiggle out of my coat, hand it over and join Charles in munching chocolate pecan caramels better known as Turtles.

"Dora, put the coats in my sewing room," Mom-Mom says, shooing her away from the nearby closet. "That closet is full of old clothes I'm giving away." Beaming, she claps her hands. "Wash your hands so we can eat."

We file into the small dining room. Sitting before us on a pressed linen table cloth are mounds of greens, candied yams, cranberry sauce, macaroni and cheese, turkey with stuffing, Virginia ham, string beans, and homemade buttered rolls. We hold hands and bow our heads while Daddy says grace.

"Merciful Father, thank you for the food we are about to receive for the nourishment of our body on this Christmas day. And thank you for my blessed mother, lovely wife, and talented son and daughter. Amen."

"Amen." I smile at my parents holding hands, again.

We dig in, eating heaping portions of Mom-Mom's awesome Southern-style cooking, which Mom has yet to master. Everyone treats themselves to seconds and in Charles's case, thirds.

"The food isn't going anywhere, son. Slow down," Dad chides Charles.

"Let that boy be," Mom-Mom says. "He just eating so he can grow up and be big and strong like his daddy."

Mom-Mom's brown eyes narrow. "How you doing in school?"

"Fine," I say. "I'm staying out of trouble."

"She has no choice," Mom says, patting her belly. "Or no Christmas."

"How can anyone see behind you?" Mom-Mom asks, eyeing my Afro with a frown.

"I sit in the back of the class, Mom-Mom."

"As smart as you are?" She looks disapprovingly at my parents.

"I have to if I wear my hair like this. I want to look like Angela Davis."

Flinching, Mom-Mom fans herself. "Baby, she was on the FBI's most wanted list. All that foolishness with the Black Panthers. She ain't nobody to be looking up to. Don't be getting all that militant foolishness in your head like your father." She scowls at Daddy. "Charles, you know I'm right."

I don't dare mention my admiration for Malcolm.

"Momma, please. Let's change the subject or just agree to disagree," Daddy says.

"Mom-Mom," I say, "Angela is really smart. And she was innocent, that's why she was freed."

"Sssh," Daddy tells me, but Grandma is on a roll.

"Why you letting her sit in the back when we fought like the dickens to sit in the front? No wonder she's getting into all kinds of devilment."

"Momma, relax, don't get your pressure up," Daddy says.

"I bet you sit up front, Charles Jr. And no teacher calling home about you."

"Yes, Mom-Mom, in all my classes. And I never get in trouble."

I become preoccupied with my gravy.

"I need ginger ale," Daddy announces, clearly over the conversation.

"Me too." Mom rushes behind him into the kitchen.

The school nurse says I can hear grass grow every year when she tests my ears. Which is why I can hear my parents kissing in the kitchen. Mom-Mom and I exchange knowing grins.

It took a while but God is giving me the best Christmas gift by reuniting our parents. Soon we'll be under one roof. This upcoming new year will be a great one, I think, yawning. My lids feel heavy, a result of going to bed late, getting up before the sun to open presents and stuffing myself. I fall asleep imagining Daddy moving back in.

"Get up, sleepy head. Come on, show us the latest dances." Daddy shakes my shoulders. I cup my eyes from the bright lights as I shake the cobwebs away.

"Whoa, that was a delicious nap," I say. "I'm ready for dessert."

"First, show your momma some new moves," Daddy says with a deep grin. "'Cause she's been doing the same three steps the entire fourteen years I've known her."

Laughter fills the apartment as Daddy hands me a cup of steaming cider.

"Charles, you need to stop," Mom calls out from the living room. The playfulness in her tone warms me better than the yummy cider. Stretching, I trail my father into the living room, where the coffee table is pushed up against the wall.

"Now don't jump around too hard and scratch my records," I warn, setting my cider down on a paper coaster.

"Roberta, you're the main one jumping around like a Soul Train dancer," Mom giggles.

"No, *Momma* is the main culprit," Daddy chirps. Mom-Mom is heavyset and up in age, but she can mimic just about every step I do. She just gets winded quick.

"Take your shoes off so we don't mess up my grandbaby's records." Mom-Mom holds the needle above the spinning record. After we are all shoeless, she gingerly drops the needle on James Brown's "Say It Loud."

Mom sashays forward, her shoulders and hips moving to the beat. Daddy's fancy footwork matches the groove as he moves toward Mom. They continue their solo grooving until Daddy holds out his hand, Mom inserts hers and they bop the familiar two-step that Mom loves. It's her favorite dance, and, judging by Daddy's face, it's his, too. He swings her around and pulls her close. It's like an unseen hand pushes them together.

Midway through the song, Mom-Mom hits the floor, shimmying and hopping.

"Let me show you some real dancing. Whatcha know about the Lindy-hop?" she says, swinging her arms and kicking her legs.

"Go Mom-Mom, go Mom-Mom!" Charles and I chant until she whips out a handkerchief from her meaty cleavage, mops her sweaty brow, and excuses herself to the sofa.

Now it's my turn to execute some of the latest Soul Train moves. I shift into the Robot, jerking my body in a series of stop-and-go movements.

"Ah, go head girl," Mom says, admiring my mastery of the latest new dance craze.

Not to be ignored, Charles executes a deep pelvic thrust and then descends into a perfect split. We stare, stunned by a move he has never done before. He remains on the floor a beat too long.

"Son, you okay?" Daddy asks.

"I think I split my pants," Charles says meekly.

I cover my mouth to spare Charles seeing me laugh, but Daddy doesn't even try to fake it. He laughs so hard tears roll down his face. He falls on the sofa, making everyone crack up, including Charles. Daddy rolls off the sofa and collapses in hysterics on the floor. In response, Mom-Mom doubles over with a laughing spell so shrill we can't help but laugh harder at the dolphin sounds she makes.

Mom, hooting and clutching her stomach, heads to the closet by the door as the song ends. "Mom, did you say there are some old clothes in here? Any of the kids'?"

"What did you say?" Mom-Mom asks, between peals of laughter. She doesn't look up.

Maybe a minute passes before a stricken-looking Mom returns to the living room carrying a tiny pink sweater on a hanger. It takes a few seconds before Mom-Mom and Daddy notice her agitated expression.

"What's this?" Mom asks. "It wasn't in the bags with the old clothes." She looks directly at Daddy. "Whom does this belong to?"

"Now Dora, we're having a great time. It's Christmas," Daddy answers, sitting up on the floor. He looks like he does when he's late paying a bill.

"Whom does it belong to?" Mom asks, her voice gritty.

"Duke's girlfriend has a little girl. It's hers," Dad says, rising.

"Duke, eh? Stay right there," Mom snaps. She looks at Mom-Mom with red eyes. "Why would you allow Duke to bring that woman and her kid here when I am friends with his wife?" Her voice is jawbreaker hard. Her tone tightens my grandmom's mouth.

Charles and I frown at the tiny garment changing our best Christmas ever into our worst. What's the big deal? Uncle Duke has tons of girlfriends. It's not right, but everyone knows. I met at least four of them over the years. I kind of like them, too, even though they wear too much makeup and perfume and call me "sugah." I think about Peaches on the trolley.

"Birds of a feather," Mom hisses. She levels a look at Daddy that stops me cold.

My parents eye each other, and I know the distance between them is greater than the few feet separating them.

"Dora, stop," Daddy says. "It's a holiday. In fact, it's a holy day, right? Let's not fuss and fight, please?"

Mom-Mom steps in between them and addresses my mother.

"First of all, this is my house. I don't need anyone's permission about who crosses this threshold. Second of all—" Mom-Mom clutches her chest.

Daddy feels her forehead and nudges Charles. "Get your grandmother a glass of water."

"Go get my pills out my bedroom," Mom-Mom says to me.

I rush into Mom-Mom's bedroom to search for her pillbox on a bureau crowded with glass figurines, perfume spritzers, ornate boxes, lotions, pincushions, and mounds of gaudy costume jewels. I look with a quiet desperation. Mom comes in.

"Put your coat on. We're leaving."

"Mom, it's not Dad's fault that Uncle Duke is a cheater."

Mom's eyes dart between my angry reflection and hers in the bureau mirror.

"No lip. I am not in the mood," Mom says. "Be ready to go when I come out of the bathroom."

The warning in her voice is clear. Still, I can't help myself. "Happy birthday, Jesus. Merry Christmas."

Her shoulders flinch, but she keeps moving. I finally spot the pillbox, snatch it up and race to my beloved grandmother. "Mom-Mom, are you okay?" I hand her the pillbox.

"Yes, lamb, don't worry about me. I ate too much, and now I have heartburn along with my heartache over this family that I love so much." She glances at my parents. It's a three-way tie for whose face is more torn up.

"What about my pants?" Charles whines. He looks like I feel: crushed with sadness.

"No one can tell they're torn under your coat," Mom says. "We're going straight home."

Sniffling, Charles looks at Daddy, who ruffles his hair and squeezes his shoulder.

"I'll see you soon, son."

Charles rests his head against Daddy's torso, oblivious to the way the adults are side-eyeing each other. I take my turn wrapping my arms around Daddy and then with cement feet trudge to the door.

Daddy pulls his keys out of his pocket.

"Dora, take these." Daddy tosses his car keys. Mom doesn't even try to catch them. They clang, crash, and skid across the floor. "I'll stay here the night and pick the car up after I get a ride over sometime tomorrow."

"Fine," Mom says.

I pick up the keys and hand them to her.

She turns to us. "Kiss your grandmother and father goodnight."

Charles and I squeeze and kiss Dad and Mom-Mom while my parents and grandmother avoid looking at each other.

Heart dragging behind me, we leave the apartment in silence. Daddy shivers on the sidewalk as we pull off. Charles waves goodbye from the back seat. I can barely lift my hand to wave, sitting next to the negative energy force known as Mom. I feel so low that I'll need to roll my socks down in order to see.

I shift toward the window to avoid traitor Mom's pinched-up face. If I could walk home without turning into a human popsicle, I would.

Life is so unfair. I had been riding a train of hurt for the longest time, and just when I think I'm getting off, we roar past the stop. Just being so close to the conductor of my misery makes me furious because I have no idea what makes Mom detest Dad so much. He tried so hard today to be perfect. And he was, too.

I lean against the passenger door as much as possible, wishing I could fall out. Bet my funeral would bring my parents together.

This Christmas debacle raises all kinds of questions. But at this moment all I know for sure is that 1974 is shaping up to be a lot like 1973. Real sucky.

CHAPTER 18

I slide my shoes on and clomp downstairs in my Sunday clothes. Mom insists we attend church together. So the three of us dress up our dysfunction and pile in her car.

We are a mess, and things will never be the same. Going to church won't change that, because all of the praying I've been doing hasn't made our life any better. Mom-Mom sings a song about Jesus being on the main line so tell him want you want. But he won't take my calls, even though he knows, if Mom has her way, Daddy is never coming home.

Fatherless homes are no joke. That's why Mom ranted and raved about not wanting a broken home. She knew, like we know now, that they don't work because the people are broken, too.

Fragments of us are everywhere. Poor Charles pees his bed at the old age of nine. Mom had to buy a rubber sheet and may have to replace his pissy mattress. If I press my nose against his sheets, I still can smell urine.

Mom is so absent-minded these days that she had to change the locks to the house because she swore she lost her keys. After paying the locksmith, she found them in the freezer. And she's smoking again. Charles caught her puffing like a naughty magic dragon in front of her bedroom window, even though it was freezing outside.

My brokenness creates a hatred so deep I dive into it. Hope I don't drown. Some days, I see nothing but gray. I feel scared a lot, too. To mask it, I get angry.

Mom pulls up to an intersection just as the traffic light turns red. Outside, the dirty snow makes the parish look like an ugly postcard. Staring at the light, I recall the story we discussed in reading class before Christmas break. It was about a young Black teen who was smart but troubled. The story ended with him waiting for the traffic light to change at an intersection. No one understood the ending, but it was clear to me.

"He can go in either direction," I told Mr. Harvey. "He can go the right way in life or the wrong way. He has to decide."

I think I need to read that story again. Since Christmas, I've been feeling like if God can't give me what I want, maybe the Devil can. That's definitely going the wrong way. And I kind of don't care.

We occupy a pew at the back of the packed church. Charles sits between Mom and me. I watch to see if any white families will sit near us or choose to squeeze in other pews. That happens when they want to avoid eye contact and shaking our hands when we offer each other the sign of peace. Once, when Mom turned and reached for the lady's hand in the pew behind us, the parishioner said she had a cut on her finger. Mom turned red but said nothing.

I inhale the scent of burning candles. Usually, the church's perfumed aroma and beauty calm me. But not even the marble altar and statues, the soaring ceiling that tells wordless stories, or the sunlight beaming through the stained glass depicting the Stations of the Cross can make me feel better.

Charles nudges me. The pew in front of us files out one by one for communion. How I wish I wasn't baptized like Mom and could stay seated. I have no choice but to trail Charles and receive the body of Christ. The wafer dissolves in my mouth and fills me with . . . holiness? I'm don't think so. Everyone knows it's a freaking wafer.

Back in the pew, I kneel not to ask God for anything, but to admit something I've been tussling with for months. Lately, church feels familiar and uncomfortable like a favorite shoe I've outgrown and now hurts. Thinking this inside church would have made me skittish before Christmas. Today I'm okay with it. Maybe God is, too. He knows what I think and feel anyway, so who am I fooling?

After Mass, riding back home, I ask Mom if she still loves Daddy. She says yes. I know she's lying. Anger pokes me from the inside and proves church wasn't time well spent. Clearly, the Eucharist didn't take.

If our future depends on Daddy coming back home, Charles and I have a head start on being doomed—on becoming the kind of statistic Mom hates.

A recent newspaper article said most boys in gangs live in fatherless homes. Many of the knuckleheads who hang around on corners in my neighborhood fit that category.

Leticia, who lives two streets over, is fourteen and has a baby. She told me she never met her father and it was no big thing because "I'm still strong and he's long gone." She saw the disgust in my eyes. Now, when I see her pushing her baby stroller on the avenue, she acts like she doesn't see me. No matter what, that's not happening to me.

"I don't want to go to church anymore," I say.

"Go at least once a month then," Mom replies.

"Why if I don't get anything out of it?"

"How do you know? God has been good to you."

I cackle, stopping when Mom glares at me so hard she nearly runs the light.

I think about pointy-nosed Shelly, the first person to question my mother's honesty. Shortly after moving in, we walked to school together, despite her being several years older. She had four older brothers, and there was safety in numbers during those earlier years when only a few black kids attended HSB. We had to stick together for protection from the public-school bullies, white and black, who targeted us as Catholic school punks.

Short-tempered and reed-thin, Shelly had a biting tongue and witchy temper, which is why my eight-year-old self failed to haul off and hit her when she called Mom a liar.

"My mom said Santa travels in a helicopter when there is no snow on the ground," I told Shelly, who rolled her eyes and looked at me like I was slow.

"You act like every word your mother says is gospel," she yelled.

Her angry outburst made me pause on the sidewalk. "It is," I said, dumbfounded and hurt.

She rushed over, her beaky nose so close I became cross-eyed. "It. Is. Not!" she thundered. "Your mother lied; your parents are Santa."

Her news made my mouth feel like cotton. "My mom ain't no liar," I mumbled, moving out of striking distance.

"You'll learn." Shelly poked her nose in the air.

Something in her voice made me think she was talking about her own mother, a short, brown-skinned lady I knew little about since Shelly was never allowed to have company past her porch. Years later, I heard her parents padlocked their refrigerator. No wonder she was so skinny and evil.

Skinny old Shelly tried to warn me. What else is Mom lying about?

I glance at Mom's profile while she parks the car. The sharp beak like Shelly. The fair skin. Were padlocks in our future?

The first day back in school after Christmas break, everyone brags about their gifts. Not me. I'm not even faking the funk. When Sister greets me warmly in homeroom, I barely respond. She swung the wrecking ball that flattened my family. She's one of the main reasons I feel like I'm running in quicksand.

When we stand to recite the Pledge of Allegiance, I decide not to open my mouth or place my hand over my heart. My parents don't, so why should I?

Midway through the Pledge, Sister leans back to make sure I see her looking directly at me. I do, and I don't care.

After the Pledge, I sulk at my desk. I'm showy about it, too, slumping against my desk so hard it squeaks across the floor. Sister says nothing, but her watchful eyes keep finding me while she conducts homeroom business.

"A roach! A roach," Eileen screams. She jumps on her seat and points at the cockroach scurrying past her desk, which is three seats in front of mine.

The class goes crazy.

"Get the broom and dust pan," Sister says as she approaches our aisle, checking every desk bin until she reaches mine.

"Did you see where it came from it?"

"Why are you asking me?"

Sister looks down at my opened book bag. "Keep your roaches at home."

The classroom giggles ring in my ears like gongs in the karate movies. Cut to my core, all I see is grayness.

Oh no, she didn't!

Forget counting numbers, I say the first thing that pops in my mind.

"So because I'm the only Black girl in this row, I brought the roach? You just assume that? Isn't that a stereotype? Do you think my family gets food stamps, too?"

Sister flinches and her eyebrows narrow, but I can see her pause and I sense she's dialing back her response. "Watch your tone; you're not speaking to a peer. Put your bag on your desk and open it."

Taking my time, I hoist it up and drop it with a thud. Yanking it open, it's absent the usual candy wrappers since we cleaned out our bookbags and desks before the Christmas break. I smirk.

"There's another one," someone screams from the middle of the room. "I saw it come out of Larry's bag."

Larry, who sits two rows away, slumps in his desk. His cheeks and ears redden. Sister stink-eyes me as she charges over to the real roach carrier.

"Dump your book bag out in the hall. Take the trash-can," she tells him. She claps her hands. "In fact, everyone check your bags. The school was exterminated over the break. Let's keep it clean."

She turns at me with a tight smile. "It's a new year. Let's make it the best one yet."

Hello, rewind, please? Once again Sister insults me and refuses to apologize. I make up my mind on the spot. *I. Declare. War.* Why not? I have nothing to lose.

─────

Two weeks later, I enter class eager for a showdown that, because I put a lot of thought into it, makes my point without getting me into trouble. *'Cause a wise man is like a nail; his head keeps him from going too far.*

Looking around, I slowly unfold one of my poems as if it's a passed note. Every time Sister glances at me, I stop reading it and look up at her bug-eyed. The third time I freeze, like a burglar under a spotlight, Sister responds just as I predicted.

"Passing notes, Miss Forest? Come up and read it for all of our enlightenment," she pauses, "or amusement."

Even though I want to leap with delight, I shuffle up front. I stare at my shoes as if I'm busted and ashamed to share the content with the class.

Geoffrey turns and makes Three Stooges gestures as I approach, trying to make me laugh.

"Geoffrey, what fascinates me is that not only are you utterly hopeless, you are so unbothered by your hopelessness," Sister says to the back of his head. Her eyes lock on me. "Class, hold on tight. Do you feel the room spinning? That's because Roberta expects the world to revolve around her." Sister faces me with a raised eyebrow as I wait at the front of the room. "We don't have all day."

I clear my throat. "'She knew holy water and prayer weren't enough to keep the boogeymen from coming.'" I cut my eyes at Sister. She's rifling through a drawer. "'Defiant, demanding, undesirable, the monsters scared the good people away.'"

"What is this nonsense?" Sister huffs.

"A poem. I'm almost finished."

"Thanks be to God!" She rests her cheek in her hand, looking bored and sleepy.

"'People with woolly hair and brown skin,'" I say looking around at my classmates. "'People like me. People like Jesus.'"

I look at the crucifix above Sister's head and then back at her. She arches an eyebrow, grimacing like she wants to throw holy water on me. *Score!*

"This is not poetry class," she says. "Sit down and focus on doing what you've been asked to do. How about writing a poem about that? Call it 'Following Directions' and complete it in your English class."

Digging into my palms to keep from laughing, I sashay back to my desk, where I will concoct other ways to strike Sister Elizabeth without using my fists. *New year. New plan. But the old Roberta you humiliated is going all James Brown on you with the big payback.*

I'm the old Roberta who digs the old Malcolm who hated whites. The old Malcolm called Satan by his cellmates. Sister Elizabeth better take some notes. I'm about to drop some serious knowledge that I picked up from Brother Malcolm before he became a hanky-head sell-out. I'm dropping facts like hotcakes. By any means necessary.

At home, I wrestle with the notion that Jesus is Black. If that's the case, how could He let down millions of slaves and millions more Black people today, as we catch the short end of the stick, as Daddy always says?

The color of Jesus has my feelings yo-yoing between pride and confusion. What good is it even knowing Jesus looks more like me than Donna, or even Mom, when that image is nowhere to be found in our school books or any church I've visited? If I could write a letter to the Pope, and all the bishops and cardinals, I'd say: "Dear religious people, why is Jesus white with blue eyes?"

Footsteps approach my closed bedroom door. *Ah geez, here we go.*

"Whatcha doing, Silky Boo?" Mom knocks and pushes open the door carrying a small paper bag and the newspaper. She lays both on the dresser. I spot a chocolate Tastykake inside. My mouth waters.

"Just reading." I whip a book out from under the pillow and bury my head in it.

"How was school?"

"Fine." I don't look up.

"Your dad call?"

"No."

"You call your dad? Finish your homework?"

"No and yes."

"Well," she sighs. "Dinner will be ready in thirty minutes."

She pauses, shifting from leg to leg, as if waiting for something. A personality transplant? Forgiveness for destroying our family again? I meet Mom's eyes. There is no fight in them.

"What's for dinner?" I croak.

"Fish sticks, French fries, and string beans." She clearly wants to talk. I can't.

"Okay." I resume reading.

"Bring your trash downstairs," she says walking out.

Closing my book, I roll over. I'd rather wash broken dishes than have a conversation with her—or say thanks for a bribe I did not ask for.

Nothing matters when she took my father from me.

I hole up in my room, my one safe place in this whole stinking house, and *still* she invades my space. Barging in with unwanted smiles along with a hit 45 record of the week, or a new book or magazine, or soft pretzels or something else that normally makes me drool. None of it can fill my emptiness. Not even Black Jesus. My anger scorches the air around me.

I pull out my poetry book and write the fastest poem I've ever done.

So much inside has died
All my tears I've cried
Now I will strike back with delight
Tell my truth in black and white
Expose the lies
Sever the ties
Scream a question to the world

From a so-called tough black girl
Does anyone care
I hurt everywhere

Today, I fret at my desk.

My nose has been stuffy all week, and I'm worried that my family is falling apart more so than usual. Daddy never showed up to take us to the movies as he promised over the weekend. Mom acts weirder by the day. Charles sucks his thumb out of the blue while spending hours drawing goofy super villains. We hardly talk to each other, except two weeks ago, after Daddy took us to see *The Exorcist*. Charles begged me to sleep with him. I kept him talking most of the night so after we fell asleep he would not pee his bed with me in it.

"We have a guest for today's class, so mind your manners," Sister barks, looking at Geoffrey. "Brother Fred will lead today's lesson, and then he'll take questions."

Sister looks excited, almost as if she's waiting for a date.

Brother Fred knocks on the door before coming in. He is a Ken doll with a collar, handsome in a Mr. Brady Bunch kind of way with dark, wavy hair, and sparkly eyes. I can tell that Donna thinks he's cute, too. She perks up, no longer slouching in her seat, which is hysterical since he's studying the priesthood and not her poked-out breasts.

I tune Brother Fred out until class is halfway over.

"Anything you want to ask or talk about?" Brother Fred clasps his hands and glances around the room.

I raise my hand. Sister stands, arms folded.

"What is your name?" he asks with a pleasant smile.

"Roberta," I fake chirp.

"That's a lovely name. One of my favorite singers is named Roberta."

"Flack?" I ask, surprised. "You listen to regular music?"

He nods. "I enjoy all kinds of music." He smiles with perfect teeth. I almost feel sorry for what I'm about to do to him.

"I was wondering if you could tell us what Jesus really looked like. You know, instead of the popular depiction."

"Good question." He rubs his chin. "You are correct. He probably didn't look the way many people imagine. That's fair to say."

I expected leg-pulling resistance instead of friendly agreement. My heart beats so fast the vein in my neck jumps. My eyes lock on his. "Was he as brown as I am?"

"I'd say yes." He scans the room nodding. "That's a strong possibility. Especially living in that part of the world."

"And his hair. Was it straight like yours or more like mine?"

He looks at my immense Afro and then over at Sister Elizabeth, who looks like she wants to go Round Two with me. He walks toward me as he speaks. "The Bible makes reference to it being woolly. I'm not calling your hair woolly," he says with a nervous laugh. He blushes deeply.

I try not to grin like I just aced a test I thought I had failed. No one has ever said those words out loud in front of a class in my eight years at Catholic school. All those paintings, illustrations, and statues of a white-skinned Jesus with long flowing hair and blue eyes are more lies adults promote. *Malcolm was right.*

The rest of the class is a blur as I can't stop thinking about what Brother Fred said. I can't wait to tell Daddy. And Charles. On second thought, this wisdom may overwhelm Charles since I recently shared the real deal about Santa.

"Boys and girls, let's show Father Fred some appreciation for visiting with us today," Sister says. No one claps harder than I do.

Three seconds after he exits, Sister hovers above me with wild eyes. "You are trying my patience," she says, her lips barely moving. "Tread carefully."

"Black History Week is coming up. We don't learn this in school so I thought—"

"Enough! I'm talking about your attitude. Cut it out." She mean mugs me for a few seconds. I know not to gloat.

Watching her return to her desk, I imagine how tickled Daddy will be when I tell him what I got Brother Fred to admit. I'm smiling at the thought when Sister whirls around.

"So you think what I say is a joke?" She shakes her head and points to the door. "Go stand in the hall until the bell rings. And you have detention for the rest of the week."

Great. More time to figure out what to do next. I am in the doorway when she continues.

"And, Roberta . . ."

I turn.

"I said earlier that there'd be no religion homework for good class conduct." Sister looks over the rims of her glasses and wrinkles her nose. "That's true for everyone except you."

CHAPTER 19

Bonnie waits for me after school. *My girl.* She loops her arm through mine.

"Won't your parents take back your presents if you get in trouble with Sister, again?" Her mouth twists with concern.

"I don't care."

"Girl, you better care. I'd give my right arm for that bad 10-speed bike you got. And the phone, and the stereo. You're spoiled rotten," she says, jabbing my arm. She is trying to make me feel better but her approach stinks.

"I'd trade it all to have my dad home."

"He'll come back. Your mom is too pretty for him not to."

"Will you stop that," I snap. "Looks aren't everything. Come on, you know that."

"Just saying. Dag! Sue me for breathing." Bonnie pulls her arm away. We walk in silence as we approach the flagpole.

Eyeing the flag whipping in the winter breeze reminds me of Sister's sourpuss expression when I refuse to recite the Pledge of Allegiance. There's a spark of an idea brewing but when I glance over at Bonnie's mopey face, I lose my train of thought. "I didn't mean it. I'm sorry."

"It's okay." Her voice is salty.

"We should do something for Black History Week. I read that some colleges are even making it bigger and celebrating Black History Month," I say.

"Wow, we could never do that here. What should we do?" Bonnie asks.

"I don't know. A protest maybe? I'll think of something."

"You know I'm down," Bonnie says, holding up her fist. "Just say the word. Speaking of Black History Week, did you enter the *Right On!* contest?"

"You know I haven't because you'll read whatever I write, knucklehead."

"When you giving your essay to me?"

"When I write it."

Bonnie smacks her lips, blows air, and changes the subject. She drones on about some cute light-skinned boy ('cause they're never dark-skinned) she met at the movies. I tune her out until we reach the corner where we head in different directions.

"Later, girl," I turn away.

Bonnie tugs the back of my coat. "Enter that essay contest."

"Okay." I look up at a sky as gray and grim as my life and hold out my hand. A few drops tickle my palm.

I wave bye and run the rest of the way home, feeling smaller with every step. I hate going home. I hate going to school. So where do I belong?

———

Stepping into my bedroom, I slip on the latest *Right On!* that I'd left on the floor. Sprawled on my back, looking at the magazine's torn cover, I'm struck by the best idea ever. Pulling out my poetry book I write:

America has a scab full of pus
She's the land of the free
Just not for us
Her flag waves red, white, and blue
Her Pledge of Allegiance rings true
for so many folks who don't look like me
So I can't sing "My Country, 'Tis of Thee"
We're still marching for equality
While white people build equity
How can I be heard, raise my voice?
In class I'll make a daily choice

I dial Bonnie's number so hard and fast the edges of my finger hurts.

"Hello." Bonnie speaks while munching.

"I know what we can do next month for Black History Week! And honor Malcolm's legacy, since the anniversary of his assassination is February 21st. Let's get all the Black eighth-graders to refuse to say the Pledge of Allegiance."

I hold my breath and cross my fingers. Without her, my plan may be doomed.

"Sounds good, but can we get kicked out for that?"

"I've been doing it for nearly three weeks. Plus, they better not. My mom knows Mike Williamson. HSB isn't looking to make headline news. He's working on a story about racism in Catholic schools, and he's including our school, but that's a secret." Okay, I'm lying.

"What? That reporter? You never told me that. They're like friends? Your mom knows important people like that columnist? Girl, you can get an internship in high school and really be a famous writer. Yeah, let's do it!"

"Bonnie, that's a secret about Mike. Okay? Like pinky swear me."

"Mum's the word."

"Let's tell everyone at recess tomorrow. First day of BHW, it's on and popping!" I hang up feeling less miserable. But just a little. Some truth-teller I am.

I pull out my diary. "Writing is easy, life is hard. And it's never been harder than this school year." I write until I fall sleep.

I dream I am on a beach. It's unmistakably Atlantic City because chicken bones jut from the filthy sand. Mom is complaining about all the riff-raff leaving trash on the beach. Daddy, burying Charles, ignores her. Suddenly everyone disappears, leaving me alone. I'm scared. I run to the water's edge, blocking the bright sun from my eyes.

In the middle of the ocean I see a tiny island with purple sand. A freakishly tall clown appears. He cups his hands and yells, "Jump in."

"I can't, I'll drown," I scream, eyeing the angry waves.

"Just dive in and swim to me," he shouts.

I wade into the water until I am forced to swim, which I do with all of my might. Kicking and slapping the waves, I make it to the island. Exhausted, I crawl onto the island where invisible hands shake me. I open my eyes. Mom hovers above me.

"Sleepyhead, you know you're supposed to take that uniform off as soon as you get home. Get up, time for dinner."

"I'm not hungry."

Mom presses her palm against my forehead. She actually looks worried. "Come on, something is going around. You need to eat to keep your immune system up."

At dinner, I decide to tell Mom about the roach incident. I need to build up my case against Sister Elizabeth in case she calls and rats me out.

"You know, I've been thinking. Maybe Girls Academy would be a better place for you, if you can get in."

What? I squeeze my eyes to make sure I am hearing right.

"One thing for certain and two things for sure, it certainly seems like Catholic school is hindering your potential instead of developing it."

For the first time since Christmas, before the fiasco with Daddy, I hug Mom.

"Now wait a minute. I am just thinking out loud," she says. "I heard you loud and clear about not wanting to go to church. You have the grades to get in. Everything still okay in school?"

"Sister Elizabeth might be upset because I stopped saying the Pledge of Allegiance."

"I don't have a problem with that. She shouldn't either— it's freedom of speech."

"I also got Brother Fred to say Jesus looked more like me than him!"

Mom's expression straddles amusement and disbelief. "It's okay to love God, but not religion," Mom says.

"That just sounds wrong," I stammer. "How can you separate them?"

The phone rings. So do Mom's words. Cupping the receiver, Mom says, "We'll talk later. I have to take this."

Brain buzzing and body tingling, I wish the caller dialed a wrong number so our unexpected conversation can continue.

In my room, I mull over what just happened. Mom pulled a curtain off a part of my mind I didn't know was there, and the light blinds me. How long will it take before my eyes adjust and I clearly see this new fuzzy idea that both scares and excites me down to my core.

The big day is finally here. My stomach is ready to fall out. Finishing the Lord's Prayer in class, we turn to the flag to say the Pledge of Allegiance. Everything seems to move in slow motion as my classmates put their right hands over their hearts. Who will join me to make a statement for Black History Week?

I scan the room and nearly jump for joy. Raymond, the new black boy who transferred here last month, Stephanie, Karen, Clyde, Vietta, and even a nervous-looking Donna, stand silent with hands at their sides. My head swells to the size of a Macy's Thanksgiving parade float. If I hear most of the Black eighth-graders in the other homerooms participated, my ego will need its own zip code.

Right on! This is what solidarity feels like. This is Black Power. I glance at Donna. *My girl.* With white support, this protest may grow. I'm for that type of integration. Malcolm was, too, after his visit to Mecca. I imagine this heady sensation is what it feels like to march for civil rights—to try and make a difference for your people. I think of the Black Panthers and Angela Davis. I think of Shirley Chisholm, who ran for president when I was in sixth grade. I think of Malcolm. We stand on the shoulders of giants. Instead of my usual slouching, I stand straighter. *I am young, gifted, and Black.*

With great fanfare, Geoffrey keeps looking back at Donna. His rubbernecking gets Sister's attention. Sister eyeballs the six of us protestors and, with a flourish, writes something in her green grade book. *What in the Sam Hill?*

"With liberty and justice, for all," my classmates say.

"Don't sit," Sister commands and several students immediately bounce back up. "In fact, keep your right hand over your heart, if you had it there to begin with. Now, look around at your classmates. Look at who feels the need to disrespect our nation's flag and the men and women who died to protect it."

"That's not what this is about," I blurt. "We will honor the flag when every Black man, woman, and child is treated equally."

"Is that so? I stand corrected," Sister says with a smug smile. "Let me be crystal clear." Sister begins to pace. "You have the right to *not* honor the flag. But every action has a consequence in my classroom. For every day that you decide not to salute the flag, I will deduct five points off your conduct grade. Now sit!" She gives Donna a cold stare.

A quick calculation means we can hold out for a total of three days before our grade, if already perfect, drops to a B. That means only the diehards like me, Bonnie, and a few others, will stick with it for the rest of the week.

"What does one have to do with the other?" I ask.

"Raise your hand. Stop blurting out like a barnyard animal," Sister snaps.

Her anger pleases me. Malcolm would be proud. I can't wait to hear from Bonnie who participated in her class. I glance at the clock. Homeroom ends in ten minutes.

Sister rambles on about the requirements for the live Stations of the Cross performance held every year during Holy Week before Easter. Only eighth-graders can play the roles. More than a month away, it's a big production. Usually teacher's pets and other try-hards are selected to participate in the sacred communal prayer service. The only role that requires talent, other than sucking up, is Mary. That goes to the best singer.

Sister seems extra animated, doing everything to ignore me. But I'm flying on a glorious cloud, and I need her to watch me gloat. I'm in control and no longer weak, like I was when she threw me out of class after slapping the Jesus out of me while shouting that I don't belong here, but in Africa, a continent I'd know little about if I relied on HSB teaching me.

Thank God for Malcolm, who opened my eyes to my country's love affair with racism.

I want her to look at me. I remember she never apologized for any of the pain she caused. All the pretzel selling and Yellow Bird singing in the world can't fix that Grand-Canyon–sized hole she blasted into my soul. She hurt me, and I hurt my family. *She needs to look at me.*

I raise my hand, careful not to appear eager. She makes me wait wicked long before acknowledging me with a half-crazed stare.

"You want to be a part of the Stations of the Cross performance?" she scoffs.

Nervous teeters sweep the class just as there's a knock on the door. It swings open. Sister Bernard pokes her head in.

"Sister Elizabeth, can you step outside for a second?" she asks, glancing at me.

"Take out your signed forms for the fundraiser and pass them up," Sister Elizabeth says. "Eileen, please collect them." She steps outside the class, pulling the door behind her.

Geoffrey turns in his seat and scowls at Donna.

"Whatcha do that for? Your pops will kill you when he finds out."

"Mind your business." Her voice trembles.

"That was too cool. Thanks, Donna," I say.

Donna gives me a smile without showing her teeth. I hope she doesn't get in trouble.

I look over at Stephanie, who glances back with fearful eyes. I give her, Clyde, Vietta, Raymond, and Karen a Black Power salute. I am eager to tell them during the change of classes that we made a proud stand today and if they don't join me tomorrow that's cool. I can stand alone.

Sister Elizabeth returns to class, her face redder.

"It seems boys and girls, that Roberta here has managed to get every colored student in the eighth-grade to join her gang, I mean movement. You are correct, Roberta. One thing should not have anything to do with the other. It behooves me to rescind what I said earlier about deducting points from your conduct grade. During the Pledge of Allegiance, you must stand, but otherwise feel free to monitor the moonbeams for all I care. I will leave that between you and your God."

Her words barely register. I am floating above it all. *We won! We won! We won!*

By the time recess rolls around, I feel like a superstar. Black students huddle around me, everyone wanting my attention and talking at once. They congratulate me for making Black History Week meaningful at HSB. For emphasizing pride and focusing attention on how Black people are still being treated like second-class citizens, even though slavery ended over a hundred years ago. Most of the fifty-two Black eighth-graders say they will continue the protest for the rest of the month. Some say the remainder of the school year. I finally feel the way Bonnie must feel every day: like a queen bee.

On day four of the protest, I sit at my desk beaming. I can hardly contain my glee over Sister's about-face regarding the pledge. What did Sister Bernard say to convince her to leave us alone? *Who cares?* Mother Superior knows she can't suspend all of us for exercising our constitutional rights.

"Everyone copied the homework?"

"Yes, Sister," the history class robot answers.

Sister erases the board clean.

"Can we talk about current events?" Eileen asks.

Sister nods. "You know the rules. Be respectful," she says, chin in her hand.

Donna and I exchange grins. Sister is about to take a nap. We push our desks in a circle. Eileen chooses President Nixon as the topic. I listen while doing Spanish homework.

"I don't totally get the fuss about President Nixon. My dad voted for him and he says what happened to him is just a witch hunt," Eileen says, shrugging.

I perk up. Maybe Spanish vocabulary can wait.

"My dad voted for him. He says Democrats are sore losers," volunteers Geoffrey.

"How can you not believe he's a crook?" says Stephanie. "The Watergate investigations have been going on forever. I'm sick of hearing about them."

"We have to talk about it," I say, watching Sister nodding. "The problem is the most powerful man in the free world doesn't know how to tell the truth. My dad, who didn't vote for him, said he is guilty as sin and will be impeached before summer's out."

"Is your father a journalist at the *Washington Post* or a political science professor?" Sister asks, annoyed. Apparently, my words woke her up.

"No, but his friend is a chauffeur at the Pentagon and he overhears conversations while driving the political big shots around."

"Consider the source," Sister snaps.

Wait! What? I sit up. We have the floor, and did she just disrespect my father?

"'I am not a crook.'" Geoffrey throws up two peace signs, imitating Nixon.

The class laughs. I'm too mad to join in.

"Well, no matter how you cut it, Nixon has something in common with Thomas Jefferson." I look directly at Sister Elizabeth. "They're both liars. I mean, hypocrites."

Donna catches her breath. Others' gasps fill the air. Sister blinks as if something flew in her eyes. *Maybe the truth.* In a flash she rushes toward me, eyes ablaze. She looms in front of my desk, lips tight. "Out! Now! I will not tolerate your impudence."

"What did I do? We are having a classroom discussion. Everyone is giving an opinion. Why can't I? Presidents aren't perfect." *Or teachers.*

"I know what you're doing. I wasn't born yesterday."

"I'm just participating in the discussion."

"You hide behind your hair and glower and talk Black Power, but you don't even know who you are." Sister's lips wrinkle in righteous anger.

"You hide behind your religion. You're supposed to be holier, better than us. But the truth is . . ."

Sister pounds my desk. I lean back in case she swings.

"I said leave. Go stand outside the room until the bell rings."

I saunter out, relieved that she didn't send me to the main office. Another suspension, and I can kiss Girls Academy goodbye. *What's wrong with me?*

I slouch against the wall, mentally beating myself up until the bell clangs. The hall swells with chattering students, kinda carefree like I used to be. I wait for class to empty and barely slip back in to get my books when Sister hisses.

"Get over here!"

I approach her desk.

"Tell your mother I will be calling her tonight. I don't know what's gotten into you, but I will no longer tolerate it."

I grab my book bag. I'm halfway down the hall when I realize to outsmart her I need crucial information. I backtrack to class, where she's writing comments in red ink on a stack of tests. I cough. She refuses to look up.

"My mom stays on the phone after work. What time are you calling?"

Sister eyes me until I feel uneasy. "Oh, don't worry. I'll keep calling until I get through."

Jesus Christ. Operation phone-off-the-hook starts tonight.

Heading down the hallway, I decide to chill out with Sister effective tomorrow. Why not? My Pledge of Allegiance boycott now involves some students in the seventh and sixth grades. It's successful beyond anything I could have imagined. I'll lay low for what promises to be my best revenge: winning the writing contest, which kicks off in two weeks.

Imagining that first-place award in my hand gives me the same rush I felt reading my fortune cookie and horoscope eons ago. It's a gift of power. A solution. The answer that I need to fix my family—to stop a divorce.

Daddy no longer comes to the house. We see him and talk to him on the phone less and less. Mom may have pawned her new diamond ring. Godzilla can deep dive in the holes where me and Charles's hearts used to be.

It's up to me to win next month and unite us. There's nothing else I can do.

CHAPTER 20

A church mouse would have been louder than me in school the past week. Yesterday, I stayed quiet after my homeroom classmates, with the surprising exception of Vietta, caved and recited the Pledge of Allegiance. Many Black students in eighth grade still refuse to do so.

Besides, I have no need to gloat. Sister Elizabeth and I can co-exist in peace. I'm thrilled she hasn't called Mom at work since the home line stays busy. Coming up with reasonable excuses for the phone being "accidently knocked off the hook" is wearing me out and making Mom suspicious.

I watch the red minute hand circle the wall clock until the first period bell rings. I wait impatiently to file out. Feeling Sister eyeballing my spine, I glance back. Eyes shining, she flashes the cheeriest smile at me for no good reason. Chills spider up my arms. *That's weird.* I will never understand her.

I erase her from my thoughts 'cause I need room for bigger things. Today is the day! We'll learn about the guidelines for the writing contest that kicks off next week. I bolt through the corridor to get a minute with Mr. Harvey alone in class.

I jog into his room and listen to chalk clicking against the blackboard as he writes today's assignment in his sloping cursive. He stops when he sees me. An uneasiness creeps across his face. *Everyone is weirding out today.*

"There you are," he says. "Let's talk."

He studies me a beat too long then shoos me out into the hall. He gestures to the adjacent empty music classroom. We step inside, and he tugs the door behind him. He looks paler than usual. Maybe he's catching a cold.

"What do you know about the contest?" he asks.

"Nothing!" I'm so excited I can't stop fidgeting with the straps on my book bag. "I came early to find out the new rules."

Sighing, he examines his scuffed up shoes then meets my eyes. "This is difficult. Sister Elizabeth was supposed to tell you in homeroom that the contest is bigger this year and so are the prizes." Looking away, he runs his hands through his thinning hair then faces me. "You are ineligible to enter the essay contest because of your suspension."

I wait for him to deliver the punch line. But he doesn't crack a smile.

"I think you lost me. I don't understand." Shaken, I plop on top of the nearest desk.

"Since the winner will represent the archdiocese, good grades are a requirement."

"I have good grades," I say, watching the room spin.

"You failed effort and conduct in the first marking period, which makes you ineligible according to the good citizenship requirement."

The news sucker punches me. Woozy, I clutch the edge of the desk to keep from falling off. "Excuse me? Mr. Harvey, can she do that? It sounds like these rules were created just to keep *me* from competing." My voice catches. My tight throat makes it hurt to speak.

"I'm sorry, kiddo." Mr. Harvey pats my shoulder. "I can't change the rules. You know I would if I could."

"Did Sister Elizabeth?"

His silence says everything. He takes a deep breath. "Look, in a few months you'll be out of here." He holds up four fingers for emphasis. "Don't let this get you down, Roberta. You'll win bigger contests one day. Stay cool. I'm asking you to, okay?"

"Okay," I choke out in a defeated voice. "You sure you can't do anything?"

He shrugs. When did he become so weak?

"I need to be excused, please."

I break a record running to the bathroom without mowing down dozens of kids in my way. In the last stall, I pound the walls, not caring who hears. The contest was the one thing I wanted more than anything else during my last year at HSB, and Sister snatched it away with a devilish smile and an evil rule change tailored for me. Even if I hadn't won, I probably would have placed second or third and been recognized at the awards program. My family would have been there to see me. Mom and Daddy, together and proud of me.

Blindsided by Sister Elizabeth again, fire runs in my veins. She struck again, only with an invisible slap covered in thorns.

Keeping me from competing wounds me as much as her reaction when I told the truth about her beloved president. Did Malcolm feel like this when Elijah Muhammad silenced him?

I storm down the hallway and rush into class, where Sister Elizabeth stands by the windows in conversation with the latest art substitute teacher, a hunched over man and a real pushover. At least he's not cruel. She barely glances at me.

Ignoring whispered hellos from friends, I close my eyes, and try to count. I can't. I open my eyes to grayness as the sub walks around me to leave. Sister, still by the window, looks me up and down, then addresses the class.

"Hold all questions until after I give instructions for the open book test." She folds her arms. "Roberta, do you not have somewhere to be? You are interrupting my reading class."

"I have a question about the essay contest."

"I suggest you direct it to Mr. Harvey, who is in charge as you well know."

"Not really, because if he had his way, I'd still be able to compete."

Sister rushes over to her desk and slaps it. Her red marking pen rolls off and hits the floor. Bruce, who had a crush on me last year, rises to pick it up. She aims her finger at him like it's a dart. "Don't you move one iota."

Sister approaches, the insubordination pad in her hand. I back up into the hallway.

"We can't have the likes of someone like you who is completely disrespectful representing Holy St. Bridget, let alone the archdiocese. I warned you that I had my eyes on you. You blew your chance, you and your big mouth. Blame no one but yourself."

"Wasn't Jesus a troublemaker?"

"You're comparing yourself to Jesus? Nice try." She snorts, clutching her crucifix.

"It's rigged anyway." I try to sound nonchalant. "Everyone knows I should have won the last two. You can have your stupid contest any old way." We stare at each other. I sniff the air as if someone stepped in dog mess, then walk away.

"One more word and off you go to Mother Superior for holding this class hostage to your illogical outbursts and for failing to be where you are supposed to be at this hour."

"Like I care," I mumble over my shoulder.

"Go report to the main office now," Sister hisses.

My heart thwacks in my ears at being sent to the principal's office again.

I will myself to stay poker faced as I head over. I will not cry. All I have left is my pride. And it's in tatters.

After school, Bonnie waits by the flagpole. Her sad eyes search my face. I'm in no mood for pity. All I need is my father to fix this.

"I heard what happened. It's so unfair what Sister did," she says. "You suspended?"

"No, that's how I know this rule change is aimed at me. Mother Superior had Mr. Harvey talk to me. He kept asking if everything was okay at home. I told him everything will stay messed up at home now that I can't—" I swallow the brick in my throat and blink back the tears.

"I can't believe her," Bonnie screeches. "Get your parents to meet with Mother Superior. Swear to God, whoever heard of citizenship requirements for an essay contest?"

We fall behind a throng of students as Bonnie rants and raves on my behalf.

"Forget HSB. Please enter that *Right On!* contest. You see all those great prizes?"

"How am I going compete with kids around the country? I can't even win the stupid contests in our stupid school."

"Hold up." Bonnie digs in her bookbag. She hands me a stamp. "Enter."

I drop it in my pencil case to shut her up.

"Promise me," Bonnie says.

"Yes." I roll my eyes. *I will never enter a writing contest again.*

"I bet your parents can do something. Sister can't just make up rules to spite you." Bonnie kicks a soda bottle to the curb. It smashes into a million bits like my sense of self. "She was afraid you might win."

I shake my head. "No, I probably would have won second or even third place. That's what I don't understand. Why keep me out," my voice breaks, "completely?"

Bonnie's eyes glisten in sympathy. "Girl, Sister Excrement is just mad because you got Brother Fred to say Jesus was dark with nappy hair."

"And because I said Nixon is a liar like Jefferson."

"Truth hurts. She's mad because you're doing her job and teaching facts," Bonnie says.

"I'm going to talk to my dad after school tomorrow. Want to come ride with me?"

"Sure do. Girl, I hate Sister for you." Her words crack open a floodgate of tears I manage to hold in until after we go our separate ways.

Bawling, I run the last two blocks home, feeling smaller with every step. Sister erased me from the contest like I was a wrong answer. All I need to do is curl up in bed and never leave or try to write again.

CHAPTER 21

A ringing phone in the distance wakes me. Startled, I bolt up. I forgot to take Mom's bedroom phone off the hook in case Sister tries to call and rat me out.

I jump out of bed. The house rule is four rings before answering, but Charles, hoping it's Daddy, picks up sooner.

"Mom," Charles shouts downstairs, as I rush into the hallway and freeze at the sight of him with the receiver pressed against his ear. "It's Mother Superior."

My insides twist. Sister Elizabeth got the principal to call. I'm toast. Now Mom will find out I'm ineligible for the contest. Not that she'll fight for me like Daddy will. I left an urgent message for him before I cried myself to sleep. *Could I hate my life more?*

Tiptoeing into the dining room, I sidestep the new squeaky runner and eavesdrop as Mom cooks.

"How do you know Roberta instigated it?" Mom actually sounds skeptical. "I see," Mom says after a long pause. "When did all this start?"

The kitchen floor creaks on beat, which means she's pacing near the window.

"Oh, trust and believe me when I say that this nonsense stops right now. She will behave, because she can't afford to get suspended or flunk conduct and effort again. If you can get Sister Elizabeth to resume the weekly reports, I'd appreciate it. Thank you for letting me know what's going on *before* reprimanding her. Roberta can be mouthy."

I bristle. It figures Mom would side with the enemy since she hates me, too.

I tiptoe upstairs and scoot in the bathroom to buy time. I'm watching the water run from the sink faucet and rehearsing my defense speech when the door flings open.

"Get out this damn bathroom!" Mom screams. "I am so tired of your nonsense. I work hard all day and then I come home and hear how you are *still* acting the fool? Talking fresh. I will take every one of your Christmas gifts and give them away to the Little Sisters of the Poor. There are kids with nothing, ingrate. Go unplug your stereo and speakers. I'm cutting your phone off. At this rate, you'll be on punishment until after graduation."

I stomp into my bedroom, furious. I am midway through dialing Daddy's number when Mom rushes in, face flushed and eyes flaming.

"Get off that damn phone before I snatch it out the wall," she yells. She yanks the cord, and the receiver flies out my hand and hits the floor.

"You might break it," I wail, plopping on the bed.

"So what, I paid for it."

"You're going to believe everything you're told? You haven't asked me anything."

"So what happened? What's this about you being a gang leader? Never mind, that's so ridiculous and I told her so. Did you tell the Black kids to refuse to say the Pledge of Allegiance? Don't answer, because I know you did. If I wasn't so mad, I'd find that amusing. But wait, let's start with *last month*. Why were you kicked out of class?"

"Sister didn't like my poem because I said Black people were considered boogeymen even though we look like Jesus."

"Say what?" Puzzled, Mom tilts her head. "What in the Sam Hill are you talking about? Never mind," she says, narrowing her lips. "And the second time you were put out?"

"She got mad because I said Nixon is a liar like Jefferson."

Mom throws her hands up. "What's your version of what happened today?"

"Um. Well. Because Sister got mad when I questioned why I wasn't allowed to enter the contest, and she told me to stop talking. I guess she got mad because I kept asking questions because she knew it was unfair."

"Didn't she tell you if you said another word you had to go to the main office?"

"I guess so."

"And what parting words of wisdom did you tell her?"

"I just said . . . I don't know, I didn't care." I pause. "She makes me so sick."

"You're cutting off your nose to spite your face. Do you really think Girls Academy will accept you if your transcript has two suspensions and shows you flunked conduct and effort twice?"

"Conduct and effort grades don't matter. Just academic subjects."

"They matter to me! Just when I was coming around to the idea of pulling you out of Catholic school for next year, you flirt with another suspension. You really do need a disciplined school environment. I see why you can't enter the writing contest. I wouldn't want someone who can't follow the rules or act respectful representing my school either."

Everything turns dark gray. My chest explodes from what feels like a thousand firecrackers going off. I can't possibly hate Mom more than I do right now.

"And to add insult to injury, you running around lying, telling folks I told Mike Williamson about the first incident involving you and Sister Elizabeth and now the newspaper will investigate racism in Catholic schools. You've lost your ever-loving mind."

That freaking big mouth Bonnie. Did word get back to Sister Elizabeth? Is that the real reason why Sister kept me out of the contest?

"I didn't tell Sister that." I run past madwoman Mom and nearly knock down Charles coming up the steps carrying a stack of comic books. I'd give anything to disappear into one of his stories. I race past him down the steps. Missing the last two, I fall hard and scrape my arm.

"Daddy will fix it," I yell, rising from the floor. "He'll straighten out the people you always believe over me. I don't know why you hate Daddy. But you hate me because I remind you of him."

I flee into the kitchen, reach for the wall phone. Flying downstairs on her invisible broom, Mom is on my heels in no time flat. She yanks the receiver away.

"I'm sick of your sass. Say another word, and I will knock you into tomorrow."

I scoot into the corner, huffy and bold. "I want to live with Daddy," I shout. "All you know how to do is fuss. I see why he won't come back. He doesn't want to live with you, and I don't either."

Mom's eyes become slits. "Daddy will fix it? You think so?" She leaps across the room, a raised fist aimed at my mouth. Startled, I duck and close my eyes. Her punch whizzes by my ear like a bullet and lands with a sickening crunch against the wall.

I can't unhear the bones cracking as her knuckles slam into the plaster.

"Aieeee!" Mom screeches so hard she reveals the silvery fillings in her back teeth. Her shoulders are shaking, and tears drop off her chin. "Oh, Jesus," she whimpers through gritted teeth.

All the open spaces in my heart close in at the sight of Mom's agonized face. *Me and my smart mouth.*

Mom slumps against the wall, then slow motion slides down to the floor. She twists in pain.

Charles thunders in and skids to a stop at beet-faced Mom on the floor, her injured hand held high.

"Mommy, what happened?" He turns to me, eyes bleeding revenge. "What did you do?" He balls his fists. Charles. Really. Hates. Me. Now. *I do, too.*

Torn between knocking my block off and comforting Mom, he starts to kneel by her. Mom holds up her good hand for him to stop.

"Go next door. Tell Nancy I need you to stay there until I get back from the ER."

"Why can't I go with you?"

"Please, baby. Do what Mommy says."

Breathing hard, he eye-stabs me and reluctantly stomps away. When he slams the door, I spring into action. Grabbing a dish towel, I get the ice tray and dump all the cubes into it. Mom takes the bulging towel and carefully lays it on her hand. Cringing and sucking her teeth, she immediately removes it.

"I can't drive to the hospital. Walk with me to the ER. Grab my purse."

In the messy coat closet I weed through boots and old book bags in search of umbrellas. My bones aren't busted but my heart is. What did Mom ever do to deserve a loser daughter like me?

I help Mom up and into her raincoat.

"Mom, I'm so sorry. I wished you had just hit me instead. I deserved it."

"No way in the world would I punch you that hard. I'm the adult, and I'm supposed to be in control." She steeled herself. "I need to tell you something. I know why you act the way you do. You love your father and blame me for the separation." She meets my eyes. "But you need to know the truth. You are old enough to understand why I made your father leave. I wanted to protect you two, but I'd rather you hear it from me than somebody else."

I hold my breath. I can tell whatever she's about to say will make every cell in my body scream in pain.

"Your father has another family. He's been living a double life, which explains our money issues. I thought he was gambling all this time." Her voice trails off. "Silly me."

"Daddy has a girlfriend who has kids? Why would he do that?" The room spins.

"Let's walk and talk," Mom says. "I can't take this pain."

I can't either. What's worse, an uncomfortable truth or lie?

Outside, it's a wind-whipped cool night with rain pelting us sideways. Sharing my Bubble umbrella, we start the six-block walk to the ER entrance.

I have questions I'm afraid to ask. Plus it hurts to talk. I'm a giant pincushion pierced by a thousand fiery needles. Every answer is another.

Mom hooks her left arm through my right one. At the corner, we pass under a streetlight, revealing her busted knuckles have doubled in size.

She stops, gestures at my dangling shoestrings. "Tie 'em before you fall."

It's hard to loop the wet strings when I'm in a fog of pain. I can only imagine what Mom feels.

We resume walking in silence. Passing the red-and-white awning of the Hostetlers' candy store, I recall the biggest clue.

"That's why you got so upset on Christmas when you found that little girl's sweater in Mom-Mom's closet. The one Daddy said belonged to . . ."

Just like that, it all clicks. Poor Mom. A fresh wave of pain drowns me. Even my pores ache. Daddy's betrayal burns more than alcohol on a pus-filled sore.

"Roberta, the girlfriend is only part of it. Her daughter is your father's." She pauses as I whip around, bug-eyed as my soul suffocates. "She's nearly two."

"Daddy has a baby—with someone else?"

Mom tugs me along with her good hand. Since my world just collapsed, it makes sense that I stumble on uneven sidewalk. Mom keeps me from falling.

"We can't have both of us breaking bones and ending up in casts." Her tone is protective and warm, like I'm still loved.

Her kindness cracks the stone resting in the pit of my stomach.

At the corner, we step over the rainwater swirling into the sewer. *Right where Daddy drop-kicked our family.*

Hiccupping sobs hijack me just as the wind gusts snatch my umbrella away. I start to chase it, but Mom pulls me close and holds me in the downpour. It's a tie for who cries and shivers more.

"I'm sorry, baby. I know what I told you hurts real bad. The only way to get over it is to feel what you feel. Don't pretend you don't. But then you have to move on."

I have never wanted to protect and love my mother more than right now. Using my coat as a makeshift umbrella, we continue heading to the ER in silence. I want to pepper her with a million questions. But Mom's words cut like unseen broken glass. It hurts to breathe. It hurts to feel. It hurts to think. I can only take so much more bad news before I punch a wall with all my might, too.

CHAPTER 22

Back home, I rub my finger against Mom's scratchy cast propped up on stacked pillows against her headboard. She's in the middle of me and Charles, who's sound asleep. Wish I were.

Mom takes prescribed painkillers for excruciating pain. Not sure what I can take to take the edge of all the broken pieces of me. The questions I need to ask, but don't dare, add to my misery. More uncomfortable truth and bold-faced lies will smash the few fragments left of who I think I am.

"Night, Mom." I rise slowly to avoid jarring her cast. "Want me to wake him up?"

"No, leave him here."

"Charles might hit your arm. He sleeps so wild."

"Leave him. I suspect I'll be up."

In the doorway, I linger, working on getting my nerve up. "I want to ask you something, but I don't want to make you mad."

"That's a heck of an intro. Go ahead, I'm sure you have questions."

"Is Peaches, the lady I saw on the trolley, Daddy's girl-friend?"

166

Mom shakes her head. "She knows her. I think they're friends."

"I knew she was trouble." Just picturing the gum smacker makes my brain throb.

"You're a quick study." Mom searches my eyes. "How do you feel about your Dad?"

"I hate him."

"Don't say that."

"Why not?"

"Because hate weighs you down."

We stare at each other. Why didn't I know Mom's a saint and Dad's the devil?

"He betrayed us," I say. "I know how Malcolm felt when he learned the truth about Elijah Muhammad. The man he adored and loved. The man with the secret families."

"The people you love the most can hurt you the most because they are closer to your heart," Mom says, shifting into a more comfortable position. "That doesn't erase all the good memories or mean you won't create new ones. You are too young to get used to the idea of hating anyone, let alone your father."

Hating him makes my stepped-on heart less achy. I wish I could tell Mom that.

Mom continues, "Malcolm also said a person's positives outweigh the negatives. And if I recall correctly, he even used examples from the Bible."

I groan at the Bible reference.

"Now, I want you to promise me something. No more trouble in school. Just stop."

"I promise, Mom." I speak with my whole existence.

Her watchful eyes size me up. "You okay?"

"Yes," I lie, moving back toward the door. I pause in the doorway. "Can I get you anything, Mommy? Ice cream or ginger ale?"

She does a double take and her eyes moisten. We both know why. When was the last time I called her Mommy? "I'm fine. Go to bed."

―――――――――――

In my room I can't sleep, and it's just as well. My hair has shriveled into a dried out mess a quarter of its normal size. Combing it as gently as I can, I torture myself with questions.

What kind of role model is my father for Charles? Is the other woman prettier than Mom? Did hanging out with Uncle Duke, who's always saying, "I'm single as a penny and fine as a dime," cause my father to stray? When did he decide we were old playthings and he needed new ones?

All the stored up so-called hatred for Mom automatically shifted to my father, the lying liar who duped us big time. Daddy two-face. Only the venom for him is infinite and the real deal.

In bed, I toss and turn. I swim in a pool of hatred so deep I can't touch the bottom.

Jumping up, I rip my played-out Michael Jackson poster off the wall. Tearing it into pieces, I imagine I'm tearing up Daddy's clothes. Mom was right to throw his clothes into the street. I'm sick to my stomach that I picked them up. If I could, I'd time travel and undo every last one of my mistakes.

Yanking open my diary. I write:

I'm not a writer. I'm not my father's only daughter. And guess what? Daddy, no Dad, as he will be called henceforth, doesn't want us anymore. He has a new family, and the first thing he did was replace me. Correction; the first thing he did was replace Mom, who I've been blaming everything on! I made Mom break her hand trying not to punch my lights out, which I deserved. I'm a terrible role model for Charles.

I lay my head down to think of what more to say. I nod off. An hour later, I wake with a start, drooling on my pages. After changing into my nightgown, I climb back in bed and discover I'm wide awake.

I open my *Right On!* magazine and read the contest rules for the first National Black Awareness Essay Contest. In 800 words or less, contestants must write about an influential Black person who inspired them. That's easy. But I want to tie Malcolm in with the fight I had with Sister over Thomas Jefferson. There's something true about the third president that explains everything else about America, and that is his hypocrisy. Maybe that's the start of my essay. I grab my copybook and start writing a draft. Forty-five minutes pass in a snap. I drop the essay and reach for my diary. I've so much more to say. Sometimes paper listens best. I write:

I'm nothing. An insignificant blob of protoplasm. Maybe lower than that. If I die, will anyone care besides Mom, who I don't deserve? My dreams of winning the contest dried up like a raisin in the sun. Maybe I will shrivel and die from anger and leave a note blaming everything on Sister, who will not be able to attend my funeral because she will be stuck in confession for years. Dad is not allowed to come and that's all I have to say about that. Man, I hate myself. I guess this is what happens when you choose the devil instead of God.

The last sentence scares me because it's been true for a while now. And look where it's led.

Today is a good day—unlike last week, when I cried so much that I was hollowed out.

Headed to class, I fret about Mom still having trouble sleeping weeks after breaking her hand instead of my teeth.

I've pinky-promised her I'll be an angel in school until I graduate. Won't be hard. I have no more fight left. I've been gobsmacked to the moon and back. What's helped me the most is Mom not making me talk to my father until I'm ready.

I shuffle into religion class. At my desk, I fold up into myself like a broken umbrella.

It's Ash Wednesday, the start of Lent. Sister says whoever wants to go to confession can leave class twenty minutes early before getting their ashes.

The idea of going to church crosses my mind. God forgives the wickedest people, right? Prostitutes, thieves, murderers. I haven't had sex and I certainly haven't killed anyone, although I've wounded Mom in so many ways, I've probably come close.

But Jesus forgave the heathens who nailed him to a cross. So why not me? Maybe if he forgives me, I can forgive myself.

In class, I can barely concentrate these days. Out the corner of my eye I see Sister Elizabeth studying me. For what?

I want to stand on my desk and shout that I'm done trying to prove my intelligence—trying to prove my worth—trying to prove I belong. If I had a white flag, I would wave it. *You won. I give up. I surrender.*

As students line up to walk to church, I decide to go to confession. My diary is one thing. Talking to God's direct representative is another. Besides, it's been months.

Sister dismisses us in groups of five. I am the last to amble over to the line of students less interested in confession and more down with early dismissal. They've gotten used to my indifference to their friendly chatter lately. My classmates know to cut me slack. We're immature at times but we recognize when someone is wounded.

Inside church, I dip my fingers into the holy water and bless myself. The last time I was here, I was livid about the marble angels and life-size statues of the white saints I pass on the way to the confessionals. Not today. My problem is with religion, not God. I choose the confessional with the shortest line, only three students ahead of me.

I've done a copious amount of sinning. Can I remember it all?

"Oh no, Roberta is going to take so long I'll miss my shows."

I turn as Geoffrey slaps his forehead in mock horror. He is such a moronic overachiever, but he actually makes me laugh. "You're so silly," I tell him. "I can't believe I am saying this, but I will miss seeing you next year."

"I heard you're going to public school. Good luck with that. They use razors to play tic-tac-toe on kids' faces. Hate to see that happen to you."

"Stop believing the rumors," I say. "Besides, with all the lumps and bumps you come to school with, you'd fit right in."

Geoffrey laughs and shrugs.

"Go ahead, we're waiting for our friends," says a seventh-grader in front of me. She and her friends step aside.

"Hurry up, Roberta," Geoffrey says. "I got a date with my TV."

Inside the confessional, I kneel and squint through the screened partition. It looks like Father James with his puffy white hair. I think he sees my hair because he does a double take.

"Bless me Father for I have sinned. I haven't been to confession in almost . . . three months. I have been horrible to my mother and brother. I made my mom bust her hand. I'm mad at my father. I got into trouble at school. There are a whole bunch of sins in all of this! That's why I think God is punishing me."

"Have you been Catholic all your life?"

"Yes, Father."

"Then you know that God is forgiving. When you look into your heart and see the sorrow you have caused, it's only then that God's grace can heal you. Say three Hail Marys. You have your penance. Go my child and sin no more."

I recall the same penance when I confessed to stealing some penny candy a year ago.

"Thank you, Father." Making the sign of the cross, I rise off my knees and turn back.

I'm tempted to ask if I can go to heaven if I have reason to never honor my father again. But Father yawns, waiting for whoever is next.

I pull the curtain back and step out of the darkened confessional for what will be the last time. I'm done with church confessions. From now on I'll talk to God directly. I'm not so sure about religion, but I'm down with God.

"How do my ashes look?" I ask Bonnie, pulling my Afro back from my forehead as we round the corner and head home.

"Black and smeary," she says, chuckling. "Like everybody else's."

"I hope I don't forget and wipe them off." I'm disappointed I'm not feeling holier.

"I'm giving up candy for Lent," she says, handing me a full bag of penny candy.

"How do you know I'm not giving up candy?"

"Are you?"

"This is my last year at Catholic school, so I'm going out with a bang. I'm going to do lent justice."

"You really aren't going to East Catholic?"

"Not if I get accepted to Girls Academy. Besides, I know money is tight."

"How's your dad? You never talk about him anymore."

"I have to tell you something. Promise you won't utter a word. I mean it, Bon."

"Cross my heart and hope to die." Bonnie's eyes grow big. She's so eager for the juice I am about to spill her freckles appear brighter. *Can I trust her?*

"My dad has done something really, really bad."

Bonnie leans in, practically drooling.

"He has a girlfriend."

"What is wrong with him? As pretty as your mom is?"

"That's not all of it. I think he lives with her."

"Roberta, that's crazy. For how long?"

"Couple months. And—"

Bonnie's lips twitch in anticipation. She can't help herself. But I can.

"I'm asking God to help me forgive him 'cause I don't know how."

Bonnie pats my arm. "That stinks so bad. Sorry, Roberta. My Uncle Lonnie has two families, but everyone knows," she says, shrugging. "Even my Aunt Laurie."

"Please don't tell anyone. It's really embarrassing."

"Hey, what are best friends for?"

"That's another reason why I think East Catholic is out next year. Mom is definitely divorcing him."

"Girl, I know you feel bad. I am going to pray your father comes to his senses and that doesn't happen," Bonnie says. "Let's change the subject. So, what are you giving up for Lent?"

Is it a sin to say stop hating your Dad? Yes, if your best friend is a motormouth.

"Writing in my diary." But then I shake my head. "That's impossible. I tell my diary everything."

Bonnie's head jerks back. "You can tell me instead."

I loop my arm through hers as we cross the intersection. I love Bonnie, but I'd rather walk through a war barefoot before telling her I have a half-sister.

———————————

At home, I tell Mom about the priest asking me if I'm a life-long Catholic. She raises her eyebrow since I said I wasn't going anymore.

"Many of the new Black kids enrolling at HSB aren't. Wait, he asked you this during confession? How did he know you were Black?"

"You can see through the confessional partition if you try hard enough." I draw a peace sign on her cast. "Why would non-Catholics want to come to HSB, anyway?"

"You may not believe it, but parents want a safe environment for their children. You read the paper about how some public schools are ringed with police cars. All the racial fights. Girls walking around pregnant. Gangs. Students disrespecting teachers."

"You mean kids who punch teachers and get suspended like me?"

"Your situation was unique. I'm talking about kids who don't want to learn and don't want anyone else to. Yeah, it's a sacrifice to send you to HSB, and aside from your horrible encounters with Sister Elizabeth, I still feel like we did the right thing. You learn universal values in a disciplined environment. Public schools have to accept everyone. Catholic schools don't."

Mom studies with approving eyes my purple peace sign on her cast.

"Wait, let me add the finishing touch," I say. Below the symbol, I write "love, peace, and soul" in graffiti style.

"I'll get Charles to draw me a Soul Train to go with it," Mom says, laughing.

Joining in, I realize this about Mom: she's even prettier when she smiles.

CHAPTER 23

" **H**ard to have a conversation when you only say yes and no."
Dad's voice dips between disappointment and impatience.

If was up to me, I'd go another three weeks without talking or seeing him. Hypocrite.

I sit across from him, staring out the windshield of his trolley into the darkness.

We are parked at the depot, the last stop of his route. His destination sign reads "out of service" until his break ends in fifteen minutes. Then he'll do another loop that stretches from this suburb through Southwest Philly ending downtown at 11th and Market Streets, the closest stop to City Hall. Topped by a statue of William Penn, it looks like a palace, although a dingy one.

Dad is turned sideways in the driver's seat, facing me across from him in what used to be my favorite seat. It feels like an electric chair now, and I'm a prisoner counting the minutes. I'm here only because Mom drove me over at Dad's request.

It's unseasonably cold. I pull back my mitten and check my watch. The trolley in front of us boards its last passenger in eight minutes. When it pulls off, Dad will turn on his destination light and move up and open his doors. Then I'm free.

"So the essay contest is a no-go?" Dad asks.

"Yes, it's been over."

He sighs and blows on his bare hands.

I look out the window for Mom's Bonneville. She's probably driven to the grocery store around the corner. I watch a man in a short jacket pacing outside a pay phone in use. I absentmindedly pop my gum.

"You know I don't like that. Throw it away," he says, handing me a tissue.

It takes everything in me not to tell him what I don't like about his actions. Removing my mitten, I wrap the gum in slow motion. Anything to keep from talking or looking at him. Anything to eat the time.

A lady bundled in a furry coat and huge colorful scarves knocks on the closed door. Frowning, Dad opens it.

"I'm on break, you can't board just yet." He nods at the trolley parked in front of him. "He's taking off soon."

"I'm not getting on. I just wanted to know if you have a schedule. The driver in front of you is all out," she says, stepping on board and smiling at us. "This must be your daughter. She looks just like you spit her out."

I pretend there's something on my boot. Then I say, "I am looking more like my mother every day." *Praise God.*

Next thing I know she's removed a glove, and she's patting the top of my hair.

"Look at all this pretty hair. It feels lovely. I bet it keeps you warm," she coos. "You have enough hair for nine wigs."

I respond with a slender smile.

"How do you care for it at night?"

"I just braid it. Sometimes I roll the braids up for more body."

"You picked a cold night to be riding with your daddy." The chatterbox takes the schedule from Dad. "Nothing like that father–daughter bond. Wish I could spend time with my father, but the Lord called him home sixteen years ago."

"Sorry for your loss," Dad says.

"Sorry," I say.

"Good night you two and thanks." She turns and waves. We wave back.

Then Dad sits near me. He turns my face toward him and I stare at his dimple, trying to keep my expression blank. Empty. Flat. Like how he left me. Us.

"I know you are mad. I know you are hurt and confused. I wanted to see you, to talk to you. I know you have questions that I may not be ready to answer or have the answers you want to hear. You are still a child. There are some things you won't understand right now. I asked your mom to bring you here because contrary to what you may believe, I love you. I love Charles. I love all of you."

My cheeks burn at the omission of Mom. I meet his eyes. He looks sleepy and sad. And a thousand times guilty. *Serves you right.*

He waits for me to speak. I don't.

Dad creases his forehead, throws his hands up in a what-do-you-want-from-me gesture.

Nothing.

I stare wordlessly.

"Daddy isn't perfect. Being an adult is complicated. You are growing up and starting to see a bit of that."

His words force me to consider the hurt he caused. The hurt I am trying not to feel. The hurt that's bubbling into volcanic anger. My father's skin looks gray, like everything around me.

"There's nothing you want to say?" he asks.

"All this time I thought Mommy was," my voice catches, "the bad guy."

Dad's face crumbles as he watches tears trail down my cheeks.

"I don't want to talk about nothing. I just want to go home. I just—" I bury my head in my lap and heave with sobs so deep I hiccup. Dad pulls me up by the shoulders and wraps me in a bear hug. I am torn between wanting to stay in his arms and recoiling at his attempt to baby me.

You have a baby girl and I'm not her. I hate you, I hate you, I hate you.

But I don't. And I do. I don't know how to handle this pain seesawing between my head and heart. "No, stop!" I scream. "I don't want to be here!"

Dad loosens his grip and cocks his head at my snot-running face.

I wiggle away. "Let me off!" I pull the cord that signals you want to exit. Its loud buzzing mixes with my shrill cries. Passengers waiting to board the trolley in front of us turn and stare. When my father fails to move, I stomp my feet. "Let me off. Open the door! I want to get off."

"Roberta, stop making a commotion. I'll lose my job." Dad grabs my hand to prevent me from pulling the cord. He wrestles my flailing arms behind my back and I collapse against him, bawling with all my might. Like a baby. A baby girl.

"Let it out," Dad whispers.

He digs out a hanky and wipes my face dry. He kisses my cheek and inside my heart, all the open spaces I did not know remain vibrate.

"Know this if you don't know anything else. Daddy loves you and wants the best for you, Charles, and your mother, even if it means we live apart. Okay?"

"Okay." I say, feeling light-headed.

He cups a hand against the window to see past the glare of the interior lights, and peers into the parking lot. "Your mother just pulled up." His eyes light up. "No school tomorrow. Want to ride with me?"

I shake my head. "We're going to pick up Charles. We're seeing a movie tonight."

Dad's smile lacks joy. He follows me to the door as I pull my hood up.

"Goodnight. Have a good week at school. Love you."

"Night," I say, stepping off the trolley. On the last step I turn. "I do have a question."

His Adam's apple moves before he says, "What is it?"

"Do you call your new daughter 'Pumpkin'?"

Dad's eyes turn watery. It seems like forever before he speaks.

"No," he says in a half-whisper. "No one can replace you, Roberta."

"Talk to you later, Dad." I step out into the wind and scamper to Mom's idling car, unsure what to believe, but feeling lighter. Hate is a heavy load to carry.

CHAPTER 24

Now that I no longer cut up in class, Geoffrey has taken my spot, waging war against Sister Elizabeth. I suspect the constant bruises and busted body parts he's getting outside of class have something to do with why he acts out. I can relate. My injuries are invisible but they still caused me to act crazy.

Bonnie says she heard his father beats him. It's certain that someone does. I feel sorry for him, even though Sister's insults sometimes make me laugh out loud. Yesterday, she said he was an imbecile in the strictest of medical terms. I wonder if all the sisters trade insults over dinner at the convent. Sister Elizabeth comes up with the best lines.

What's new now is Geoffrey also misbehaves in Mr. Harvey's class, which is why the entire class has detention today. Geoffrey stuck wads of gum under several desks.

I'm agitated. I want to cook dinner. Mom still tries to do everything she did before breaking her hand, and it drives me crazy.

Detention lasts for forty-five minutes, much longer than Sister Elizabeth's. As we file out, Mr. Harvey calls me over.

"How you doing, kiddo?"

"I'm fine. Staying out of trouble."

"Just checking. A good friend of mine will teach English at East Catholic High next year. She's a wonderful teacher. She'll be heading up either the school newspaper or the yearbook. I told her to be on the lookout for you."

"I may not go there. I'm praying Girls Academy accepts me." I cross my fingers.

Mr. Harvey knits his brow and rears back in his seat. "They'd be crazy not to accept someone so bright and talented. You know I will write a glowing recommendation. So you decided after this year no more sisters, eh."

"Well . . . I had some unreal stuff happen this year."

Mr. Harvey gives me a knowing nod.

"Plus, my parents are divorcing. Money will be tight." *Dad has two families.*

"Sorry to hear that, kiddo. There are East Catholic scholarships by the way. And why do you think you won't get into Girls Academy?"

"I got Fs on my transcript. Girls Academy only accepts top students."

He shakes his head. "Conduct and effort aren't academic subjects. Outside of here they don't amount to a hill of beans. Yes, they were used against you for the contest. But don't put too much stock in them. Now, I've kept you long enough. Go home."

I step into the hallway, and he calls after me.

"Girls Academy will be lucky to have a student of your caliber grace their doors." He clenches his fist in a Black Power salute.

I raise mine, too.

"Shut the door," he says. "I'm here for a while. I'm not taking work home today."

At the water fountain for a quick drink, I hear, "Pssst."

At the opposite end of the hall, six classmates crawl in a line outside Sister Elizabeth's room. Geoffrey, crouching like a cat burglar, is against the wall moving slowly toward the edge of the slightly ajar door. He peeks through it for a few seconds, then jerks his head back and slaps his knee.

I glance around. Every other class is gone. School let out nearly an hour ago, so whatever they gawk at better be worth it. I tiptoe toward the creepy crawlers then kneel.

Donna whispers so low I can barely hear her. "Wait for the signal." She eyes Geoffrey, who is behaving like a chunky James Bond.

"Someone in there doing it?" I whisper.

"Even better." Donna grins.

Geoffrey motions it's my turn to see what everyone here has witnessed.

I inch forward, imagining myself a panther stalking prey. I ease myself along the wall and pause in front of the door. Chalk dust dances in the sunlight of the open space.

Familiar and squeaky small noises greet my ear. *Kids are having sex*? That's so nasty. I've never actually witnessed anyone doing it. I just heard my parents, even when they turned the music up. But that was a long time ago.

I pause before peeking in. I'm not sure how I feel about actually seeing this. Then I recognize the sounds. *Someone is crying.* What loser is using the classroom for crybaby central without shutting the door? I look back at my detention crew. They smile like game show contestants. Geoffrey winks and mouths, "Hurry up."

Pulling my massive telltale hair back from my forehead, I peep inside. Hunched over her desk, Sister Elizabeth sobs while holding a crumpled tissue in one hand and clutching her rosary beads in the other. Sister's glasses rest before her on the desk. How is she so oblivious to our prying eyes? The hushed titters and whispers? She's totally off her game.

A current of weirdness swooshes through me and I stiffen. That happens when I see something shocking. Sister blows her nose. Her gold ring glistens in the afternoon sun.

Blood rushing, I survey the funky state of the room. Dirty erasers line unwashed blackboards. Rows of desks form squiggly lines on a littered floor. No trace of Sister's demand for order.

A part of me wants to whoop with glee, but another part says no. I turn away. What could force Sister, of all people, to fall to pieces here? But then, if not for detention, our floor would be empty at this hour. She'd be free to cry all she wants in peace. *Has she done this before?*

Retracing my crawl, I point toward the other end of the hall.

"Be quiet, Mr. Harvey is still marking papers," I whisper. Geoffrey follows me with a joker-sized smile.

Out of earshot of our teachers, I turn to Geoffrey. "Is she being transferred?" I ask.

Geoffrey smirks. "Never thought we'd see the penguin lose her cookies. Man, if this had happened during recess, we could have sold tickets." Geoffrey whips out his palm for me to slap him five. "Too bad I found out too late."

"Found out what?" I ask, leaving his palm hanging.

"She has feelings. Her brother kicked the bucket."

"How do you know?"

"My cousin heard Sister Benard talking about it outside the faculty room. Get this, no one knows why she only visited him in the hospital once. He's been in and out since school started. Who does that? She's a strange fish."

The hairs on the back of my neck stand. Heat fires up my cheeks. "Her brother died?" I ask. "That's the punchline?" I glare at my classmates. "Get out of here!" I grunt. "Or I'm telling."

Everyone except Geoffrey scatters. They look back at me with questioning eyes. A frown punctuates Geoffrey's doughy face. He folds his arms and stands wide-legged like a pint-sized Mr. Clean.

"What's come over you? You're acting nuts."

He clearly does not know me. Maybe I am a stranger to myself, too.

"You hate that battle-axe. Why spoil the fun? It's not like she hasn't made you cry."

I point to Mr. Harvey's room, disgust etch-a-sketching all over my face. "Go or I'm reporting you."

"Forget you." Geoffrey throws up his hands and storms off. "You've been weird lately."

I stand there, mind racing. I think about Charles. I think about Malcolm. I think about the story we discussed in reading class that ended with the boy waiting at the traffic light. I said then in class that he was thinking about which way to go. Now I wonder: When he finally moved, was he astonished by the direction he chose?

CHAPTER 25

Grinning so hard he's squinting, Charles hugs Mom and rushes out the front door. His excitement feels like a betrayal. I peek out the kitchen window. Dad's horn beeps twice as he drives off to shop for Easter suits—as in plural. As in one for himself to accompany us to Mass like he used to. *What in the Sam Hill?*

My stomach clenches. Except for me, everyone has a short memory about my father's sinful ways. Why is it an option he's even invited?

Coast clear, Mom gestures for me to remove Charles's Easter basket from its hiding spot in the storage bin by the sink. There's enough candy for five baskets. Mom insists that I share in the bounty despite the number of silver fillings hugging my back teeth. I insisted I'm too old for a basket. I'm giving in, but she doesn't know it. I need to hold out longer. For general principle and all.

"When are you getting your Easter outfit?" I ask.

Cleaning the oven, she pauses to examine her handiwork. Then grins at me.

"Anything I wear looks new since I haven't been to church in a while." She shrugs, removes her gloves and examines her healed hand.

"Does it still hurt?"

"Not too bad."

I pile the basket and assorted candy packages on the table, debating how much to say about my father, the bold-faced liar. "Still, everyone else," I pause to emphasize my point, "is getting something new to wear."

Stooping in front of the oven, Mom looks back at me. "What's eating you?"

"I just don't understand how you can talk to him like he is not a bold-faced liar. Act so nice like nothing happened." My stomach hardens.

"It's called maturity—something I hope you experience sooner than later." Her voice has an edge, and her eye twitches. She checks the gleaming oven for nonexistent missed spots.

Instantly I feel bad. I didn't mean to insult Mom. I'm always on her side.

"It's just that he was so heart-stoppingly wrong. You are a saint to forgive him," I snap my fingers, "just like that." I'm trembling.

"Heart-stoppingly? Yup, you're my little poet."

Mom rises, shuts the oven door and adds water into a small pan. "Forgiveness is a process. And no matter what, he is your father. We—you, Charles, and I—will always have a relationship with your father. Of course, my relationship changes." Mom looks like she wants to say more.

I do, but don't. 'Cause, immaturity. I'm thirteen, not thirty. I sit at the table.

"When is your grandmother taking you shopping for your outfit?"

"Tomorrow. Are you still mad at her since she knew Daddy's secret?"

"She didn't know everything. We're cool. I've learned to let go what's gone."

Her words stop me cold. Mom talks like a poet sometimes. I want to tell her. Instead I change the subject.

"I don't even want to go to church." I shift into my Thinker pose, based on the statue I finally saw at the Rodin Museum on Benjamin Franklin Parkway on a field trip. "You think God cares that so many people only come to church on Easter and Christmas? All decked out in their finery, folks who normally wouldn't be caught anywhere there like my father—" I stop, instantly regretting mentioning him. Mom searches my face.

"People go to church for different reasons on holy days and holidays," she says.

"That's why I stopped," I say. "I just wasn't feeling . . ." I shrug. "I don't want to talk about him."

Mom nods and gazes with affection at the packages of yellow marshmallow chicks eyeing the ceiling. They remind me of the song, "Yellow Bird."

"Do you think Sister became a nun because some guy broke her heart?"

Mom tilts her head, pondering my question, then tosses her head back and howls like I just told one of Charles's jokes. Shoulders shaking, she struggles to catch her breath. Her laughter lifts my sagging spirit. I join in, my high-pitched chortles mixing with Mom's squeals. We sound like a laugh track on helium. We rock back and forth, cracking up a good while before Mom regains her composure. I can't recall the last time we belly laughed until our stomach muscles felt sore.

"I don't think it works like that," Mom says, setting aside a packet of purple dye and wiping her eyes. "Men can make women do all kinds of things, but I'd like to think really important decisions like that are deeply personal. More women are choosing how they want to live and work. Even though the Equal Rights Amendment didn't pass, change is in the air. Your generation will benefit from a shift in thinking about what women want and need."

"I already know I'm never getting married. I want my own apartment, car, and career." I get a bowl and pour in the dye. Mom removes eggs from the refrigerator.

"I'm all for you having a career but I do want some *grand-babies,* and for that to happen I expect you to be married."

I shake my head as I add boiling water to the dye. "Maybe I'll become a nun."

"Yeah, right," Mom says, setting the carton down. Then she gets tickled again. Body rocking, she bursts into another round of glass-shattering cackles. This time I just watch, mesmerized at how happy she is. And because I am responsible.

The next day, I sit next to Mom-Mom, who groans as she bends to touch the tip of the new kicks I am dying to buy. The slingback suede sandals with espadrille wedge heels are shoe heaven perfection. The clerk has already measured my feet, but Mom-Mom has her own sizing process, which requires pressing my big toes to gauge if there's room—a half-inch exactly—for my toes to grow into. I study her cleavage—jeez, 'll never understand what's so desirable about big boobs.

Mom-Mom pushes the top of my shoes and grunts her approval. Yay!

"Promise me two things," she says, sitting upright, slightly winded. "Always buy leather shoes and get the right size. Nothing like having bad feet. It catches up to you."

"Promise." I giggle. If she had checked the last pair, I wouldn't have gotten them a size too small. The sales clerk sidles over.

"We'll take them," says Mom-Mom.

The clerk boxes the shoes and heads to the cash register. Cash in hand, I rise to follow her. Mom-Mom tugs me back into the seat.

"What's this about you halfway talking to your daddy and not spending time with him? In my day, I could never tell my mother I didn't want to see my father. Your momma done spoiled you all rotten. Who ever heard of such?"

Mom-Mom's words carry arrows aimed at Mom. Wrong target. I stiffen. "It's not Mom's fault he did what he did, and it's not my fault I feel the way I do."

Mom-Mom rears back as if I've just tried to clobber her. Her pained expression confirms my words have done the trick. Her mouth forms a tight O and her eyebrows nearly touch. She leans in close, her lemony perfume tickling my nose.

"We'll discuss this when we get home," she whisper-screams through lips that barely move.

Ah jeez, do we have to? I will myself not to sneeze.

"You hear what I said?"

How can I not? "Yes, Mom-Mom."

I trail behind her to the counter, thankful she's mad *after* I spent all of the Easter cash she gave me. I even have a new floppy hat she purchased in hopes I'd get my hair pressed bone straight and curled for church. *No way, Jose.*

I've ticked off Mom-Mom so much that the entire time we ride the bus she is in a constant state of agitation. She disapproves of everything I point to out the window and say I like: tight dungarees with a crease sewn down the middle of each leg the girls wear, cute boys with huge afros, and colorful bubble graffiti. She says graffiti is a sign of the devil. If I was as fresh as she claims, I'd say, "Add your son to your devil list." But I have good sense.

I dread the upcoming lecture as we walk up the steep, narrow staircase to her apartment. Inside her apartment, the aroma of cinnamon and vanilla greets me.

To my relief, Mom-Mom darts to the bathroom and maybe falls asleep. I'm glad I don't have to use the bathroom anytime soon.

I dial Mom several times to ask her to pick me up but the phone just rings. Mom-Mom walks into the living room as I hang up for the fifth time.

"Who you on the phone with? That fast-behind girl? Is that why you so mouthy?"

"Who? Bonnie? She's not fast. When did you stop liking her?"

"I never said I didn't like her." The plastic covers squishes as she sits next to me. "Forget Bonnie. You need to forgive your daddy. You know what Easter means, don't you?"

"Jesus died so our sins can be forgiven," I say robotically. I slouch, and peer at a photo of Dad in his cap and gown perched on the credenza facing us.

She pokes my side, and I sit up like I'm in school. "So Easter teaches you about what?"

"Easter teaches us about resurrection and forgiveness." Impatience coats my tone.

"Do you understand the words coming out of your mouth?"

"Of course."

"Then act like it."

"Can I be honest?

Mom-Mom pauses then nods.

"I know what Easter is supposed to mean but it doesn't mean that to me. It's just another Sunday, and I really don't want to go to church."

"'Cause you don't want to go with your father?"

"'Cause I'm not sure there is . . . a God," I blurt.

Mom-Mom freezes, squeezes her eyes and bows her head praying for my wretched soul. When she looks up, tears glide down her face. She cups my hand. "Roberta, you blaming God for what ails you is misdirected anger. You too young to be full of vinegar, child." She wraps her arm around me, and I wish I could erase what I said. Mom-Mom taps my left breast. "Anger corrodes the vessel it's carried in. Remember that."

Eyes glistening, she points to a crucifix hanging on the wall, near the photos of Jesus, John F. Kennedy, and Martin Luther King. "All of them martyrs. You're upset that you've been lied to? They lied on Jesus! Nobody's nailing you on a cross. Jesus forgave; why can't you?"

My body tingles. It's like some of the darkness in me gets a little light. I bet anything that Mom-Mom prayed for the spirit to pinprick my vessel of hatred, which would be . . . my heart? "I'm sorry. I get so mad and confused sometimes. I know there's a God. Mostly." I look upward, feeling guilty. "I'm just not sure He hears me anymore. You know, Daddy . . ."

My throat knots up, and I collapse in a nose-running sob.

Mom-Mom strokes my hair. I bury my face in her warm bosom and hiccup-cry until my head thumps. Mom-Mom grabs a flowery tissue box off the side table, snatches a handful. Sniffling, I use half. She uses her stack to dry the river of my tears running down her blouse.

I lean back, feeling lighter since I sprung a leak and let it all out. The anger, fear, guilt, jealousy, selfishness, and hate; all the stuff that cooks up confusion—it's out now.

"Were you trying to call your mother earlier to take you home?"

"Yes, but I'm staying."

"Want some milk and cookies?"

I nod, even though I'm thirteen.

Mom-Mom gives me a knowing smile and rattles around in the kitchen while I search for the reason that turned me into a sniveling crybaby. The answer nags at me like a name on the tip of my tongue but out of reach. A shiver runs through my body when I realize the trigger for my crying jag: I had said Daddy like I used to. Before I had to hate him.

I lay all of my new clothes on the bed, including my bra and panties. I take my time dressing, savoring the freshness of wearing something for the first time. I rub scented lotion on before sliding into my pants and matching combo jacket with the top that ties in the back. I slip into my four-inch wedges and admire my taller physique in the mirror. I shape my Afro one last time and float downstairs.

"You look pretty in pink," Mom coos.

"You look pretty, too," I say, admiring her purple dress with the red slash that accentuates her tiny waist and high, round booty. Men can't help but rubberneck when Mom walks.

Charles thunders down the stairs in his beige three-piece leisure suit. It fits him so well he could model in the husky section of a Sears catalogue. He's beaming, Mom's glowing, and I'm bouncing out of my skin with eagerness to get to Easter Mass.

"Where are my keys?" Mom twirls, looking high and low.

Charles scoops them off the top of the television.

We file out of the house, heads high in our Easter finery. My mood is so good I don't even argue with Charles about whose turn it is to ride up front. I ease onto the back seat just as Charles turns to Mom.

"Is Daddy meeting us at Mass?"

Mom shakes her head. I catch her glancing in the rear-view mirror at me.

I hold onto my smile despite waves of disappointment.

In the pew, I sit between Mom-Mom and Charles. Mom invites Bonnie to join us, and Mom-Mom gives Bonnie a warm smile and a thumbs up for her outfit, which matches mine except it's blue.

"Is your dad coming?" Bonnie whispers. I shake my head. Concern clouds her eyes.

"Believe it or not, I actually hoped he would," I murmur.

Bonnie slides a piece of gum in my hand. I pocket it. She raises her eyebrow but I lack the words to explain. Today is full of surprises, including the peace I felt as soon as I entered and dipped my fingers in the holy water—the peace that fills me as I celebrate that Christ has risen, the peace that comes with knowing that I am changing. The fact that I wanted to see my father is proof of that. Besides, I'm tired of breaking commandments.

After communion, I join the entire pew as it kneels to pray. It's the first time I've been to church since confession. I have a lot of atoning to do. I know God is listening.

I thank the Almighty Father for protecting Mom and Charles and helping us even when we forget to thank him. I thank him for my friends and family. I pray for his guidance, forgiveness and love. I apologize for doubting him like Peter and wishing hell and damnation on Dad. I get lost in my conversation with God. I am the last one to stop kneeling and sit.

On the ride home, I think about how I initially wanted to attend church to show off my Easter outfit. Instead, I revealed my heart to God. Like Malcolm, I'm changing. I think God approves.

CHAPTER 26

When something juicy and forbidden happens in class, there's an unmistakable buzz. If certain sounds are only heard by dogs, that's true for kids, too. It's a faint hum that happens all at once. Plus, you feel it.

I pause from translating my poem into Spanish. I look up.

Donna watches me with a sly smile. She nods at her textbook, which she holds upright on her desk and mouths, "Wait."

My row eyeballs me with goofy grins. Donna cranes her neck to check on Sister. Earlier, when I passed her desk, she was red-inking papers and adding scores to the grade book.

Donna turns her textbook around to reveal what's inside: an adults only comic book is making the rounds.

Unlike clueless me, students sitting in my row have been waiting the entire period to get their grubby hands on the nasty drawings. Sometimes sitting in the last row stinks.

Some classmates brag about fooling around. Not me. Nobody's getting my cookie anytime soon. Bonnie and I pinky-swore to remain virgins until we graduate high school. Still, I'm eager to see what's on the pages that's causing half the class to blush.

Apparently, through the grace of God, Sister looks up and catches Donna smiling at me and me smiling at what's within her textbook.

Busted, Donna begins erasing the spine of her book, which is a sure sign foolishness hides between its covers. "Erasing graffiti, Sister." Donna scrubs imaginary ink.

I pinch the underside of my arm to keep from cracking up at Donna's bad acting. I imagine falling out of my desk and rolling down the aisle, cackling to the heavens only to be stomped on by Sister Elizabeth. I almost laugh out loud at the thought, then cough, and stare at my poem, waiting for the fireworks. *This will be better than the Movie of the Week.*

"What are you hiding inside that textbook?"

Squirming and squinting, Donna acts mute.

"In the time it will take you to answer me I can walk the earth and cure world hunger."

"A magazine," Donna whispers.

Sister Elizabeth puffs out her cheeks and points her marking pen at Donna.

"Are those teen magazines going to help you pass your weekly religion test, which you desperately need to do judging by your poor performance to date?"

"No, Sister."

"Donna, come to the front of the room and show the class exactly what is preoccupying you and Roberta's attention." Sister returns to grading papers.

Donna shuffles to the front of class with the X-rated magazine that will be included in dozens of upcoming confessions. Even though she's known for having the best posture in the Etiquette Club, Donna slumps like a dry plant.

Sister prods her. "Show us the long-haired heartthrob you two nincompoops are drooling over."

"It's not that kind of magazine." Donna tentatively shows Sister the cover.

Sister cocks her head until it registers she's looking at filth. She snatches it and thumbs through. Her face grows scarlet, and she clutches her crucifix. I bruise my arm to stifle my laughter and avoid being kicked to death by her.

"This is the kind of filth you bring to my class? Is this yours?"

Big-eyed Donna shakes her head.

"Whom does this belong to?" Sister asks through clenched teeth.

"It was passed to me."

Sister slaps her grade book closed. "I'll wait." She rolls up the sex magazine and places it on the edge of her desk like it's radioactive.

Grimacing, she walks up and down each aisle scrutinizing every face for a clue. After circling the class, she returns to her desk and claps her hands.

"Alrighty then, class detention today."

Groans, teeth sucking, sighs, and other sounds of unhappiness erupt.

"I expect to hear a pin drop," Sister says, glancing at the clock. "Sit up straight with your hands folded and your feet on the floor. We may be here for a long wretched time." Sister Elizabeth grabs the magazine and zips to the trashcan. "This is where it belongs."

Geoffrey raises his hand. "Sister, that's my father's. Please don't throw it away. He'll kill me."

Sister Elizabeth hovers above Geoffrey. "It's time we had another meeting with him. I will return it then, and not a moment before."

Geoffrey palms his face.

Sister grabs his ear. "Face your classmates and apologize for speaking up too late."

"I'm sorry," he mutters, looking like a cross between Dopey and Grumpy.

The bell rings. But not for us. We slump in our chairs, listening through clenched jaws to the hallway echo with the sounds of joy and freedom that come at the end of the day.

Some students, like me, get a head start on homework. Others daydream. Sister resumes grading papers. The class is beyond quiet.

After fifteen minutes, a miracle occurs.

"Sarah, lower the window shades."

"Yes, Sister Elizabeth." She bounds up and grabs the window pole.

All that's left is to clean the board and erasers. Five minutes and we're out of here. Yay!

"Cut it out!" shouts David Green, a pimply-faced boy who has yet to experience his growth spurt. He sits across from Geoffrey, who enjoys picking on him. David finally decides to stop suffering in silence, but at the wrong freaking time. Apparently, Geoffrey beaned him with an eraser.

Sister stares at Geoffrey as if he is two-headed. "Boys and girls, thank your class clown," she wags her finger at Geoffrey, "who has the audacity to misbehave mere feet from me for adding another thirty minutes."

Our unhappiness fills the air.

"I have a stack of logic-defying essays to wade through, and since many belong to this class, it makes sense for you to suffer with me. Another outburst? I'll add thirty more minutes."

I lower my head onto my desk, then bolt up before she accuses me of napping. Sighing, I picture myself clobbering Geoffrey, who'll keep me from seeing the After School Special. I glare at the back of his sweater dotted with lint balls and hope he can feel my disgust long distance. I pity his freshmen teachers and classmates.

Twenty minutes later Sister Elizabeth says the magic words. "Class dismissed, starting with the first row. No running," she says without looking up.

The last person out of class, I race to the end of the hallway and into the stairwell where a commotion below echoes. Taking the steps two at a time to the second-floor landing, I arrive as Geoffrey shoves David. A circle of kids egg the fight on.

Geoffrey turns, sees it's me, and continues his bullying. "You sissy, you had so much to say in class."

"I'm reporting you," David shrieks.

He heads for the steps, but Geoffrey blocks him. Geoffrey pops him in the jaw. David's head snaps back.

Rather than fight back, David bends over and covers his face as Geoffrey beats on his back like it's a human drum. David tries to run. Geoffrey grabs his shirt tail, and David's buttons fly.

"I only have three school shirts," David shouts as buttons skip down the steps.

Attacking his shirt fires David up. Head down, he charges into Geoffrey, who wrestles him to the floor. I hope David kicks Geoffrey's behind.

Geoffrey straddles David, who lets out a horror movie scream as his classmate pummels him.

"Better let him go," I tell Geoffrey, whose radar for teachers often malfunctions.

I want to pull him off David, but if he accidently hits me, I'd have to give him the Batman to Robin punch I already want to. Obeying Mom and avoiding trouble trumps everything. I look over at Donna to join me, but she won't meet my eyes. I walk away as everyone else from detention instigates a fight.

I head down the stairs and am about to push open the door to the yard when I hear Sister's heels. The taps on her shoes sound like Click-Clack balls.

"Get up off that floor." Sister Elizabeth's growl fills the staircase.

A few students jet past as I tiptoe upstairs to peek at Geoffrey getting a well-deserved smack down from Sister.

On the landing above me, Sister peers down at both boys. "Geoffrey, on your feet. Now!"

As Geoffrey starts to rise, David elbows him. Geoffrey wrestles him back to the floor and they roll dangerously close toward the steps. Sister leans over and grabs the back of Geoffrey's sweater just as David accidentally grabs the folds of Sister's habit, knocking her off balance.

It happens in a snap, and I instantly jump back against the wall. Entangled, all three bounce down the steps as Sister Elizabeth's glasses fly across the stairwell. Her white slip flies up revealing fat legs in black stockings. I cover my eyes because I was raised right. The sound of bodies tumbling down twenty-two steps shoves a lump of ice in my stomach.

When the falling stops, I peek between my fingers at three bodies sprawled in a messy heap several feet away from my frozen legs. Donna scrambles to a motionless Sister Elizabeth, whose head rests near David's torso. Dazed and moaning, Geoffrey lies across him. My knees wobble like jelly at the unimaginable sight. Someone broke a neck. I just know it.

Students cover their mouths to stifle laughter. Some ask, "Sister, are you okay?"

"Yes," Sister says, grabbing her crucifix and gesturing for Donna to hold off helping her up. "Let me get my bearings. Where are my glasses?"

I pick up Sister's glasses from the corner. A lens is cracked.

"Geoffrey and David, are you okay?" Sister asks, sitting up and straightening her veil and habit, which thankfully landed below her knees.

"Yes, Sister. Sorry, Sister," they answer.

I start to carry the glasses to her just as Geoffrey moves off David, who fails to realize the tail of Sister's long veil is wrapped around his leg. As he stands, he accidentally tugs on her habit and it tumbles off her head.

I halt, gawk, and choke at the image in front of my eyes.

Shock forces my saliva down the wrong way, closing my windpipe. I cough and struggle to breathe because Sister Elizabeth is not bald. Far from it.

Plenty of hair covers her head, it's just not the kind expected. Her thick, bushy hair looks just like mine except it is a few inches high and a golden brownish color. Absent the black and white habit surrounding her face, I strain to recognize her. And then I do.

Squinting, I shiver. I feel like I did when I stuck a bobby pin in an electrical socket.

It can't be.

"Did you swallow your gum?" Donna asks, patting my back. She takes Sister's glasses from my frozen hand.

What looks so familiar to me looks out of place on Sister Elizabeth's scalp. It's like seeing fur on a bird. *Why does Sister have a small Afro?* All of the dots connect and an "aha" moment so powerful hits me like a stinging slap to the face. Sister Elizabeth is Black. Like me. Just really fair like Mom's side.

CHAPTER 27

Mom always said we can spot other Black people no matter how light or keen their features. Sometimes it's the shape of the nose or the fullness of the lips or the not-quite-white complexion. Or the hair. That was often a dead giveaway, especially if bushy. Oh my God. Mind blown. Now her unusual coloring makes sense. She was mixed with her blue-eyed, high-yellow self. Didn't matter. The one drop rule made her Black. Seeing her teeny-weeny Afro, which we jokingly call TWA for short, makes it as clear as cellophane. Mom would've known if she had seen her.

Mouths agape like the letter O, we gawk. No one scrutinizes her harder than me. Do the others know what they see? Of all days for Stephanie to be absent. I'm the only Black girl here.

This is the biggest scoop in the fifty-year history of our school.

In a flash, Sister stands, yanks Geoffrey up by his collar, shoves him against the wall, and beats the living crap out of him. We watch in petrified silence, fearful any one of us could be next. No doubt she took mercy on me big time when we fought in September.

Sister alternates slaps and punches, each more powerful than the previous one. She stops when his nose bleeds. Geoffrey drops in a heap on the stairwell, covering his face.

"Every last one of you better be out of my sight in two seconds," Sister bellows. She grabs her veil off the floor. She's so outraged her cheeks look burgundy.

We swarm out of the building as if it is the last day of school. Discombobulated, I bolt into the sunshine and stop next to the Blessed Virgin Mary statue. I just cracked a mystery I didn't know needed solving. I feel otherworldly. And powerful.

Karma crowned me queen today. Talk about payback for not allowing me to enter the writing contest. I cannot wait to tell Bonnie, my parents, and every Black student about Sister Elizabeth's secret, which explains so much.

Some classmates pass by, laughing about "Brillo pad" hair and the need for Sister to shave it off. I follow behind them to see what else they have to say.

"Was that the wildest thing ever?" asks Donna, running up behind me. She glances back to see if Sister followed us outside. Not yet. We quicken our pace.

"I can't believe it. Her hair," I say.

"I know! Me neither. You think she . . ." Donna whispers, ". . . has cancer? My aunt's hair was just like that after she got sick."

"That's what you think?" I stop in my tracks.

"What are you waiting for?" Donna asks, glancing back. "Sister Elizabeth is on the warpath. She'll be headed to the convent any second."

I'm in shock and speechless. Just as I'm wrapping my brain around discovering a deep secret, Donna introduces something else. Doubt.

Donna blathers on about the need for everyone to treat

Sister better in light of her impending death. She's not joking, adding to my confusion. I keep my thoughts to myself. At the corner she heads home in one direction and I turn in the other.

I'm so deep into thought about Sister's Afro I cross on a red light and step in front of an oncoming truck. Someone screams, "Watch out!" I jump back as the driver slows down, shakes his fist, then makes monkey noises out the window.

"Not cool," shouts a Black male teen a few years older. He's cute in a geeky way. We smile at each other as he disappears down a side street.

I turn my attention back to Sister as I pick up my step. My father once said some self-hating Black people light enough to pass for white go out their way to put Black people down. Maybe Sister was like that mulatto in the movie, *Imitation of Life*. No wonder she became enraged when I asked about her brother. Was he darker?

This is totally unreal. Sister Elizabeth is Black? My feelings flip-flop. I'm overwhelmed with confusion, disgust, bewilderment, and anger. She never said she was white. She just acted white.

If this is her secret, she's still a mystery. A bigger one. What do her parents look like? Did race play a role for her not visiting her brother in the hospital?

Trying to figure it out will kill me. I nearly collide with a Volkswagen. The squeaking brakes of the yellow Beetle startles me. An old Black lady drowning in moles pokes her head out.

"You nearly gave me a heart attack. Get that hair out of your eyes."

"Sorry," I yell, breaking into a run.

I barge into the living room winded and gasping for air. I collapse on the couch.

"What are you running from?" Mom asks, getting up to peer out the front door.

"You are not," I pull my knees up to my chest, huffing, "going to believe this." Mom's alarmed face makes me hold up both hands. "It's not about me or Charles."

"Oh, you scared me. Charles is at a program for prospective altar boys and Mr. Roberts hasn't called to say when he's dropping him off. I thought something happened." She settles on the couch that now has a mystery stain since she removed the ripped-up plastic covers we detested.

Between ragged breaths, I tell Sister's secret. To my disappointment, Mom fails to react in the way I imagined.

"Are you sure?" She flashes a skeptical smirk.

"Mom, cross my heart and I hope to die. I know what I saw."

"You know I don't like you saying that." She frowns. "You're too young to talk about dying, even in jest. Roberta, hair can be a tricky business. I had a white friend in college with thick hair who used to relax it with the same perm Black women use." She shrugs then she reaches for our thick family photo album with her good hand.

I dart up and grab it for her. She opens it up to a grainy black-and-white photo of her as a little girl with her parents. As a child, I thought my mom and her parents were the whitest-looking Black people on the planet.

"You were little—you probably don't remember meeting your grandfather before he died." `

We study the photo. "Didn't he have blue eyes?"

Mom nods. "You can't tell in this picture, but yes. You know Black people have blue eyes, green eyes, blonde hair."

"And noses like yours that are so pointy they can harpoon a shark," I say, repeating Dad's joke.

Mom pokes me good-naturedly with her elbow. "If Sister really is Black—" she pauses off the look I give her. "Okay, let's say she is. That's her cross to bear."

"Really? That's all you have to say?"

"Yes, and you don't need to be going on and on about it. You've been doing so well lately, avoiding trouble in school. No need to open that can of worms."

"But, Mom, it explains so much. Why she treats me the way she does. She says I have too much pride because she has none!"

"I hear you. Just feel sorry for her. If she is living a lie . . ." Mom's nose turns pink. "Sometimes truth has consequences we are not ready for," she nearly whispers.

I lean back against the couch feeling wobbly. Between Sister Elizabeth's fakery and what Mom is and isn't saying, I will have a field day with my diary tonight. Mom looks as uneasy as I feel.

"Charles should be here any minute now." Mom glances at her watch. "I highly suggest you don't mention this to him. You know how fast rumors spread in a school. And speaking of rumors, you know as well as I do that Bonnie has a big mouth." Mom gives me a knowing grin.

"Awww, man! She's my best friend. How can I keep this front-page news from her?"

Mom gives me her you-know-better-stare.

I throw up my hands. "Okay, I'll wait until after graduation, deal?"

Mom chuckles and nods.

"I have the biggest story ever, and I can't tell it," I wail. I punch a sofa cushion then put my chin on the back of my hand like the Thinker.

"It has happened more than you know," Mom says.

"Mom, I heard of Black people passing. Do white people ever pass for Black?"

Mom stiffens. Weird. With difficulty, she removes the old photo of her with her parents from the sticky album and hands it to me. I hold onto the white border of the photo to keep it free of fingerprints.

"How old were you here?" I ask, smiling at my Mom younger than I am now.

"Judging by the dress—and I didn't have many—I'd say about ten." Mom pauses, then looks me in the eyes. "My father was so poor growing up in Culpeper, Virginia, that Black people helped them out from time to time. White folks looked down on them. Called them trash. So when he left to come to Philly and met your grandmother, he never said he was Black. But he never said he was white either."

"Wait, what? You mean, he *was* white? You are half-white?" I ask, mouth gaping like a goldfish out of water. "My mom is a *mulatto*?"

"You know the one drop rule. I *am* Black. My husband *is* Black and my children *are* Black. I know who and what I am. You don't be confused about who you are."

Mom heads into the kitchen as my head whirls like Charles's spinning top.

I follow her into the kitchen, flabbergasted and feeling less Black and beautiful. "Mom, this is huge! You didn't just tell me what we're having for dinner. You dropped a bomb. You could have told us before now."

"Now you know. So what? What does it change? Do you feel differently about me or your grandfather who you barely knew? Most Black families have white relatives in the family tree. You go back far enough, you'll find more of us related than anyone wants to talk about. Heck, my mother always said there's a bunch of red-haired, light-skinned Black people in Culpepper all related to your favorite person."

"Who?" I contort my face in confusion.

"Thomas Jefferson."

"Ugh." I toss my hand up. I'm already dealing with enough. "Mom, I always thought you were the Blackest light-skinned person I know. You are always quick to let people know you're Black and—" I pause as something profound registers. "Now I know why you can't wear an Afro."

Mom snort-laughs so hard, she can barely catch her breath. Her gut-belly laughter forces me to join in. I fall to the kitchen floor buckled with laugh pain. Mom drops in a chair and slaps the table, squealing.

"I guess I sounded kind of dumb making the hair comment," I say, clutching my stomach.

"Kind of," Mom says chuckling. She rises and places a pot of water on the stove. "Get me that box of rice."

I rise off the floor and search for the rice in the crowded cabinet all the while thinking about how Mom is right. She is Black even if she is mixed, although now I have to question what being a Black person really means. Or being a white person.

The phone rings, and Mom gets lost in conversation. She motions for me to add the rice and then leaves the room. When she goes upstairs to talk, it's top secret.

Waiting for the water to boil, my mind reels. There's so much to ask Mom. Maybe I'll start with what's bugging me right now. It's a weird two-way tie. What happens to Sister Elizabeth when word gets out? And why in the world do I care? Good thing I have the weekend to think about it all.

CHAPTER 28

The next day, I lay across Mom's bed removing her pink toe-nail polish. Mom reads information about evening college programs. I eye balls of colorful yarn in a basket in the corner.

"Mom, when your hand feels stronger, will you teach me how to knit and purl?"

Her eyes glimmer. "Of course. Someone just told me that yarn is on sale up the avenue. We're losing another store. The Knit Palace is going out of business. We'll go pick out some colors you like. Oh, get the bag of books your father brought to my job. There's one for you," Mom says.

I open the plastic bag on her dresser and spot a brand-new copy of *The Autobiography of Malcolm X* and two other paper-backs for Mom. I squeal. "Awww, I'm ready to read it all over again, especially the last part. I guess I have your permission."

We laugh. I open the book and inhale its new smell. I place it next to me as I paint her toenails.

"Malcolm's mom was half-white, which explains his red-dish complexion," Mom says.

I glance up, ready to discuss her bombshell since she fell asleep early last night. Malcolm hated the red hair he inherited from his white grandfather. I don't look like my Mom or her father. If I did, would I feel differently? I stare at Mom's profile. She could compete and win in any kind of beauty pageant, white or Black, with her wash-and-go hair, perfect skin and dewy almond shaped eyes. Her looks are a gift from her parents, who she couldn't choose. I don't hate any part of her or my white grandfather. He clearly loved my Black grandmother, although now I wonder about her DNA.

"Is it possible Grandmom is mixed, too? She's about your complexion, although her hair is thick like mine."

"I'll never know since she was adopted."

"Growing up as a mixed girl, did you ever feel like a racial lone ranger?"

Mom cackles. "No, silly. Again, I'm not confused. I am Black. Do you feel differently knowing you are part white?" She looks amused.

"Nope, because I *look* Black." I hold my toasted beige hand against Mom's pale leg. "Come on," I tease, "were you ever tempted to try and pass?"

Mom sighs and leans against her headboard. "What I wanted more than anything then—hell, now too—is for skin color not to matter so much. Our people sometimes are the worst with this light-skinned versus dark-skinned nonsense. I hope our Black Is Beautiful movement truly changes our own screwy attitudes about color. Charlie has done a number on us."

Mom's nickname for white people always cracks me up. Thumbing through my Malcolm X book, I recall how it helped me make sense of this school year. His light skin was a non-issue. I cup my chin.

Mom's eyes light up at me in the Thinker's pose.

"Frederick Douglas was half-white and so were some of our other great leaders," I say. "Do you think mixed or really light-skinned Black people feel they have to work harder to prove their Blackness?"

Mom sets aside a brochure from Temple University. "Depends. Some people swear by the one drop rule, but that's because of laws, which were created to benefit slave owners, who fathered biracial children but wanted to profit off them. A lot of that went on, which is why we're so many different complexions. As for me, I don't feel the need to prove anything. But yes, I know light folks who need to be the most revolutionary person around to solidify their Black card. The bottom line? People define themselves how they want. What matters is how they treat others."

"I've been thinking about this," I say. "Race, like truth, is really complicated. It's not just Black or white."

Mom nods and grins. "I'm impressed you think about these issues and ask such insightful questions. Keep your grades up, and go after your dreams. This is a terrific time to be a Black student with a good head on your shoulders. All kinds of opportunities exist. That's why I'm so hard on you."

I study her smooth face. "Mom, you're still kind of young." This tickles her. I pause as she covers her mouth, filtering girlish laughter that fills the bedroom. "I wasn't trying to be funny when I said that. What are your dreams?"

Mom takes a deep breath and stares at something I cannot see. "My dreams are for my children to be happy and successful. To defy the odds of a broken home."

Her words sting. Both of us. I'm poker faced while her eyes dim and her lips flatten. I change the subject.

"Wouldn't it be cool if I became a famous writer like Judy Blume or Alex Haley? Or maybe a journalist? If I could write for my job, then it'd be like getting paid for a hobby, right?"

"That's a great way to look at it." Mom brightens. "You want to enjoy your career."

I steer the conversation back to her dreams. When she talks about her younger days, I see the girl in her face. "What did you want to do when you were my age?"

She sits up straighter. "I thought I wanted to be a nurse, work in a hospital with babies. But in high school, I think I was around fifteen, I met a professor who I thought had the coolest job in the world. So I went to college planning on being a teacher, maybe even a professor. I was in my second semester when I met your dad. I didn't go back after I had you." She grins.

"I can see you as a nurse, Mom. But you would make a better teacher."

"Well, that's water under the bridge. As for you," she tosses me the *TV Guide*, "I'm saving space on the living room book shelf for your books."

"Mom!" My voice catches. "That's the nicest thing you've said all year!"

Holding her healing hand high to protect it, she tickles me on the bed until I cry uncle.

It takes most of the afternoon to write my latest poem. My mind swirls with questions about race. There's so much to say. So much no one wants to talk about. So many secrets, lies and half-truths. I amble into Mom's bedroom and hand my poem to her.

"Why don't you read it to me?" she says.

"It's called *In Between*." I read:

Malcolm X's grandfather was white and so was mine
When it comes to race, Mom could blur the line
Yet she's so proud to say out loud she's Black
When it comes to color, what's false, what's fact?
The one drop rule defines the Black race
But some Blacks want to live in white face
If Sister is pretending to be white

She's living a lie, a sin, that's not right
When people are mixed, must they always choose
To become mysteries with missing clues

Mom's reaches for my work. "You didn't write that," she teases.

"It's just the first draft, Mom."

"That's so good."

"Maybe I'll ask Sister Elizabeth if she's mixed," I blurt.

Mom's head jerks up like I just cursed. She gives me a don't-be-fresh-stare. It's been a while.

"On the last day of school, Mom. I'm not crazy."

"I can't wait to meet her at graduation." She pats the bed for me to come lay beside her.

I place my arm, the color of tan sand, next to Mom's. "I'm in the middle. I'm not light or dark."

"That depends. Some people will call you light and others will say you're dark."

"Well then, as you say, I can't win for losing," I say, shrugging.

"You win when you don't act better or act less because of your skin color or anyone else's." She hands me the *TV Guide*. "Find us a good movie."

I take forever to find something worth getting up to change the channel. I just want to stay nestled against my mom all night.

On Monday, the yard buzzes with exaggerated accounts of the fight. Word is Sister wears the old-fashioned habit because she has "pubic" hair, which angers me to no end. No one even acts like they suspect Sister's race. Bonnie is upset she missed it. While I fill her in on the details, I leave out the main one.

As the days pass, I am sure about one thing: Sister Elizabeth knows I know. The air between us sizzles with this electric fact.

She behaves differently in the tiniest of ways. While she looks at most students like they are freewheeling idiots approaching a cliff, whenever our eyes meet, I see question marks where declarative sentences used to be.

This school year taught me what uncertainty looks like. I recognize it in my own reflection.

Dad says, "Fake it until you make it," but your eye game must be tight. They are a dead giveaway to doubt and fear. It's one way to tell who will hit you back or not in a fight. Now that I'm looking, I see it in adult eyes. When I watched the documentary about Malcolm X, there were some interviews where he seemed less sure of what he was saying, especially after he broke with the Nation of Islam. I chalked it up to being tired. Now that I know he wasn't always brave and sure, I admire him more.

Today, Sister feels me watching her. She looks up from the papers she's marking. Something odd, just different, flickers across her eyes. We look at each other in a way we never have before. At least, I think so. Then Sister blinks, and the blue brick walls return.

I wonder how the students, priests, other nuns, and parishioners would react if they found out she is Black? Even a tiny bit.

How can Sister love God if she doesn't love herself? As mad as my father makes me, I'd visit him in the hospital. Does she visit her parents? I shudder. One thing is certain and two things are for sure, Sister needs prayer as much as I do.

The bell will ring any second for lunch. All I have to do is tell Bonnie. Then it's a wrap.

I think of the short story we read that ends with the Black male teen waiting at the traffic stop trying to figure out which way to go. And then I think of what Mom said. *"I hear you. Just feel sorry for her if she is living a lie."*

Her words tug at my smugness. They open a space I first felt when I saw Sister crying after her brother died.

I look at the crucifix above Sister's desk. Jesus forgives everyone, even those who sentenced him to death. *Have you forgiven me for hating Mom, then Dad? For punching Sister?*

I think about Malcolm and how he transformed from a high school dropout and criminal to a Muslim leader and a global social justice champion. He used to think all white people were devils until he saw them as brothers while praying with all races in Mecca. He even took on a new name, El-Hajj Malik El-Shabazz, when he broke away from the Nation of Islam. Too bad Franz Kafka has a lock on the word "metamorphosis," because that's exactly what Malcolm achieved. I think about my own struggles during the school year and something stirs deep inside.

I gaze out the window at lime buds sprouting on a tree. Changes are all around. Inside me, too.

Thanks be to God.

In a matter of months, I plan to attend a high school without uniforms, crucifixes, or statues of saints, without nuns, priests, and visiting seminarians.

I scribble on the last page of my copybook: *Girls Academy. Same suit, different tailor.* Then I add a question mark.

The bell rings, but Sister holds up her hands for us to remain seated.

"President Nixon will make a major address to the nation tonight," she announces. "I urge you to watch so we can have an intelligent discussion tomorrow."

As *Scooby Doo* says, "Rut roh." I'll just sit back and listen. Nothing good can come out of my participation. Nearly every adult I know says Nixon is a sweaty-face crook. But what we really dig is that a Black man, a security guard, set in motion events that bought everything to light.

I add my homework to my book bag. I'm eager to watch

Nixon's speech with Mom. Last night, she said we'd make popcorn and listen to the president lie. Then she winked at me. I wished I had known way before now how cool Mom is.

That night, I remember the year before when I snuggled on the sofa watching President Nixon sweat as he spoke. Even if he wasn't guilty as sin, he sure looked the part with beady eyes and a wet upper lip he constantly wiped with a hanky.

"Today, in one of the most difficult decisions of my presidency, I accept the resignation of two of my closest associates in the White House, Bob Haldeman and John Ehrlichman, two of the finest public servants it has been my privilege to know."

"If they are so fine, why are they resigning?" I asked the TV.

"Shhh, let me hear this," Mom said.

I halfway listened as he droned on until he mentioned he had replaced the attorney general and his counsel, too.

"That's four people gone," I said.

"Where there is smoke, there's fire," Mom said knowingly. "He'll be the fifth."

So now, I'm on the sofa listening to Dan Rather. "This is a special report from CBS News in Washington, where the president of the United States is about to address the nation."

Mom sets down a tray with bowls of Jell-O and fresh popcorn.

"I bet Nixon hates those two *Washington Post* reporters," I say. "Sister said they are responsible for telling the story about him breaking the law that may lead to his impeachment."

"You'd be a good reporter with your nosey self." Mom turns up the volume.

"It was almost two years ago, in June 1972, that five men broke into the Democratic National Committee headquarters in Washington," Nixon says. "It turned out that they were connected with my reelection committee, and the Watergate break-in became a major issue in the campaign."

We listen to Nixon explain why he released the transcripts but not the actual tapes. My mind drifts back to the day I called Jefferson a hypocrite. Our current president is one, too.

"Do you think fifty years from now some kid, like me, will get in trouble for calling any of our presidents a hypocrite?" I ask Mom.

She tilts her head, weighing the question. "I'd like to think future presidents will fall in love with the truth instead of power and corruption. But history has a way of repeating itself. Maybe if it happens again, you'll be the reporter to expose him. Or her."

I beam at the possibility.

CHAPTER 29

Spread out on my bed, I read newspaper articles about the slaying of Dr. King six years ago this month. A photo of him catches my eyes. I fly down the steps to show Mom. Seated on the couch, Mom works her knitting needles overtime on an oddly shaped reversible scarf for Charles.

"This happened when I was four," I say. "Look at all the nuns in the crowds!" I show Mom the newspaper photo of Dr. King giving a speech to 10,000 people at 40th and Lancaster in West Philly.

She nods. "I didn't just send you to Catholic schools for discipline. The sisters have often marched for civil rights."

"Sister Elizabeth wouldn't have." I roll my eyes.

"Well, two more months and you will never have to see her again or wear another uniform for that matter." Mom peers over her reading glasses at me. "Unless you choose to do so."

"Fat chance of that. I'm sick of hypocritical people."

"You think you won't find them in public school, or anywhere else for that matter?"

"Yeah, but at least they aren't disguising themselves as holy people, having us believe they are better. Just like the president. If you hold that office, you should be better."

"Better than what?"

"Most people."

"Fairly sure few saints walk the earth." Mom fixes a dropped stitch.

"I'm not saying you have to be perfect, Mom. But if you are in a position of power and people are looking up to you, you have to take that seriously. It's heartbreaking to know adults who you think are great can mess up just like you." I realize I'm cutting it close to the bone. I swear I didn't mean to do so, but I can't shut up.

Mom stops knitting and watches me with intense eyes.

"Nixon and Jefferson, probably all of them prove my point," I say in a quivering voice. "Every kid is told to work hard and one day you may grow up to be president, as if that's the greatest role model." I chew my lip, stunned by the sadness hijacking my body. "It's not just politicians but other leaders, like Elijah Muhammad. Really, any adult you look up to." I pause to swallow the firebrick blocking my windpipe. "Like . . . Daddy. It's hard understanding that people can do great things and wrong things at the same time. That really messes with my head." I turn to hide fat tears that spring from somewhere deep and refuse to stop flowing.

The knitting needles clank on the table. "We all struggle with that, because nobody is perfect," Mom says softly. The warmth in her voice tells me she knows I'm crying. She also knows not to mention my father even though I just did.

The silence ticks on longer than it should.

The sofa squeaks as Mom rises. She turns the TV to a news special about Dr. King's assassination. I listen while retying my perfectly looped sneakers. I need to pull myself together.

The anchor says Bobby Kennedy broke the news about Dr. King's death in a stunning speech to a crowd in Indianapolis. Just last week in history class we discussed how Bobby's assassination occurred two months later. I glance up as Mom starts to turn the channel.

"Can I hear what he said?"

Mom lifts her hand from the dial. "Sure, baby."

On screen, Kennedy spoke while holding a piece of paper. "I have some very sad news. Martin Luther King was shot and was killed tonight in Memphis.

"He dedicated his life to love and justice, and he died in the cause of his effort to promote peace and love. For those of you who are Black and are tempted to be filled with hatred and distrust of the injustice of such an act, maybe feel against all white people, I can also say I also felt in my own heart the same kind of feeling. I had a member of my family killed, but he was killed by a white man."

My mouth falls open at Kennedy's conclusion. I scoot to the edge of the couch, listening hard as he recites a poem about pain falling "drop by drop on the heart until comes wisdom through the awful grace of God."

I can't stop blinking.

"This is why I love poetry," I say, as a lump in my throat swells.

Mom holds up her finger for me to be quiet.

"What we need in the United States is not division, hatred, and lawlessness," Kennedy continued, "but love, wisdom, and compassion toward each other and a feeling of justice toward those who still suffer within in our country whether they be Black or white."

"Wow, do you think he memorized all of that?" I ask.

Dabbing her eyes dry, Mom looks directly at me. "What do you think, poet?"

"I think he made it up on the spot, because it sounded like it came from the heart."

"I think you're right."

"I was surprised he said he felt like he knew the pain Black people were feeling toward whites because a white person killed his brother."

"That shows you how smart he was," Mom said. "He was real with the Black people hurting in that audience. He connected. I don't think it was a coincidence that there were no fires in Indianapolis that night."

"I liked the poem he read, too. I'm going to look it up in the library."

"The part about pain turning into wisdom through God's grace is deep," Mom says.

"So deep I'm ready to write a poem." I chew my lip. Something stirs inside.

In my room, I pull out my diary and write:

Drop by drop,
pain will stop,
when we live,
to forgive,
the human race,
through our God's grace.

I dedicate it to Dr. King and John and Bobby Kennedy. And Malcolm. Slouched against the headboard, I daydream. I see a great leader, maybe a president, comforting an audience in pain by reading one of my poems when no other words will do.

CHAPTER 30

"Roberta, come here please."

I peer up at Sister Elizabeth, then glance around the room to ensure she's addressing me, as if there's another Roberta. I'm in the middle of my last history test and I want to ace it to get straight As on my report card. Soon, fingers crossed, I'll get my acceptance letter for Girls Academy, one of the city's best. Grudgingly, I get up and avert my eyes from my classmates' answers as I pass by their desks.

"You are wanted in the main office," she says low.

Caught off guard, I say loudly, "I haven't finished."

Some students look up. Sister presses her fingers to her lips for me to dial my volume back. "You'll have time to finish it tomorrow."

"Am I in trouble?" I ask in my best library voice.

"Not if you have no reason to be." Sister returns to marking paper with a hint of a smile.

I hurry out the class. Just when I think we are co-existing in peace, she may have hopped on the danger train again. If I'm summoned during a test, this is something major.

When I enter the office, the office aide perks up. "Mother Superior is expecting you. Follow me, please."

I trail behind, ready to defend myself against God knows what. Rounding the corner, Mother Superior's profile is visible as she talks to someone I can't see.

Mother Superior waves me in.

"Sister Elizabeth said—" I pause. Seated a few feet away is a petite nun bent over collecting papers that have spilled from a folder. When she looks up, her face is brown and behind her blue veil a small Afro pokes out. My knees nearly buckle.

She smiles. "This must be Roberta."

I stare, mouth hanging open like I have no home training. Because, mind blown. Bonnie really didn't make her up.

"Roberta, take a seat. This is Sister Carol. She wants to talk to you about something important." Mother Superior pats my arm then closes the door behind her.

Tongue-tied and heart racing, I plop on a chair as Sister Carol sorts her collected papers. I'm psyched lunch is next. Bonnie will flip out when I tell her I met the Black nun.

Sister Carol adds the papers to a clipboard, turns to me with a huge smile. "I've heard a lot about you."

I nod. "I've heard, well not a lot, but my friend Bonnie told me about you. I thought she was pulling my leg. I've looked in the yard for you for years."

"I don't spend much time in yards," she says, chuckling.

I instantly like her. The clipboard slides off her lap and crashes to the floor. I pick it up and spot my name, school, and grade on a list. Puzzled, I hand her the clipboard.

"Are you familiar with the archdiocese's Bridges Program?" she asks.

Bewildered, I shake my head.

"We train students who are leaders at their respective schools to help work on race relations in their high schools. You saw your name on this list because you were nominated, which is an honor. We only choose students with certain attributes. Interested?"

I breathe with ease for the first time since being summoned. "Yes. I'm curious about the attributes. What are they, please?"

"We want young people who are outspoken, fair, and independent thinkers. I also look for students who have something extra. Students with grit and grace."

I have never felt so flattered. Then desperate. "Can I still participate if I attend a public high school?"

Sister Carol remains smiling but her eyes don't.

"There's prejudice there. Everywhere, really." I lean forward with enthusiasm.

"I thought you would be attending East Catholic? I agree the program is needed in public high schools, too, but that's not our focus."

"I'm going to Girls Academy." I cross my fingers. "If I get accepted."

"I've seen your records. You are an exceptional student. I'm sure you'll get in. But why are you leaving Catholic school? If it's the tuition, we can help with that."

"May I be honest? It's the racism. And hypocrisy. Those are biggies for me."

"That's not confined to Catholic schools. I'm the first Black nun in my order. I know." As if reading my mind, she says, "My faith is stronger than any obstacle." Sister Carol looks directly at me and takes my hand. "You've had some painful lessons this year. I've learned truth is often seen from different lens. It's a challenge to live in a religious world you don't always feel invited to. God called me to do this work— from within. I forgive those who hurt me to heal myself."

Her words make my throat tighten. "Do you know what happened between me and Sister Elizabeth?"

She nods.

"We're almost at the end of the school year, and Sister Elizabeth still hasn't apologized." I speak low, straining not to tear up at a familiar rawness I thought was long gone.

"Forgive Sister Elizabeth anyway. Sometimes people express their regret in other ways. I can tell you with confidence she is sorry." Sister Carol fishes in her bag and hands me a tissue.

"Thank you," I say, surprised my eyes remain dry.

"When I was about your age, my father told me that when you stay angry at someone it's like being a bucket full of acid. And you know what acid will do."

"Corrode my insides."

Sister Carol nods. "Don't do that to yourself. You're a special young lady. As far as your high school selection, maybe we can make an exception and still allow you to participate in some capacity. As you know, the church needs to do a lot of work to bring people together. Of all faiths. We'll see."

I am surprised at how her presence soothes me. "Will the student leaders in the program meet with you?"

"Yes, once a month at East Catholic, where I teach. I'm the advisor to the Black Studies Club, which I started five years ago. East Catholic provides many opportunities for girls with leadership potential. You'd have your pick of potential colleges in four years. Although you certainly will at Girls Academy as well."

"Does the Black Studies Club discuss Malcolm X?" I ask.

"Of course. His book is very popular with high school students."

"I read it twice this year. Malcolm said one book could change your life. That's exactly how I feel about his autobiography. I'd love to encourage students, Black and white, to read it."

Sister Carol nods. Her Coca-Cola colored eyes glow. She hands me a brochure. "Read this and call me if you have any questions about the Bridges Program." She glances at her watch and adds the clipboard to her bag.

"Did you graduate from East Catholic?"

"Yes, way before you were born. I was the second Black student there out of 2,200."

"I know it was difficult."

"At times. But then I thought about Sister Theresa Maxis Duchemin." Off my blank expression, she tells me about a founding member of the Oblate Sisters of Providence in Baltimore, the first Black order, who also co-founded the Servants of the Immaculate Heart of Mary (IHM). Turns out Sister Duchemin was exiled for many years after a bishop she angered revealed her mother was Black. "She lived with an order in Canada before returning to Pennsylvania. But she never lost her faith."

"So she was passing?" I ask, head about to explode. Is Sister trying to tell me something without saying it outright?

"She was very fair. Clearly at one point she identified as being Black with the Oblate Sisters of Providence. When she left Baltimore, maybe she found it easier to stay quiet."

"I never heard of her." What else could I learn from Sister Carol, I wonder.

She hands me a small envelope and tells me to open it when I get home. Then, she hugs me and I never want to let her go. I take in her Afro so proudly displayed and think of Sister Elizabeth's. Maybe when Sister Carol and I get to know each other better, I'll ask her how well she knows Sister Elizabeth.

I'm at the door when I turn with a sheepish smile. "Sister Carol, if you're not in a hurry, can I ask you for a favor?"

A crowd of students, Black and white from all grades, encircle Sister Carol while she jumps rope with Bonnie. One hand holds down her crucifix, the other clutches her habit. Sister Carol's sturdy shoes keep pace with Bonnie's monstrous platforms.

My girls, along with lay teachers and other Sisters, cheer and clap for the odd duo moving in sync. More teachers watch from their class windows.

Bonnie deftly jumps out to allow Sister Carol to continue alone. Bonnie hugs me as Sister Carol jumps on one leg.

"This is better than Shock Theater and the Soul Train line!" Bonnie slaps me five.

Sister Carol motions for me to jump in. I rock my body to the beat of the ropes. Timing my entry with perfection, I join the first Black nun I ever met in a game of double Dutch. Sister knows the moves. Our brown eyes glimmer with glee while our Afros bob to the rhythm of the ropes.

Later that night, resting against my headboard, I open the envelope from Sister Carol. I pull out a small card headlined "The Serenity Prayer." I read it: "God grant me the serenity to accept the things I cannot change, courage to change the things I can, and the wisdom to know the difference."

I hear the front door shut. Mom is back from getting us hoagies and fries for dinner. Today's the 69-cent special. I smell the onions from here.

"Mom, can you come upstairs for a minute?" I yell.

I hear her footsteps disappear into the kitchen then head my way. She arrives with a paper plate overflowing with French fries.

"Just because I'm eating upstairs, don't you do it, too. You know Charles follows behind you. What's up, buttercup?"

I grin at Mom's new nickname for me. "Today, I met Sister Carol, that mysterious Black nun."

Mom's eyebrows rise, but she doesn't say anything.

"You know, the one I thought Bonnie was lying about since third grade. Sister Carol called me a leader."

Mom munches on a fry. "Congratulations! I'm happy but not surprised. You're smart and outspoken. You got dozens of students to refuse to say the Pledge of Allegiance for valid reasons." Mom hands me her plate.

"She says I should seriously consider attending East Catholic."

"I'm not surprised."

"Well, she says I can get a scholarship to help with tuition."

"This is an interesting development. You must like her if you are considering it."

"There's a program for student leaders to address racism. The Bridges Program. She wants me in it." I nibble a fry. "It's overwhelming."

"It's an honor," Mom says.

"Not that. For months, I thought God stopped answering my prayers. Stopped listening and talking to me. But it was me who stopped. I thought he had forsaken me, our family. The broken people. But he fixed us, right? God bought us through."

"Roberta, that's beautiful," Mom says, her tone a combination of love and pride. "This has been a doozy of a year for you. For all of us. But we've come through, yes, thank God. Sometimes faith is all you have. To God be the glory."

"I still don't believe it rained forty days and Noah built an ark," I say.

"Oh, I knew I was speaking too soon," Mom says laughing.

"But I believe in God. I love God, just not religion," I say chuckling. "And Catholic school is far from perfect. But I'm not afraid to stand up for myself and others. To speak the truth to power."

"Or forgive," Mom says. "How many girls your age would let Sister Elizabeth's secret remain? Of all the things you have done, that one right there speaks volumes about the young lady you are becoming."

"Thanks, Mommy."

She does a double take. She gives me a quick hug and then grabs my dirty clothes off my floor. "Unfortunately, some habits are harder to change," she says with a wink.

We laugh together.

CHAPTER 31

Hate to admit it, but I am bona fide jealous of Charles. Four years younger and he manages to win a first-place award for his grade in the annual science fair.

I shake my head at myself in the mirror. I'm not just jelly, I'm super proud, too. He gets to add a top award to Mom's curio. Looking in the mirror, I pick out my hair and admire my denim outfit.

"Come on, we're running late," Mom yells upstairs.

In the car, Mom-Mom and Mom beam as if Charles is the Second Coming. Charles fidgets with happiness in the back seat next to me.

I nudge Charles. "Now you'll be pressuring yourself to win every year. And you know what?"

"What?" Charles's eyes narrow.

"You will! Mom will run out of room to display all of your awards."

Mom-Mom looks back. "Praise God! That's beautiful, lamb!"

She watches Charles hug me. Mom smiles at us in the rear-view mirror. Warmness spreads inside. I'll clap until the insides of my palms turn red when Charles walks across the stage.

"I hope Daddy isn't late." Charles checks his watch. "We get our awards first."

"Good," Mom says. "We can leave early and get something to eat." Mom double parks. "Go ahead, we're right behind you," Mom says. Charles and Mom-Mom get out so he can line up since fourth-graders do their presentations first.

I spot a parking spot directly across from the church. "There, hurry," I say pointing.

Another driver sees the coveted spot, slams on the brakes and starts to back in. Lead-foot Mom swoops in, causing me to apply imaginary brakes.

"Whiplash," I shout, laughing. I stop when the driver who wanted our parking spot backs up next to us.

He flicks his middle finger at Mom then peels away, a cloud of rubber his *hasta manana*. Mom shakes her head along with several nuns watching from across the street.

I scan the crowded sidewalk for my friends huddled with their families. Carrying a bouquet of roses, Eileen approaches a group of nuns by the main entrance. Leaving early, after Charles gets his award, spares me from watching her receive the first-place award as the winner of our grade's essay contest. Still, I'm proud of myself for congratulating her for winning second place in the archdiocese competition.

Her father trails her with a camera. One sister steps away from the cluster to pose with Eileen. When they turn to face the camera, I gasp. Sister Elizabeth said she would be out of town during the awards ceremony.

"Mom, there's Sister Elizabeth." I speak louder than intended, especially with the windows rolled down. "You finally get a chance to see—" I whisper, "—she's Black."

"Which one?"

"The tall nun with Eileen, the girl holding the flowers."

Mom looks at Sister, and time stands still. I nearly tip out my seat, I'm so eager to hear what she thinks. Mom turns back to me, eyebrows knitted. She shrugs.

"It's hard to say, especially from here. Not all white people are the same pale shade, just like all Black folks aren't the same color."

She studies my overeager eyes and seems amused. "My supervisor is taking evening classes. She's writing a paper about 'internalized racism,' a five-dollar phrase for self-hating. I told her maybe my daughter would write a poem about it. She said she'd love to read it."

I feel like I just won an award. "Wow, I never had someone say they want to read a poem I haven't written yet."

Mom looks back at Sister then faces me.

"I don't care if she's Black, white, or polka dot. What she said to you was racist. Wrong is wrong, but look at all that has happened that turned out right. Talk about turning lemons into lemonade, Miss Soon-to-Be High-School Leader." She pats me on my shoulder and grabs her keys and pocketbook. "Part of growing up is knowing when to let go of what's gone."

There's an odd glint in her eyes, and my gut clenches. I don't know if she's referring to my obsession with Sister possibly passing as white or if she's talking about Dad, who waves at us from across the street.

Sadness waters down my happiness every time I see him now. I hope such feelings fade with time. He's handsome in the brown suit he picked out when he took Charles Easter shopping, so the few Black mothers and grandmothers attending the awards program watch him head in our direction. We wait by the car so we can all walk in to together.

He smiles at Mom and pecks me on my cheek.

As we cross the street, Sister's eyes light up at my parents and linger on Mom. No doubt she is surprised by how little I resemble Mom, whose face remains unreadable as Sister approaches us. Mom sizes her up in a casual way, the kind that sees everything in quick flashes without letting on that she's scrutinizing the person down to their pores. I do the same thing, and I get it from her.

"It's a pleasure to finally meet you, Mrs. Forest." Sister extends her hand.

Watching Mom and Sister greet each other, I compare their complexions and features. Aside from sharing different shades of pale skin, they look nothing alike.

"After all of our conversations." Mom voice is all business.

"Good to see you again, Mr. Forest."

Dad nods. "Evening, Sister."

I wonder if everyone feels as uncomfortable as I do.

"You must be so proud of your son's win and Roberta being accepted to the prestigious Bridges Program."

"Yes, we are." My parents say in stereo. We all chuckle.

"Thank you, Mr. and Mrs. Forest for your responsiveness this year." Sister looks directly at Mom. "And all of the conversations."

Mom starts to respond, but stops and nods.

Sister and Mom look at each other until Sister breaks her gaze first. "I'll see you good people inside."

That's the cue for Sister to continue making her rounds with other families.

I wait until we get beyond her earshot. "So, what do you think now about my theory?"

"She still looks as white as the driven snow to me," Dad says. "She doesn't sound like a sistah, either." I know he means a Black woman, not a nun. He shrugs. "Race is funny. I work with Italians whose wives look Blacker than your momma."

I sidle up to Mom, whose opinion I most need.

"It's hard to say. And it's not like she would ever admit it. If she is and doesn't want the world to know, she picked a good place to hide."

I mull that over as we move up the steps to celebrate my brother, whose award unites us, if only for a celebratory dinner.

On the landing, Mom gives me a full-on Mom look. "Always be true to yourself, no matter where you are, who you meet, or what you do."

And I wonder, was that the biggest lesson I needed to learn this year?

―――――――――――

Unable to sleep, I turn on the light and grab my poetry book. I've been mulling something since Sister met Mom. I'm now unsure about Sister Elizabeth's race. On one hand, if she's mixed, maybe she's hiding it to avoid excommunication like Sister Duchemin dealt with. I'm kicking myself for not asking Sister Carol if that still happens. Doesn't seem godlike. I hope not. Understanding what's swirling in my head requires a poem. It takes three attempts.

I once thought truth was black or white back in the day
Before life turned complicated and truth turned gray
Growing up sure is challenging, it can be so tough
One day I'm certain, the next not confident enough
There's a puzzle I've yet to solve, one that makes me feel dense
When it comes to racial identity, some math makes no sense
People with a drop of Black blood are considered Black, they say

What about white people with drops of Black
blood, same rule in play?
Sister's hair is "Black" and my Mom's is "white"
What makes one race "wrong" and the other "right"?

Me gusta. I turn off the light feeling satisfied even though the answer about Sister's race remains elusive. The truth sometimes is.

CHAPTER 32

I am lost in a racy book I swiped from Mom that I have no business reading when the phone rings. "What's happening," I say coolly, expecting to hear Bonnie's breathless voice spilling the latest gossip.

"May I speak to Roberta Forest?" a woman's prim voice says.

"This is Roberta." I sit up, with a puzzled frown. *Whose mother is this?*

"Hi, Roberta. This is Donna Nelson, editor of *Right On!* magazine."

I grip the phone tighter.

"It is my great pleasure," she continues, "to let you know that you won first place for your age category in our National Black Awareness Contest."

My jaw drops. I stare at the magazine's glossy pin-up posters on my walls. "Oh my God, I can't believe it!" I squeak.

"You deserve it, young lady. We read many compelling entries, but yours stole our hearts. Your writing conveyed a lot of emotion. It's unfortunate that your teacher said those things to you, but it looks like you made lemonade out of lemons. We need to verify your address so we can send you all of your prizes."

"Can you hold on for one second, please, Miss Nelson?"

Holding the receiver away from my mouth, I cup it with my hand and go for broke as a screaming human jumping jack.

"Mom, Charles, come quick!" I grab the latest issue of the magazine off my bureau.

Mom and Charles zoom up the steps and rush in. Worry lines crease Mom's face. I hold the magazine up and mouth, "I won the essay contest!" When the news sinks in, Charles and Mom slap each other five.

"Miss Nelson, can you tell me the prizes, again?" I share the phone with Mom. "I am so excited I can't remember."

"You might want to sit down. You have quite a few."

Mom and I exchange grins, our heads pressed together as we listen.

"You won a first-place engraved plaque with your name inscribed on it along with $100."

I make the sign of the cross, look heavenward and mouth, "Thank you, Jesus."

"We also thought a budding writer—and you are quite talented with a mature perspective—should have an electric typewriter."

"Ooh," escapes my lips.

Charles giggles. Mom's eyes shimmy with pride.

"You also won a set of encyclopedias and a year-long subscription to the magazine."

"Thank you so much!"

"Wait, there's more. We need you to send us a photo for the article announcing the winners. We need it within two weeks."

"You want a photo of me to put in the magazine?"

Miss Nelson chuckles. "Everyone will want to know who won all these great prizes, right?"

"I can't believe it! First place," I say. "Thank you. I love the magazine!"

Miss Nelson laughs. "Keep writing. Can I speak to either parent for permission to use your photo?"

"My mother is here. He name is Dora Forest." I hand Mom the phone. I'm elated I've done something to make Mom swell with pride.

After a short conversation, Mom hangs up. We scream and dance like Mom-Mom's church people. Mom and Charles hug me, depositing wet, sloppy kisses on both cheeks.

"This calls for a celebration," Mom announces. "We're going to dinner in a couple of hours. Let's get dressed up, go somewhere nice. Invite Bonnie, tell her it's my treat." Then Mom's bright eyes turn serious. "It's okay if you want to invite your father."

"Okay, I'll call him," I say.

"Can we order anything we want?" Charles asks.

"Anything."

Charles dances out of my room. Mom turns to me with a proud smile.

"You sounded so cool and collected. I was impressed listening to you."

"Can you believe the editor called me? If I acted professional, it was because I was pretending I was you on the phone."

A soft "Oh" slips from Mom's lips. Her surprised reaction swells my heart, too. I see her nose turning pink, which means waterfalls are coming. Seeing Mom cry, even happy tears, bothers me to the tenth power. 'Cause, I'm immature.

"Gotta call and tell Bon the good news." I bolt out the room.

I love Mommy to death, but unlike my dad, we're not the real hug up type. And it's okay. Cause we're working on our own way of sharing feel-good vibes.

I call Bonnie from the kitchen phone to share the news, thank her for encouraging me to enter, and invite her to dinner.

"Wait, before you hang up, I just got to say I am happy for you but a little upset, too."

"Why?" I ask

"You are not supposed to keep secrets from your best friend."

What does she mean? I think about never telling Bonnie about Sister Elizabeth possibly being Black or about my half-sister. "What secret?"

"You never told me you even entered," she whines.

"Oh," I say, heady with relief. "I didn't tell you because I didn't think I would win. Girl, I used your stamp to mail my essay. Get your butt over here."

"See you soon," she says, chuckling.

I hang up and think about when to disclose my other big secrets. Maybe in due time, as Mom always says.

Back in my room. I lie on my bed fuzzy with happiness—the kind that makes your cheeks hurt from smiling so hard. I like that kind of discomfort. I look out the window at a sun-hugged day.

I tuck my diary under my arm and scurry to the front steps to write in the sunshine. It feels glorious outside. I throw my head back and bask in the warmth dancing on my skin.

I write: "Today is the happiest I've been since turning thirteen. Maybe the best day of my life. I won *Right On!*'s contest about Black awareness, which was about one of my worst days. How cool is that? Who knew something good could come out of that awful fight with Sister?"

A honking car temporarily distracts me. I resume writing. "It's so ironic that by calling Thomas Jefferson a hypocrite, my face will end up in *Right On!* Ironic that my own father is a hypocrite, too. But we all are. Good thing I didn't know all that before I entered the contest. Try summarizing that in 800 words." I draw a smiley face and close the book.

I squeeze my eyes as the steps seem to transform. The air thins. On the cusp of ninth grade, I am floating on ribbons knitted with joy, gratitude, and faith. My heart beats smarter, stronger. Confidence and coolness ooze from my pores. Far from the loser kid I used to be, I know this: I feel ready to roller skate in the sky to whatever's next.

A car door slams and I turn my head to see Dad approaching, beaming his dimpled smile. His eyes flicker with pride. He carries a bouquet of baby roses, and his camera to take my photo for the magazine.

We have a lot to work out as a family and as father and daughter. But still, he has a lifeline to my heart. Holding my breath, I wait to hear the one word that will take this perfect, sun-framed day over the moon.

"Congratulations, Pumpkin," he says.

The last week of school is like a movie starring me. Mother Superior announces my win during morning announcements. My classmates applaud, and the next day, Sister Elizabeth allows my friends to bring in supplies for a party. Stephanie fixes homemade cupcakes. Donna brings cute party hats and napkins. Vietta picks out the prettiest card and has everyone sign it. And Raymond gives me Mallo Cups.

Since school's out by the time the issue with my photo hits the stands, Mr. Harvey, who knows reporters, has the neighborhood weekly interview me.

"That way you have something to show around school before you leave," he says. I suspect he did it because he was thrilled by my decision to attend East Catholic and he felt guilty for not fighting to keep me in the school essay contest.

On the last day of school, I carry the article like a prized forty-five record. My story is only a paragraph and it's buried on page 7, but to me it's a front-page story above the fold, which Mr. Harvey says is reserved for the biggest news.

I am in a newspaper. Huddling around me, my friends read it before the bell. Bonnie cleared out all of the copies from the newspaper box nearest school and handed them out to our jump rope crew.

In homeroom, my article gets passed around, making me feel like a celebrity.

Since it's the last day, we remain in homeroom until dismissal, shooting the breeze, discussing summer plans and vacations.

We take turns exchanging our colorful autograph books, where we write cheesy farewell messages to each other. This year's notes will be more heartfelt. I won't see many of them again. Most of my classmates are moving to the suburbs over the summer. About half will attend East Catholic for Girls or the Boys school, which is several blocks away.

Stephanie wanders over. "Coming to my birthday party?" she asks again.

"You know I am. Why are you acting like you won't see me next week?"

"I'm just going to miss seeing you every day."

I pull a pack of Now and Laters out of my pocket and hand them to her. I have an entire box, a graduation and farewell gift from the Hostetlers, my sweet neighbors who moved last month.

"An early birthday present," I say. She beams.

Donna hands me her autograph book and takes mine. Thumbing through it to find a blank page, I write: "I will miss you, Donna, one of the coolest chicks I ever met. Cher has nothing on you! Have a great summer. Roberta '74." I draw a peace sign under my name.

"Read mine later, Roberta." Donna closes my book and lays it on the desk. "I could hardly find room to write something, Miss Popular." She slings her hair back. "I hope we stay in touch. I know you will have some interesting stories to tell."

Donna's beautiful eyes look shiny and sad. Why aren't we friends outside of school? Why don't we go to each other's birthday parties?

"Give me your book," I say. She hands it over, and I add my phone number under my comments. "That's my number. Call me anytime."

"Roberta, you have your own phone?"

"Yes, how did you *not* know that I got it for my birthday?" She shrugs.

I know. Outside of school we live in different worlds. Black and white.

"Well, now you know. Call me sometime."

"I'd like that," she says as Geoffrey scampers over.

"Yo, Roberta. Sign my book anyway you'd like."

I write: "To my favorite class clown, I hope you grow up to become a famous comedian and perform on the Johnny Carson show. P.S. Make peace not war."

"Don't write anything crazy in mine," I warn him.

He writes: "Stay cool! Don't fight any more nuns. I won't."

I laugh when I read it.

Out the corner of my eye, Vietta sits alone, watching everyone. I head over and in her book I write: "Thank you for standing with me to the end. Come over sometimes. Bonnie and me will teach you how to jump rope." Her grateful smile makes me want to kick myself for not doing so when the weather broke and we started jumping rope again during recess.

"Hey everyone, Vietta saved a page just for me so nobody better write on it," I challenge.

Soon a cluster of classmates wait to sign her autograph book.

The class grows rowdier as the clock ticks toward dismissal. I peek at what Donna wrote. She's right. I should have waited. I'm choked up.

"Dear Roberta, I will be the first one to buy Angel Dressed in Black and the first one in line for you to autograph it. I learned a lot from you. Always your friend. Love, Donna."

The bell rings and the class cheers. Most of the students dash for the door. I hurry around a few classmates who stop to tell Sister Elizabeth goodbye, but when I get to the stairwell, I make a U-turn. I need to say a few things to Sister Elizabeth. I wait in the hallway until my classmates leave.

The room is now empty except for her, and she is staring out the window.

"Sister Elizabeth?"

She startles, then searches my face as I wait in the doorway. "Did you forget something, Roberta? I haven't yet checked all the desks."

I enter, unsure what I may say. This is not planned. "I just wanted to ask you . . ."

Her smile fades. She forms a teepee with her fingers on her desk.

"What answer did you expect when you asked the question about Thomas Jefferson?"

"Ah, that. Let's not revisit that day," she says, her voice suddenly cheery. "That was a low point in my many years of teaching."

I wait, unsure of what I want. Deep down I know she would not tell me what I am dying to know. Suddenly a thought occurs.

"Did you ask Sister Carol to meet with me?"

"I did, with permission. Sister Carol will be a terrific mentor for you." Her eyes soften and for a second I think she will finally apologize. She starts to speak, sighs, and then looks down at her folded hands. Her bare nails are rosy and shiny. I never noticed her nails before. Not even when she slapped me. We stare at her hands until she clears her throat, rises from her desk, and shoves them into her pockets.

"Have a great summer, Roberta," she says, winding up our awkward farewell. "Do well next year. I expect to hear great things about you at East Catholic."

I struggle with what to say, until it hits me that I am wrestling with the old Roberta. The part best left behind. "Bye, Sister. I hope your class next year is easier than ours."

Sister makes a squishy face and chuckles. "Me, too."

I look around the classroom that I will never forget. I wave at Sister Elizabeth, whose face is impossible to read. She waves back. I walk with a bounce out the door, elated to be moving on. I feel her eyes on my back, watching every step. I refuse to glance back. Sometimes you just have to let go what's gone.

CHAPTER 33

Sprawled on a sheet I covered the sofa with, I snap my fingers to the beat as Soul Train comes on. I like this bouncy theme music, now a hit record by the Three Degrees, one of Philly's female groups. Man, everyone digs TSOP (The Sound of Philadelphia).

The doorbell rings.

"That's Lee Lee, I'll get it," Mom says, barreling down the stairs and out the door.

Great, 'cause I'm not moving from such a comfy spot on Day 1 of summer vacation. Without its squeaky plastic covers, the sofa is perfect for daydreaming during commercials about upcoming splash parties at the swim pool in my maternal grandmother's siditty suburban neighborhood. I'm old enough to go now.

I sniff the lemony sheet, courtesy of the new fabric softener I picked out. I chuckle recalling Mom's reaction after I told her I use the sheet to protect the sofa from my oily hair. She did a double take and said, "You are truly growing up." I reminded her I'm nearly fourteen and proved it by not rolling my eyes at her surprised reaction.

Mom and Lee Lee's happy chatter about shopping specials and clipped coupons spill in from the porch, drowning out the theme song. The hippest trip in America requires a higher volume, but I'll strain to hear it 'cause I'm not getting up to turn up the TV. Nope, not happening. All the nopers in Noperville say nah.

Seconds later, Mom returns, tossing me a thick bag with our new blue dungarees.

"Mom, can you hold mine up so I can see what they look like?"

"You are spoiled rotten. I feel sorry for your husband," she says, unfolding the pants. She holds them up by the waistband for my inspection.

"Ooh, Lee Lee is nothing but the truth," I say, referring to our new neighbor who runs a seamstress business from her basement. I had her sew a seam down the middle of each leg. Called "tracks," every girl who considers herself impossibly hip—like me—wears the figure-flattering look. Mom even got a pair. "She did a good job. I'll try them on later, okay?"

Folding my pants, Mom shrugs off my Saturday sloth. "Lazybones, you don't need my permission."

The word "permission" flickers in my head like a lightning bug on a summer night.

I sit up in the Thinker position as Mom starts up the steps. "Mom, when I asked Sister Elizabeth yesterday about calling Sister Carol, she said she had permission. Did she get it from you?"

Mom comes back downstairs and stands by the curio. "You and Bonnie went on and on when she spent the night about this mysterious Black nun. Your father and I thought you should meet a sister who is a sistah," she says with a hint of a smile. "But I did not have a nickel in that dime regarding the Bridges Program. I can't take credit for that."

"Wow. Until we spoke, I figured Mr. Harvey called her."

"He may have for the leadership group. He always saw your potential. It's nice to have so many people watching out for you, isn't it?"

Her compliment reaches deep, all the way into my corpuscles. It ripples from my toenails to scalp. Mom removes Charles's trophy from the curio and cradling it, stands in front of me. "And it's nice to be a role model, isn't it?" She holds up the trophy.

"What?" I cock my head.

"I didn't stutter. Charles does his best because he sees you trying so hard."

I inspire Charles? I guess I dwell on my own problems so much that sometimes I don't see anyone else. Looking at the trophy in Mom's hand, one bigger than any I've ever won, I think it's all my brother's doing. Isn't it? I look at the pride in Mom's eyes. I recall in this same room one afternoon how tugging on one of Charles's beloved rosary beads unraveled them all.

I thought the first day of no school couldn't get any better than lazing on the sofa and doing a marathon with the TV. Mom just took it over the top. I haul myself up and bear hug the best mom ever.

CHAPTER 34

Today feels even better than the last day of eighth-grade. The July *Right On!* featuring my photo with a roundup of essay winners will arrive any second in the mail. Since winning a subscription, I get the magazine a week before it hits newsstands.

In the warmth of the sun, I wait for the mailman with my diary on my lap. Thumbing through it, I find the entry I wrote after Sister Carol asked me to consider making a speech when we go back to school. I wrote:

> *Dearest Diary: I am a nervous wreck. Sister Carol wants me to speak at an assembly during the first week of school. But you know what? I'm going to do it anyway. I have a lot to say but the gist of my message will be we know we are growing up when we realize that truth isn't always as simple as black or white. Or even people for that matter. What's true and who we are can be complex. Sometimes we all take turns as walking contradictions. But I plan to do my best to be honest and focused as a member of*

the Bridges Program. Our city needs to improve race relations. There is no racial justice without racial equality. As high school students, we can make meaningful changes. I'll share that Malcolm X said some of the best revolutionaries are teenagers. I'll urge them to read his amazing book. Wow, now I'm getting excited about speaking!

I underline Malcolm X and draw a heart above his name.

The screen door squeaks. I turn around. Charles stands in the doorway, a comic book tucked under his arm. I pat the concrete space next to me. He bounds down the steps, my unspoken invitation lifting his chubby cute face with delight.

"Mom says he should be here any minute," he says, wiggling next to me.

Charles opens the comic book, where he keeps his clipping of the local article about me winning the national essay contest. Mommy collected as many copies as she could to share with friends, family, and her co-workers.

"I'm starting a scrap book for you," he says.

I plant a wet one on his cheek so he can pretend to be grossed out. Then I pick up the clipping. In the margins are elaborate drawings of superheroes.

"Charles, did you draw these free-hand or trace them?"

"Free-hand. You like them?"

"You're really good. I love them."

"So when you write your children's books, can I draw the pictures?"

"They are called illustrations," I say, nodding.

"Yup, that," he says. Charles throws back his head and lets loose a deep laugh at nothing in particular, but everything good.

A car approaches, blasting my latest jam. Our heads bob and shoulders sway to possibly the best summer house party groves ever. The car's occupants, grown folks my parents' ages, smile and give our seated boogie movies a thumbs-up.

"Young sister and brother, get up and show us what you working with," the bearded, bald-headed driver says. His booming voice is equal parts admiration and amusement.

"Dance with me, Charles."

My brother looks like he would rather wash broken dishes.

Feeling self-conscious, I respond with a shy giggle. I wave to the old-head admirers and they wave back, then the car rounds the corner.

"All I need now is a piece of gum or—" I snap my fingers. I reach into my pocket and pull out the last two pieces of apple Now and Laters. We slap five and rip off the waxy wrapping. Mouth watering, my nails and teeth scratch off the paper in record time. I bite down on the most fantastic sweet-sour candy in the free world and taste a good time.

Charles struggles to open the wrapping with his chewed-up fingernails. I scrape my long thumbnail across a stubborn stretch. His appreciative slurp is the best thanks.

Shoulder to shoulder, we chew with our mouths open while shielding our eyes from the lemony sun. A low-flying plane zooms overhead, leaving white streaks.

"They're called contrails," Charles says, pointing.

My eyes sting from watching the plane, so I close them. I inhale the heady scent of Mom's potted gardenia.

"He's here," Charles says, nudging my side.

I open my eyes as the mailman bounds up the stairs.

He hands me a big manila envelope for Mom, some bills— and my magazine! I set the other mail on the step and tear the wrapping off the July *Right On!* In the corner a red headline reads: "Black Awareness Essay Winners Inside." I open the magazine and flip the pages looking for my photo. It's on page 33 in the lower right-hand corner.

I become a human pogo stick screaming at my black-and-white image. This magazine has featured every Black celebrity known, and now I'm in it.

"That's me!" I read the caption, "'First-Place Winner Roberta Forest, 13, Philadelphia.' I'm in the same magazine as Michael Jackson!"

"First place in the whole U S of A," Charles yells and shimmies.

When we calm down, we lean against each other, scrutinizing the photo Dad took of me with my brand-new electric typewriter. My photo is the only one shown of the first-place winners from three age categories. We read the article detailing all of the prizes awarded.

"So neat you beat kids older than you, including twelfth-graders!" Charles is giddy with awe.

A tingly sensation starts in my heart and spreads all over. Perfect moments do that.

The screen door creaks open, and we turn to find Mom standing at the top of the steps in her new jeans matching mine. She smiles with her whole face at us cuddling and enjoying each other's company. Her mood lifts me higher. Soon I may float away on a cloud of joy.

"Mom, it's here," I say, waving the magazine. "You got mail, too."

She scans the large sized envelope. "This is information about evening classes at Temple," she chirps. "It can wait. Let me get a look at *my* daughter's photo. The famous writer. My buttercup."

I hand her the magazine folded open to the article on the contest winners. Mom's eyes widen and grow glassy at the photo of me with the typewriter and in the Easter hat Mom-Mom bought. She shouts and hops so high Charles and I lapse into a giggling fit.

"I am so proud of you." She dabs her eyes on the back of her hands. "It feels good out here. I think I'll join you two."

Mom slides next to me, and I realize it's been years since we've sat on the steps together. Why has it taken so much and so long for this to happen again?

Mom hugs me and pecks my cheek. She smells like the best nose candy ever.

"Mommy, your perfume smells better than those flowers," says Charles.

"I suspect that's indeed what you are smelling, but thank you, baby." Mom ruffles Charles's hair and pats my Afro. She threads her arm back into my mine as I loop my other arm with Charles's.

Entwined like a human pretzel, we watch a trolley push a broken one down the avenue, electrical sparks shoot overhead. Horns blare from the backed-up traffic. Wherever they're going is going to take longer than expected. Don't I know it.

Still, I feel weightless, free of the anger, dread, and uncertainty that dragged me down so much of eighth grade. I close my eyes and let the sunshine nuzzle my upturned face. I feel radiant, strong, loved, and capable.

Here, at this moment, one thing is for certain and two things are for sure: I am exploding with happiness and anticipation for what comes next. I'm so ready.

I exhale as the dazzling rays grow warmer on my skin. Pleasure bubbles from the inside. Joy feels like this.

Shaking with belly-hurting laughter, I hold on tight to Mommy and Charles. I am Roberta Forest, an award-winning writer. For a few seconds, everything shifts and tilts as the whole world revolves around me.

A NOTE FROM THE AUTHOR

The racist comment that kicks off the story happened when I was 11 and in sixth grade. As the daughter of the indomitable Dolores Farmer, I shared her resiliency and bounced back from the traumatic experience. My coping strategies included losing myself in books and writing poetry. And while I did write about the racist encounter—in an essay that won first prize in *Right On!* magazine's first national Black Awareness Essay Contest—much of the story is fictionalized.

What remains emotionally true are the life-affirming lessons about truth telling, family bonds, spiritual quests, and forgiveness that I hope readers of all ages ponder, discuss, and when appropriate, act on.

My harrowing classroom experience launched my journey from institutionalized religion to a more spiritual trek, one I continue today. The incident also shaped the trajectory of my career, solidifying my desire to write for a living while pursuing truth. As a journalist, I am happiest scrutinizing powerful institutions, holding the mighty accountable and amplifying the voices of the marginalized.

I first wrote this story as a screenplay. Unable to sell it, I adapted it into a novel.

I hope Roberta's story speaks to young readers struggling with that elusive thing called truth, a feat even harder in this age of alternative facts. The issues gripping the nation today are the same ones I grappled with over 45 years ago. Much work remains.

ACKNOWLEDGMENTS

I am grateful to Malcolm X and Alex Haley for collaborating on an autobiography that enlightened and empowered me and inspired this novel.

To Michael Paul Williams, the husband of my dreams and the writer I most admire, I love you to infinity. To Dolores Farmer, tons of love and appreciation for teaching me to read and write at age four. I told you in second grade I wanted to write as a grown up and you said I could. To Aluster "Chuggy" Farmer, your faith in me since childhood is a gift. Love you. A special thank you to the following wordsmiths doubling as awesome people: Padma Venkatraman, Heidi Durrow, Lauren Francis-Sharma, Anne Westrick, Maya Smart, Meg Medina, Ginger McKnight-Chavers, Jenn Stroud Rossman, Patty Smith and Bonnie Winston. For years of encouragement as I worked this story, much appreciation to Kristin Swenson, Stacy Hawkins Adams, Anne Westrick, Gigi Amateau, Ellen Brown, Laura Browder and Virginia Pye. Tons of hugs to my early Beta readers: Sonia Johnston, Anne Westrick, Bianca Farmer, Maya Shaw, and Chad Martin.

Nothing but love to my homegirls: Laronda Jenkins, Wanda Reese, Kenyatta Haley, Laurie Bundick, and Bernita Mapp. Thank you for your friendship for over 45 years and for championing this story. Incredible residencies at the Rowland Writers Retreat, the Virginia Center for the Creative Arts, and the Djerassi Resident Artists Program allowed me to elevate my manuscript while befriending many exceptional artists. I am fortunate to have honed my writing and editing skills as a proud member of James Rivers Writers and the Virginia Screenwriters Forum. I stood on a mountain of nos to get the yes to publish *Malcolm and Me,* a winner of the 2019 She Writes Press and SparkPress Toward Equality in Publishing (STEP) contest. I'm so appreciative of the opportunity and everyone who worked behind the scenes. I want to give a special shout out to Brooke Warner, Samantha Strom, Julie Metz, and Laura Matthews. And to you dear reader, thank you for spending time in Roberta's world!

ABOUT THE AUTHOR

Robin Farmer is a national award–winning journalist and the 2019 She Writes Press and SparkPress Toward Equality in Publishing (STEP) winner. At eight, she told her mother she would write for a living, and she is grateful that her younger self knew what she was talking about (many young folks do). Her other interests include screenwriting, poetry, movies, and traveling. She's still hoping to write stories about young people for television and film. Robin earned her degree in journalism from Marquette University. The transplanted Philadelphian lives in Richmond, VA.

Author photo © Clement Britt

ABOUT SPARKPRESS

SparkPress is an independent, hybrid imprint focused on merging the best of the traditional publishing model with new and innovative strategies. We deliver high-quality, entertaining, and engaging content that enhances readers' lives. We are proud to bring to market a list of *New York Times* best-selling, award-winning, and debut authors who represent a wide array of genres, as well as our established, industry-wide reputation for creative, results-driven success in working with authors. SparkPress, a BookSparks imprint, is a division of SparkPoint Studio LLC.

Learn more at GoSparkPress.com

SELECTED TITLES FROM SPARKPRESS

SparkPress is an independent boutique publisher delivering high-quality, entertaining, and engaging content that enhances readers' lives, with a special focus on female-driven work. www.gosparkpress.com

A Song for the Road: A Novel, Rayne Lacko. $16.95, 978-1-684630-02-8. When his house is destroyed by a tornado, fifteen-year-old Carter Danforth steals his mom's secret cash stash, buys his father's guitar back from a pawnshop, and hitchhikes old Route 66 in search of the man who left him as a child.

The House Children: A Novel, Heidi Daniele. $16.95, 978-1-943006-94-6. A young girl raised in an Irish industrial school accidentally learns that the woman she spends an annual summer holiday with is her birth mother.

The Leaving Year: A Novel, Pam McGaffin. $16.95, 978-1-943006-81-6. As the Summer of Love comes to an end, 15-year-old Ida Petrovich waits for a father who never comes home. While commercial fishing in Alaska, he is lost at sea, but with no body and no wreckage, Ida and her mother are forced to accept a "presumed" death that tests their already strained relationship. While still in shock over the loss of her father, Ida overhears an adult conversation that shatters everything she thought she knew about him. This prompts her to set out on a search for the truth that takes her from her Washington State hometown to Southeast Alaska.

The Frontman: A Novel, Ron Bahar. $16.95, 978-1-943006-44-1. During his senior year of high school, Ron Bahar—a Nebraskan son of Israeli immigrants—falls for Amy Andrews, a non-Jewish girl, and struggles to make a career choice between his two other passions: medicine and music.

Colorblind: A Novel, Leah Harper Bowron. $16.95, 978-1-943006-08-3. Set in the hotbed of the segregated South, Colorblind explores the discrimination that an elderly African-American sixth-grade teacher and her physically challenged Caucasian student encounter at the hands of two schoolyard bullies.